The Sunlit Days

The Sunlit Days

Jane Julian

PIATKUS

For
Sally and Deborah

Copyright © 1990 by Jane Julian

First published in Great Britain in 1990 by
Judy Piatkus (Publishers) Ltd of
5 Windmill Street, London W1

British Library Cataloguing in Publication Data
Julian, Jane
 The sunlit days.
 I. Title
 823.914 [F]

 ISBN 0-7499-0018-0

Phototypeset in 11/12pt Compugraphic Times by
Action Typesetting Limited, Gloucester
Printed and bound in Great Britain by
Mackays of Chatham PLC, Chatham, Kent

Chapter One

A sound had broken the silence and Caroline Trevarth opened her eyes. She got up stiffly from her chair and went to the window, thinking it was her cat, Samson, wanting to be let in from the cold. But he was nowhere to be seen and she decided she must have heard the mewing of a gull. She pulled her shawl about her shoulders; the wintry landscape seemed to bring a chill into the room.

She looked from the window of her drawing room out to the spreading lawns, now frost-sparkled, past the naked rose bushes to the bare boughs of oak and elm and beech that made up the woodland at the river's edge. Even now, in the depths of winter, she liked this outlook, though it was summer that brought its full magic home to her.

Her husband's forebears had planted well, landscaping the gardens so that, between the trees, the house commanded a prospect of the river and beyond to the bay and the open sea. She was grateful for their planning and had kept faith with them, allowing few changes to be made. But change would come, for the fortune on which the house and gardens had been designed was fortune no longer; the mines had closed long since, the smelting houses too, and the port on the North Cornish coast built by Thomas's great-grandfather lay idle, the once-busy harbour silted from disuse.

Her daughter Maud loved this view too, as did the grandchildren. They would be with her in a few days, spending the Christmas holidays here in Trecarrow, filling the house with song and laughter. Christmas was a time she loved, with the family once more around her; she even enjoyed being pampered and fussed though she pretended to be irritated by it.

She heard the door open and turned to see her housekeeper, Mrs Prideaux, a thin, pinched, black-gowned angular woman, stooped with years, her once raven-black hair now silver-white. Caroline knew she should have let Ada go long since; she expected little of her now, knew she could not hope to manage so large a place, though she still had her forbidding ways. She is showing her age, Caroline thought, forgetting for the moment that Ada was younger than her by a couple of years.

'Yes, Ada?' she asked.

'The family? When are they due? I need to know what you have in mind for them.' Her voice had never lost its local accent and intonation.

Caroline smiled to herself. Ada always was a stickler for the proprieties. 'You don't need me to tell you, Ada. They will go where they always go. Joseph will want the old nursery of course, Simon and Sarah their usual rooms. They would hate to be put anywhere else. They have a good view of the river from them. And Maud next to me.' She was sorry Maud's husband would not be with them this year. He was already in uniform and in France.

Mrs Prideaux did not seem to be satisfied, wanted more precise instructions perhaps, and Caroline felt herself getting irritated. She suppressed the feeling. She had no right to be impatient, merely because Ada was so much slower than of old; she had good reason to be grateful for the years of devoted service her housekeeper had given to the family. She had often wondered why Ada had stayed so long; was it really almost sixty years?

Caroline found it hard to believe so much time had passed since she had taken the housekeeper into her employ. The years had flashed by. Yet time did not go by without leaving its mark, and a host of memories. She need do no more than close her eyes to relive the excitements and secrets of the past. How could it all be so vivid? Was this a gift granted to everyone or was it just she who, at a blink, could conjure up such rich visions?

'Will you want to see them as soon as they arrive?'

'Of course.'

'Especially Joseph, I suppose?'

Was it so obvious Joseph was her favourite. Could not Ada see why? She should know.

She wanted to be left alone and was glad when Mrs Prideaux went. She sat again in her high-backed chair, the only one in which she could find comfort these days. Sitting there she could see out to the water and catch a glimpse of the small fleet of oyster dredgers as they passed down river. Were they manned by the same families as of old? she wondered. She supposed so; things changed so slowly here in Cornwall, and she was grateful for that. But war always brought change, already had; several of the fishermen were at sea with the Royal Navy, and more than one young man from the village had been called up into the Army or the Royal Air Force.

Joseph too would soon be in uniform. How unfair it was that two major wars should be visited on her generation, to say nothing of the minor battles and skirmishes that brought such misery. Perhaps Joseph would be spared, to find a safe billet in Whitehall. She did not think it would be in his nature to settle for that; he would seek danger rather than avoid it. He was too like his grandfather.

Thought of his grandfather brought a moment of the past and she let it comfort her for a second, so that she fell asleep, still with the vision in her mind.

She woke, startled by Samson leaping to her lap. She put him down. He was too heavy for her and the brief doze had somehow stiffened her joints. She raised herself in the chair and tried to make herself easy. She supposed this pain was a penalty of age, but, apart from the difficulty of getting moving if she sat too long, there was nothing seriously wrong with her. She had outlived her husband and would see most of her friends into the grave, she was sure.

What had come into her mind a moment ago? She could not recapture it, but she was left with a feeling of disappointment that she could not understand. She had nothing to be disappointed about; was, in so many ways, a woman fulfilled.

Yet there had been a time when that was not so, when the future had looked empty and barren, when she and her

3

husband Thomas had ceased to hope for children and she herself was discontented and restless. Thomas, dear Thomas, whom she still missed, though it was seven years since he died; strange how difficult it was to call his image to mind, how she needed the prompting of a photograph to see him clearly.

She went to her writing desk and took up a silver-framed photograph and went back to sit at the window. The photo was of Thomas and herself as they had been fifty years ago. She stared at the picture and saw a frock-coated man, serious, heavy-jowled, with sidewhiskers – dundrearies, they had been called, and out of fashion even then. She studied her own clothes in the picture with amusement; there was a certain elegance to the close-fitting bodice, tight sleeves, and the skirt with its bustle, but how uncomfortable they were, and how she disliked the restraint of the corset, so essential to the figure of the day. Young women nowadays were fortunate to be spared that.

Yet she had been pleased with her appearance then and so had Thomas. He had his hand on her shoulder and, instead of gazing into the camera, was looking down at her with pride and love. Mr Ellery, the photographer who had come from Truro to Trecarrow to take the picture, had been very taken with the pose.

Even then Thomas looked old. He had always seemed older than he was, and had behaved so: sedate and serious, weighty and considered in his views, a man to be reckoned with, a man of property and influence, whose only regret was their childlessness.

It had been her failure, she was sure then. He had not blamed her, but at the time she could not help blaming herself. For them sex had been a sterile affair; she had learnt to submit to it from duty and in the hope of one day becoming a mother. After fifteen years of fruitless marriage they had given up hope and she had been doomed to be no more than a decorative nonentity, denied any worthwhile role, a cipher even in her own household.

She was amused at the turn her recollections had taken. It had not turned out quite like that. She had after all found contentment, had been blessed with a child, her daughter Maud; Maud, who in spite of a wayward nature had settled down to become a dutiful wife and an indulgent mother to her three children.

And they would soon be here to spend a long Christmas holiday at Trecarrow. She must try not to show her favouritism, must greet Joseph no more warmly than the others. But it was hard to avoid.

Samson jumped to her lap again and pushed at the photograph, trying to get her full attention. 'No,' she said. 'Get down. You're too heavy.' Not like that sweet little tortoise-shell female of those days long past. What had she been called? The name escaped her and then suddenly came to her with the clarity that often accompanied her flights into memory.

Claudia. How well she remembered her and the part she played in their lives.

Chapter Two

1

'Claudia,' she called. 'Claudia, come here.'

The little cat looked up at her but continued to groom herself, ignoring the call.

'Claudia,' Caroline Trevarth commanded, 'come here.'

Slowly the cat came forward, looked up and waited to be picked up. 'Why!' said Caroline. 'I do believe you're going to have kittens.' She stroked her and Claudia responded by purring, intermittently at first and then steadily, with smug content.

Caroline was glad Mr Ellery had gone, with all his photographic impedimenta and his young assistant. She could change into something more comfortable than the clothes Thomas had thought proper for the portrait. She would choose a cotton day dress, much more fitting for this hot day. But she felt indolent, too much so even to ring for Prudence to help her change.

She sat with Claudia and stroked her, talking aloud to her. 'I envy you,' she said. 'Everything about you, Claudia. You'd look funny in a corset. I don't suppose it would suit you at all.' She did envy the cat, she realised; it was no pretence. Why? The easy comfort of Claudia's life? But then she too was pampered and cossetted, petted and fondled. Her independence — was that it? Perhaps so, for she could come and go as she pleased, do what she wanted in her own way and her own time, without having to conform to convention.

But that was not why. She knew why, as the cat, sleek

and self-satisfied, began to knead, rhythmically clawing at Caroline's skirt. 'You're going to have kittens. You are, I'm sure.'

That was why. Why should the cat be so blessed and she so denied? She pretended she no longer minded being barren, but it was not so; she cared with an intensity that was almost unbearable, that came over her whenever she saw another woman with a baby, or as now, with a mere cat that gloried in its motherhood. She found herself gripping the cat's fur until the poor animal miaowed in protest. 'I'm sorry,' she said and began stroking again, reassuring her.

Caroline resented her fate deeply, and more so the feeling of guilt that came with her sterility. To be so much less than a real woman she must unknowingly have sinned. She had prayed to God to bless her with child but He had refused her. She must be at fault; her husband was man enough, there could be no doubt of that.

She put Claudia down and went to her room and called her maid, Prudence, to her. She was sick of self-examination, was too prone to such indulgence. She needed some occupation to distract her, something other than the merely nominal authority she held as mistress of Trecarrow.

When she and Thomas took their places for dinner she spoke diffidently about her need to find an interest outside her present sphere.

'I hear that women are admitted as members of local School Boards. Don't you think, Thomas, that I might be of some use there?'

He was amused at her proposal. 'My dear,' he said, 'you know nothing of children.' She bent her head to hide her hurt, but he had seen her flush. 'I mean,' he said, 'children of the common classes. And you would have to submit yourself to the whims of the electorate. That sort of thing is quite unfitting for a wife of mine. Any woman involved in that is bound to be tainted. I cannot allow it to happen to my Caroline.' He smiled and would have patted her shoulder consolingly if he had not been at the other end of the dining table. He bent to his soup.

'Charity work, my dear,' he said. 'That's the answer if you

7

wish to have something to occupy you apart from running the house as you do.'

He knows very well, she thought, that I have no real say in how the house is run.

'Mrs Prideaux manages things excellently without me.'

'Charity work, my dear,' he repeated and seemed satisfied he had found an answer to her need for occupation.

She nodded her head but kept her own counsel. She had helped the ladies of the Cornwall Distress Committee, visiting families in need, dispensing charm and blankets, a Lady Bountiful. The poverty she was faced with in that dreadful town of Redruth so grieved her that she found it difficult to act her part again.

She looked along the table to Thomas. He smiled at her and nodded in approval of her apparent acceptance of his judgement. He treated her like a child, or like one of his precious porcelain figures. She had no other purpose than to look elegant and reflect credit on her husband's taste and refinement. For most women perhaps that would be sufficient and it should be so for her. But it was not.

Thomas interrupted her thoughts. 'Has Mrs Prideaux said anything, my dear? Has she mentioned her brother?'

'I did not know she has a brother.'

'No, I suppose not. She would want to forget him, I have no doubt.'

'What do you mean?'

Thomas said no more until they had finished dinner, the servants had taken themselves off, and they were alone in the drawing room.

'You find Mrs Prideaux satisfactory, my dear?' he said. 'You have no reason to doubt her good sense?'

'Of course not. She's all I could wish for,' Caroline said, hiding the envy she felt for her housekeeper's authority over the household. 'Why do you ask? Is she in some sort of trouble?' She could not imagine what sort of trouble could come to that calm and competent person.

'Not she herself, my dear, but her brother. He's a soldier. Not a very good one it seems, always in conflict with authority. And has now escaped from custody while awaiting sentence for some offence or other. Don't be

8

alarmed but it's possible he might make his way here to his sister.'

'I'm not alarmed, Thomas. All this has nothing to do with me.'

'No, indeed. I'm sure you'll be quite safe. But I'm told he's a violent young man, so we shall have to be on our guard. I think perhaps you should have a word with Mrs Prideaux, warn her that her first loyalty is to us and the law. She must tell us if he tries to get in touch with her.'

'I shall speak with her,' she assured him, but for some reason she could not clearly identify she felt uneasy. Perhaps it was the mention of "a violent young man". How could such a man be brother to the imperturbable Mrs Prideaux?

2

Ada Prideaux, housekeeper to the Trevarths, ran the household at Trecarrow with firm authority. The servants knew their place. Not one of them had dared to mention her brother to her, though she was certain they must know of his escape from Bodmin barracks and the hunt for him. It had been reported in the *West Briton* and was common knowledge.

He would try to reach her, might even now be near at hand, for where else could he go but to the sister who had always protected him? She was not sure she wanted his dependence on her. There had been a time when it comforted her to know he needed her, but that had changed. She had another charge now: her mistress Caroline.

She was not sure how she would answer if he came to her for help. He was no longer a child to be shielded from the consequences of his folly: he was a man possessed of all the arrogance and stupidity of his kind. That stupidity had led to his present troubles, his womanising, his refusal to accept authority, his violent impulses. Once she had admired his sturdy independence, encouraged it; now it was an embarrassment to them both.

Ada Prideaux hoped her mistress knew nothing of him. She must try to keep from her the fact that she was sister to such a man. She felt threatened by a relationship which she had once cherished.

9

She tried to clear her mind of him by busying herself with her household duties. There was that brazen young girl Jessica to deal with, for leading the stable boys on. She had the girl brought before her to rebuke her for her misconduct.

The girl was quite unabashed. ''twas only kissin', she said defiantly. ''twas nothin' more.' And she smiled as if the recollection pleased her. That smile, as much as her behaviour, determined the housekeeper to get rid of her. The mistress need know nothing of the circumstances, would probably see no harm in the girl, did not understand the raw passions that led such hoydens astray, was too unworldly to guess at such things.

Ada Prideaux looked coldly at the girl. How could she have demeaned herself so? She was a pretty thing, dark-eyed, square-faced, with a comely figure, but she was wayward and thoughtless. She would go the way of all such girls, become pregnant — if she were not so already — and regret it for the rest of her life.

'There's no place for you here. You'll leave tomorrow,' Mrs Prideaux said. The girl seemed surprised at the decision and for a moment the housekeeper thought she was going to appeal for a stay of justice, but she shrugged her shoulders and, with an insolent pout of the lips, left the room.

Ada Prideaux felt a sharp sense of satisfaction at her summary dismissal of the girl. For form's sake she would report it to her mistress but Mrs Trevarth would not question it, would accept, as always, that her housekeeper knew best.

Mrs Prideaux appreciated such trust, was grateful for the privilege of serving so lovely and sensitive a woman as Caroline Trevarth, could wish for no better reward in life. It was her duty and privilege to protect Caroline from the world's harsh realities. She and Caroline's husband, Thomas Trevarth, agreed on that as on most things and conspired together to spoil and cosset the woman they loved.

She thought again of her brother George. He could not be allowed to endanger the peace of Trecarrow and intrude on Caroline's well-being. At all costs he must be kept away, or, if he came for help, he must be persuaded to go quickly and leave them alone.

Perhaps her fears were ill-founded. Perhaps he would not

come. He might turn to others for help, to one of his former friends, to that woman, Molly Sullivan, she suddenly thought. She had once resented George's intimacy with so brazen a creature; now she hoped he would look to the Irishwoman for salvation, rather than to her.

'Pray God he leaves us alone,' she said aloud and felt only a twinge of guilt at her wish. He must not come here. If he did, and there was any risk to her mistress, she told herself she would not hesitate to give him away. That was her duty, however hard it might be.

She smoothed her dress down, straightened her hair under her cap, swung the keys at her belt, and left the room. She must let her mistress know of her decision on Jessica.

3

The evening still held the warmth of the day and Caroline was drawn to take a stroll down to the river which ran beyond the woodland at the bottom of the terraced lawns. Swifts swooped and screamed. Auguries foretold a summer of lazy heat.

Whenever she felt restless – and she had often felt so recently – Caroline enjoyed the peace and solitude she found here, along the river bank. Sometimes, as now, the oyster dredgers would be out on the water, coming back from the beds further down river. She waved to them but no one answered, no one had even seen her. She was as unnoticed here as elsewhere, a nonentity, lost in the shadow of the trees.

Yet the peace of the scene did something to restore her well-being and she returned to the house in more cheerful mood, only to find Mrs Prideaux waiting to speak with her.

'Yes, Mrs Prideaux?' she said. The title was a courtesy Ada Prideaux demanded. It gave her word added authority; cook, maids, garden staff, coachmen – all accorded her the respect due to a widow, though in fact she had never married. Prideaux was her maiden name.

As Caroline waited for her to speak she studied the woman. She had gypsy blood, maybe, for she was black-haired, olive-skinned, with dark and secret eyes above an aquiline nose. She missed beauty only by the stern set of her lips and a disfiguring birthmark on her cheek. Caroline had never dared to probe her background, and it was Thomas who had taken up her references. It had been a shock to learn she had a brother.

'I feel we must dismiss one of our young laundry maids,' the housekeeper announced. 'Jessica, ma'am.'

Caroline could not place the name. She supposed she had seen the girl, but had no recollection of her. 'Was there something unsatisfactory about her work?' she asked, trying to show an interest, knowing Mrs Prideaux liked to maintain the fiction that it was her mistress who had the final say in matters of appointment and dismissal.

'She is quite unsuited to a house of this kind, I'm afraid,' Mrs Prideaux said.

Caroline wondered what it was that unsuited her. She brought the girl to mind. 'She seemed willing enough,' she said.

'Too willing, ma'am.' Mrs Prideaux pursed her lips. 'Altogether too willing. She's a disturbing influence. We have our responsibilities to the young men who work in the garden and the stables. We can't allow that sort of thing at Trecarrow.'

'You know what's best, Mrs Prideaux,' Caroline said. 'But I think I ought to see her before she goes.' She was curious to know what it was about Jessica that made her so disturbing an influence.

'There's no need to bother, ma'am. She doesn't deserve such consideration.'

'I shall see her before she goes.' Caroline was surprised to hear herself speak with firmness. 'I shall speak to her myself,' she said, trying to assert a confidence she did not feel. She did not suppose Mrs Prideaux would take any notice of her wish to speak with Jessica. 'And what of your brother?'

Mrs Prideaux turned away as if she had not heard.

'I did not know you even had a brother,' Caroline continued.

'There was no reason why you should know.'

'He's on the run from the army, Mr Trevarth tells me.'

Mrs Prideaux went to the door without speaking.

'What will you do if he comes to you for help, if he comes here?'

'I know my duty, ma'am.'

Caroline could see the housekeeper had no intention of confiding in her. 'You'll remember I want to see this girl Jessica before she goes?'

'I'll see to that.'

To Caroline's astonishment Mrs Prideaux kept her word. Jessica presented herself the next morning. The girl was no longer dressed for service, but wore an outdoor coat – too big for her and shabby – over a cotton print dress.

'Mrs Prideaux said you wanted to see me, ma'am,' she said nervously.

Caroline looked at her with interest. She seemed a strong girl, nice-looking, with wide eyes and full lips.

'How old are you, Jessica?' she asked on impulse. 'Seventeen? Eighteen?'

'Fifteen.' She had a soft voice. 'Fifteen last birthday, ma'am.' She looked her former mistress in the eye and smiled in an open and friendly way that took Caroline by surprise. Servants usually showed an impassive face to her.

'What did you do to make Mrs Prideaux dismiss you?' Caroline asked.

The girl smiled again, but this time a secret smile, hinting at a memory private to her.

''Twas nothin',' she said.

'Won't you tell me?'

''Twouldn't be fittin', ma'am.'

'What will you do?'

'I didn't like service anyway,' the girl replied. 'I'll get work over to the mine, I do fancy.'

'The mine?' She wondered what sort of work was suited for a girl in the mine.

'They still need bal-maidens over to Wheal Agar.'

I must ask Thomas what a bal-maiden is, Caroline thought, and found herself envying the girl as before she had envied her cat Claudia. Jessica, it seemed, had freedom to choose, more than she herself had. *She* was bound, by duty and obligation, to live out a fruitless existence, mistress of a house that owed nothing to her, wife to a husband who loved her but who showed it by treating her as a decorative ornament, fragile as the Dresden figures he secured in their glass cabinets. She too was encased, kept inviolate.

She saw Jessica in front of her, one-time laundry maid, bal-maiden to be, and envied her.

'You may go,' she said, then called her back, drew a sovereign from her purse and gave it to the astonished girl.

4

It had been easier than he imagined. His escort had been so stupefied with the routine of drill that they had been taken by surprise when he leapt over the table, scattering the papers, falling on Captain Roberts, and knocking him to the ground by the force of his charge. He was out of the door before they had recovered their wits and was running and dodging out of the barracks, heedless of the shouts that followed him into the narrow streets of Bodmin town.

'Prideaux,' he heard a distant yell behind him. 'Prideaux! Stop, man!' But he ran on.

He had hidden till dark in a coppice, not far from the main road from Bodmin to Truro, and then when the sun went down, he set off walking westwards, instinct pointing him to the familiar ground of his youth. He would find help there, either with one of his old miner friends, with Irish Molly, or with his sister.

It was of his sister he thought most as he trudged through the night, of his sister Ada who had watched over him as a child, nursed him in sickness, protected him from danger, and loved him. She would not forsake him now. It gave him courage to picture her welcoming him, finding him a hiding-place until the hunt died down. That would not be long; he was of no consequence, only one of many army deserters.

For a moment the thought of Irish Molly came to mind, Molly Sullivan, the woman who had first seen the man in him. He smiled at the recollection and began whistling an

14

Irish ballad which had been one of her favourite songs. He stopped, realising his vigilance had slackened. He was passing through the village of Fraddon and people were stirring. Imperceptibly almost, day was breaking and the world was on the move. He hastened on, thoughts of Irish Molly gone, the need for watchfulness returning.

He left the road and climbed a hedge into a field of rough pasture where a couple of ponies grazed. One of them trotted over to him and the other followed. He spoke to them, patted them and was tempted to mount one of them and ride the rest of the way to his sister. But he did not want to add the crime of horse-stealing to his desertion. He left the ponies and, keeping close to the hedge, walked until he again found a patch of woodland in which he could safely rest.

He stayed there again during daylight and moved at dark. He had taken drink from a stream. He was hungry, but he was used to hardship. He could get by, until he reached his sister's place. He called to mind what she had written to him about her employment. The house was called Trecarrow, set in grounds bordering the Fal river, somewhere between Truro and the mouth of the river, a part of Cornwall of which he knew little.

His Cornwall was the Cornwall of tin and copper, the mines that burrowed the land from the North Coast near St Agnes, along the once rich seams to Chacewater, Carn Brea and Cusgarne. He longed to see them now and wondered why he had ever been foolish enough to leave them. He would be there still if Wheal Kitty had kept going. It had been knacked, like so many others and he, in a fit of temper at the way he and his fellows had been treated, had enlisted in the Duke of Cornwall's Light Infantry, a folly he had come to regret.

Perhaps it was to one of his old miner friends he should go first. They were men who faced danger every day of their lives and who knew what it was to be hungry and at odds with authority. He remembered old Joe Beskeen, squat and solid and broad-shouldered, a hard-rock man in every fibre, too old at the closing of Wheal Kitty to hope to work again, a man of piety and courage, a comrade he could trust.

He would go to him first. He would still live in his tiny

15

cob-walled cottage along the valley from St Agnes, with his little patch of land. George Prideaux lay back under the trees and thought of his friend.

Joe would help. He had never turned anyone away.

With nightfall he was on the move again, filled with determination to reach Joe Beskeen's cottage by dawn; to stay there — if Joe were willing — through the day, until he could get across country to his sister at Trecarrow.

His plans did not take him beyond that. It would be enough to reach Ada; that way led to safety.

It took him longer than he thought to reach Joe's and it was full daylight when he got within sight of the cottage. A policeman was at the door talking to a woman standing there. Though he could not be sure at that distance, George thought he recognised Sarah, Joe Beskeen's daughter.

The policeman turned away, the door closed on him and George waited until the man was out of sight over the hill, before making his way across fields to the rear of the cottage. There a stream ran, crystal clear and burbling merrily. George was heartened by the sound, somehow so reminiscent of his boyhood.

He walked up to the back door but before he could raise his hand to knock it was thrust open. Joe's daughter stood there, hands on hips, face set in a scowl. 'What do you want, then?' She had recognised him but there was no welcome in her.

'Joe?' he enquired.

'What do you want with Joe?'

'How is he?'

She laughed mockingly. 'What do you care? Is that what you're here for? To ask about him?' She moved to shut the door but he put out his hand and held the door ajar.

'How is he?'

She opened the door wide and let him pass, then closed it quickly after him and turned to face him. 'Don't think you can fool me. You've not coming thinking of Joe. It's yourself you've a mind for, no one else, like all men.'

'Except Joe,' he said. 'He'd never a thought for himself.'

'More fool he,' she said.

'Where is he?'

16

She glanced towards the stairs and then moved to the foot of them to bar his passage upstairs.

'They're after you,' she said. 'The police have been here. They thought you might come to your old friends for help. Well, there's no help for you here. You can go. Take yourself back where you belong, to the army. That's the life you chose.'

'Joe? Is he ill?' He followed her example and kept his voice low. 'Is he upstairs?'

There was a sound from above, as of someone putting a foot to the floor.

'There, I knew you'd disturb him,' Sarah said. ''twill do you no good to see him. He can't help you. I don't suppose anyone can.'

Footsteps, slow and unsteady, moved above, then Joe appeared at the head of the stairs, a frail ghost of a man, grey and gaunt where once he had been strong and rugged, but his eyes lit with pleasure when he saw who was there.

'George Prideaux,' he said. 'By all that's magic. Are you real then or am I dreaming?'

'He's real enough,' Sarah said. 'More's the pity.' She went to help her father down the stairs and sat him down before the empty hearth. 'He's not staying,' she said firmly. 'Just came to see how you were and he's off now.' She challenged George to contradict her.

Joe shook his head. 'D'you think I'm soft in the head? I know why he's here. He's come for help. He's on the run. Eh, George?'

'I'm on the run,' George confirmed.

'He's not staying,' said Sarah.

Joe's eyes lifted to her; he smiled, so that George saw something of the Joe he had once known, the Joe who had seen him through those hard first days down the mine.

'I'll not stay,' he said. 'I don't want to bring trouble on you.'

'I'll not turn you away,' Joe said. 'You need help. You'll have it. Take no notice of Sarah. She's thinking of me, not of herself.'

His daughter snorted with impatience and turned her back on them both.

17

'But I'll not stay. I'd be grateful for a bite to eat and then I'll be off. I'll find somewhere to hide for a day or two till the heat's off. No one's going to bother their heads about me for too long.'

Joe began to cough and his daughter turned back to him and then, accusingly, on George. 'You see,' she said. 'That's how he is. You asked about him. Now you can see.'

Slowly the coughing subsided and Joe sat back in his chair, took a deep breath and spoke. The words came slowly and through pain. 'She'll give you bread. At least we've got that. And a candle and lucifers. We can spare those. You'll need them to hide down old Kitty.'

'Wheal Kitty?' George was surprised at the suggestion and then saw the sense of it.

'You'll be on your own ground there, boy,' Joe said. 'Johnson's shaft and Prior's. No one do go there these days. You'll be safe, I do reckon, leastwise safe as anywhere.' He had exhausted himself. Sarah stood beside him, arm on his shoulder, looking down at him with deep concern.

'I'll go now,' said George.

'Bread and candle, Dad said. Then you must go.' Sarah went into the linny at the back of the house and returned with a small canvas pack. 'Here,' she said, thrusting it at him. 'And good luck.'

'Wheal Kitty,' whispered Joe.

'Wheal Kitty it is,' George said and turned at the door of the cottage to raise his hand to his old friend.

'God bless!' he heard Joe say.

Chapter Three

Mrs Ferris, who came in from the village to help in the kitchen, brought news that an enemy plane had been seen approaching Falmouth. Everyone had expected bombs to fall but it had turned tail when the anti-aircraft battery at Pendennis Point had gone into action.

Caroline had heard the sound of the guns but had taken no notice. They were too distant to be alarming, and who would want to drop bombs on Trecarrow? There was nothing here to interest the Luftwaffe, merely an eighteenth-century house, neglected grounds and outbuildings, and a couple of old ladies.

She did not like to think of herself as an old lady but she knew that was how others regarded her. She was old, of course, as years went, but years as such were meaningless. Her heart was still as young as ever, still as likely to be moved as when she was a young woman, open to love and beauty and dreams.

She heard a flutter outside among the bushes in the flower beds and, drawn to the window by the noise, saw her cat, Samson, leaping at a magpie which taunted him from a safe distance. Caroline rapped on the window to distract the cat. He was a hunter and could not be changed, but, at the sight of her, he lay down, pretending no interest in the bird. The magpie was more startled than the cat and flew away and out of sight.

She looked at the clock and was surprised how little time had passed since she had last looked. How oddly time moved, swiftly or haltingly, impossible to guess what made it change its pace so. How slowly it dragged when there was something to look forward to, like the visit of the family.

She hoped nothing would prevent their coming, but so much could happen in these hazardous times. Yet she would surely know if anything serious happened to Joseph. She always knew when he was ill, whatever the distance separating them. She could not explain it, made no effort to understand it, merely took it for granted.

She rang for Mrs Prideaux. 'Is everything ready for the family?' she asked.

'Of course. I know what has to be done,' Mrs Prideaux said with unaccustomed sharpness, revealing her own anxiety. 'I hope nothing happens to stop them coming. And it would make life a good deal easier for everyone if you allowed a telephone in the house, then we might know just when they were due.'

Caroline ignored her. She hated the instrument. Thomas had had one installed as soon as the lines reached Cornwall. On his death she had it removed. It brought nothing but bad news.

Bad news still came of course, but more slowly, and without that shrill and insistent ring to jar the nerves.

Mrs Prideaux would not be denied her protest. 'I know Miss Maud agrees with me. She worries about you. She could speak to you whenever she wanted. And we could call the doctor quickly.'

'Who for? I'm not ill.'

'And we could speak to Master Joseph too, telephone him on his twenty-first birthday, wish him many happy returns.' She moved about the room, needlessly plumping cushions, examining surfaces for dust, clicking her tongue in annoyance at the papers her mistress had at her feet.

She could speak to Joseph, that was so. There were times when she would welcome that, but his voice had a disturbingly reminiscent quality, a depth and resonance that reminded her too strongly of the past, that distant yet ever-present past.

'How old are you, Ada?' she said impulsively.

'You're not going to talk about pensioning me off? I do my job, don't I?'

'Of course I'm not thinking of pensioning you off, as you

20

call it. I should be lost without you. But you're no longer young. Neither of us is.' She had noticed how much more slowly Ada moved about the house, how often she failed to hear what people said to her. She still had the illusion that she ran the house, but these days Caroline herself gave Cook her orders, watched over the household accounts, kept an eye on things. Yet it was true she would feel lost without Ada; she too was part of Caroline's past, held an important place in her memories; how much less fulfilling life would have been if she had not been part of their lives.

'Do you ever think back to that time?' she asked.

The housekeeper looked suspiciously at her mistress, then a haunted expression came into her eyes, almost as if the question frightened her. Caroline saw then that the past she brought so vividly to mind was one that Ada was glad to forget.

'You look tired,' she said and sent the housekeeper away to rest. She herself was ready for her afternoon nap but found it difficult to relax. She heard a sound on the gravel drive and went to the window to see a policeman on a bicycle riding slowly towards the house.

Her heart gave a lurch. Policemen, like the telephone, brought bad news more often than not. Something had happened.

She turned, expecting the worst when a knock came at the door and Mrs Prideaux showed the Constable in. He was a broad and bucolic man, whom she knew, whom everyone in the village knew. He stood awkwardly before her, helmet in his hand, shuffling his feet.

She sat down. 'What is it?' she said.

'The black-out, ma'am, that's what it is,' he said.

She did not understand.

'The black-out. I've had complaints. 'tes dangerous leaving all those lights showing. Folks are mighty put out about it. Your lights can be seen way out in the Bay.' He had said what he had been told to say and now wanted to be gone.

'I shall make sure we're specially careful,' she said, and heaved a sigh of relief. 'There are so many windows. It's so easy to forget. But I'll see it's done properly.' She turned to

21

the housekeeper. 'See Mr Harvey has a warm drink before he leaves. It's bitter, isn't it?'

The policeman nodded and his face broke into a large smile. 'I'm sorry I had to speak like that,' he said.

When he had gone she sat back in her chair and dozed, letting her thoughts wander idly, thinking of her daughter Maud, remembering how wilful she had been as a child and yet how lovable too. Thomas had indulged her every whim and the servants had adored her. She should have grown up to be a spoilt and selfish woman, but was thoughtful and considerate, at least where her mother was concerned. She had been a pretty child, an attractive young woman, and was now a handsome matron; strange that she bore no trace of her father in her appearance. The strain was there though, in Joseph.

She heard a sound on the drive again and got up to see who it was. It was Constable Harvey riding back to the village. As she watched him she saw, quite distinctly, another policeman, in another time. It was good news he brought too, though at the time it seemed anything but good. It came so clearly to her, that feeling of alarm. How could she have been so blind?

Chapter Four

1

Caroline watched her little tortoise-shell cat Claudia scampering after a leaf in the rose bed and, hearing a horse on the gravel drive, turned to see a police superintendent riding round to the rear of the house. She tried to bring his name to mind. He was an acquaintance of Thomas's. Groves, she thought, Superintendent Groves. What could he want? He must know that Thomas would be at the works at this time of day.

It was no concern of hers what he was doing here. She had no wish to see him, had taken against him when Thomas first introduced him, disliked the way in which he seemed to be on duty even when paying a social call, his eyes following every movement, as if he saw in everyone a potential law-breaker.

She sat down and picked up her petit-point, bored though she was with it, but needing something to occupy herself while the world went by.

She turned at a knock at the door and Mrs Prideaux came in to announce that Superintendent Groves wished to speak with her.

'What does he want?' she said impatiently.

'He wouldn't tell *me*, ma'am,' Ada Prideaux said and showed her annoyance at the slight.

The superintendent followed Mrs Prideaux into the room. 'May I have a word, Mrs Trevarth? I shall see your husband at his place of work but I thought I ought to warn you of

23

our intentions.' He looked pointedly at the housekeeper. 'I wish to speak with you in private, if you do not mind?' he added.

Mrs Prideaux looked at her mistress for her agreement before going from the room. The policeman closed the door after her and stood with his back to it for a moment as if listening for movement outside. Eventually, satisfied Mrs Prideaux had gone, he turned to Caroline, 'It is to do with your housekeeper.'

'What on earth can Mrs Prideaux have done?'

'Not what she has done, but what she might do.'

Caroline did not understand. 'I can't imagine what you mean. Mrs Prideaux is the most law-abiding of women.'

'Indeed,' said the superintendent. 'So I understand, but circumstances alter cases. I trust what I have to say will go no further than this room?'

She did not answer. He could think what he wanted.

'You may have heard of the presence of an army deserter in these parts,' he went on. 'A dangerous man, a violent man.' He glanced at her.

'Violent?' she asked and felt a tremor of alarm.

'And very dangerous. He's probably hiding down Wheal Kitty. He knows it well, it seems.'

'You mean my housekeeper's brother? My husband mentioned something of the kind.'

'George Prideaux. We know him of old. He was always a trouble-maker, even as a youngster. A hard character. Not a man to be trifled with.' He looked around as if to sit down but she had no intention of inviting him to be seated. The sooner he went the better.

'I shall be asking Mr Trevarth for permission to post men in your grounds,' he said. 'We have reason to think he may make his way here.'

Again Caroline felt a tremor of fear at the thought of this man of violence drawing near to Trecarrow. It could not be. 'Mrs Prideaux would do nothing to help a criminal, even her brother,' she asserted.

The superintendent slowly shook his head. 'You may think so if you wish, but I know when to trust my judgement. I hope you will allow my men to do their duty and that you will tell your Mrs Prideaux to give us every co-operation. I shall warn her we are watching her. If he shows his face here he'll be taken, you may be sure of that. I wouldn't like any member of your houshold to get into trouble with the law.'

She took his remark as a threat and her indignation mounted. 'Is that all?' she asked dismissively and turned to ring for him to be shown out.

'One final word,' he said. 'He's a dangerous fellow, has already half-killed one man and would not baulk at attacking a woman. Warn your staff to be on their guard, especially the women. Let us know immediately if he is seen anywhere about. He is desperate and if he's cornered he'll turn on anyone, anyone at all.' She noticed how fleshy yet cruel his lips were. She wished he would go, but she recognised he was there to protect her and her household. She must force herself to be polite.

'How shall we know him?'

'By his hunted look, I reckon. I'm told he was handsome enough as a lad. Dark, swarthy complexion, gypsy-like you'd say, with a gypsy's insolence.'

He went to the door. 'I'll be seeing your husband. But in the meantime I'll arrange for a couple of my men to search the stables and the outbuildings.' He took her agreement for granted and, much though she disliked the man, she was grateful for his presence and that of his men. The thought that the man Prideaux might be near at hand frightened her more than she had imagined when Thomas had first mentioned it.

She rang for her housekeeper. 'You know why he came?' she asked, but did not wait for an answer. 'Your brother.' It sounded like an accusation. 'The police think he may come to you for help. They are setting a watch on the house. I trust you will do nothing to make things difficult for us.'

Mrs Prideaux stood before her, head lowered, saying nothing.

'You would be foolish to protect him.'

Again the woman said nothing, gave no clue to her intentions.

'They say he is dangerous,' Caroline said.

25

Ada Prideaux looked up, smiled at her mistress and said, 'Yes, so they say.'

'And is he?'

'Who can tell what has happened to him? Men change.'

Caroline was glad when Thomas returned. She felt safer with him at home and she greeted him with more than her customary warmth. His serious face lightened and he held her away from him to look at her.

'What is it, my love?' he said.

'Superintendent Groves came,' she began.

'Ah yes, the deserter Prideaux. Does Mrs Prideaux know?' She nodded.

'I'm afraid the young man is no credit to her. I'm told she brought him up when their parents died. You must have a word with her, tell her not to get embroiled in his affairs.'

'I have spoken with her but I think a word from you would carry more weight, Thomas.' She was curious to know more. It was rare for events from the outside world to intrude upon her, rare and alarming, but also intriguing.

'What sort of trouble was he in to make him desert?' she asked. 'Mr Groves spoke of violence.'

Her husband picked up the newspaper, sat down and looked at her over its pages. 'It's a sordid business, my love. You don't want to know any more.'

Her curiosity was whetted. She waited a moment and approached the matter indirectly. 'I cannot imagine a brother of Mrs Prideaux doing anything disreputable.'

'Men are not like women, Caroline. They have brutish instincts, especially men of his kind.'

'What kind?' she was moved to ask.

'It is hardly a fit subject for us to discuss.'

He returned to his newspaper while she pretended to give her mind to her embroidery. At length she said, 'Mr Groves said he was dangerous.'

'Yes, so he tells me, and a powerful young man with it, so let's hope Mrs Prideaux has sense enough not to get involved with him. Or, even more to be desired, let us pray he's taken before he can do any more harm.'

'What harm has he done?'

26

Thomas Trevarth sighed, put his newspaper down and frowned at his wife. 'He almost killed a man in his unit. They quarrelled over some woman, if you must know, my dear. I told you these men have brutish instincts. You can imagine the sort of woman it would be.'

No, she thought, I cannot, but she did not speak.

'This fellow Prideaux got away from custody and was seen making his way west from Bodmin. Groves thinks they have him cornered. I don't think there's any cause for us to be alarmed. The police and troops between them won't let him slip through their fingers. You need not worry your pretty little head about him. You'll be safe. I'll see to that. I've agreed with Groves that he should post men to watch the house until the fellow's taken.' He looked at her over his eyeglasses. 'Satisfied, my love?'

She was not satisfied but said nothing. Thomas would tell her no more, she was certain. There *was* more to tell and more she wanted to know. What did he mean, they had fought over some woman? And what sort of woman was it? How would such a woman be different from her? Did not all women have the same feelings? What did Thomas mean by "brutish instincts"? It was a closed world to her and she was angry at her ignorance, at the way in which she was shielded from the larger world that lay behind the walls of their estate. Even when she visited that outside world, for calls upon her friends or charitable visits to the needy, she was still wrapped in Thomas's protective concern, still sheltered from reality.

That was reality outside, she suspected, not this stifling cocoon of comfort and well-being. She had never thought like this before, she realised, and did not understand what made her think it now.

Thomas was looking at her with concern. Had she spoken her thoughts aloud? She did not think so.

'You mustn't worry. I'll have another word with Groves, get him if need be to post extra men to guard us. You'll be quite safe, my love. I shall make sure of that. And I shall have a word with Mrs Prideaux, tell her she must let us know if that brother of hers gets in touch with her. We cannot allow danger to come near you.' He put his paper aside and walked over to rest his hand on her shoulder. 'Believe me, Caroline, we have nothing to fear from this man. He belongs to another world.'

2

Dark held no terrors for him; he had an instinct, almost that of an animal, making him aware of objects near, could always sense them; and dark was never total even on the blackest of nights. But that was above ground. Here there was nothing, not even a sparkle from the water running down the rock walls; here dark was solid, tangible. His eyes were open but he might as well have been blind; only touch held true, the feel of his hands along the rough sides of the stope, of his feet over the waste that cluttered the drive.

He dared do no more than hold to the sides. If he moved a stumble might reveal his presence to the men after him. They could not be far away, for he had heard a voice and another and another, some close by, seeming within a yard or two, others remote and vanishing into the mine and up the shafts, away into the fresh and gusty air above ground. Down here the air was foul and stagnant and he wondered how long he could survive in it.

Foul air and dark were not the danger. His enemies were the men searching the deep mine, thrusting flares and lanterns into each drive, probing the dead workings, peering into every crack and hole. He could almost pity them, these open-air men, sweating in their army serge, gasping in the thin air, fearful in their knowledge of the weight of rock close upon them. They were uneasy, these brave troopers and riflemen, timid with dread in this foreign element. He could sense it in the voices, the way they called one to the other as they moved from drive to drive, level to level.

He had the advantage over them in that. He knew these ways of old. Wheal Kitty was a familiar friend. He trusted her to protect and shelter him, while his pursuers chased a shadow here, an echo there, up Johnson's shaft, down Prior's until, confused by the soft noises of the mine, they became disorientated, 'mazed' − the local word returned to him — and then terrified, and desperate to get back to grass and open sky.

He stood motionless, listening, breath shallow, exuding sweat from every pore. Sounds of pursuit had faded and he was about to take the candle from his pack and light it to find his way out when some instinct made him hesitate and, in that moment, he saw a faint flicker of light come and go and come again. They had reached this level, the four hundred, after all. He had not thought they would venture so far down, but here they were. And here they might trap him. Yet he dared not move; a careless step might bring a tumble of stone to tell them where he was. He pressed back against the rock, hoping that if they cast their light into the stope the shadows would confound flesh with stone and keep him hidden. Water trickled down his hair and neck until he was as wet as the walls. He saw a dark bulk behind a light at the entrance to the stope and held his breath. The light passed and with it footsteps; then the steps paused and returned and light shone for a second glimpse into the narrow working.

'Likely as not he's up and away, out of this hell-hole,' he heard Sergeant Greenwood say, voice slow and breathless from the close air about him.

'He's gone to ground somewhere. Here's as likely as anywhere. It's where he worked, they tell me.' That was Corporal Rennie. So, he was out of the sick bay and eager for revenge, it seemed. 'I hope the bastard rots down here,' he said.

The sergeant did not reply but the lamp swung back and forth penetrating the gloom, throwing scintillas of light from the damp rock walls.

George Prideaux stood stiff and silent, eyes closed against discovery, waiting for Rennie's cry of triumph. But none came. Steps moved away, voices faded into the distance and he heard, faintly, an oath from Rennie as the man stumbled. He opened his eyes and dark remained.

So, Rennie had recovered, but no doubt would bear for life the marks of their quarrel. He could expect no mercy if they caught him, for he had compounded his offence by assaulting Captain Roberts when he broke out of barracks.

They would not catch him. He was determined on that. Nor would he rot down here as Rennie hoped. There were ways of escape and he knew them. Fumbling out of the stope he reached the drive. It was familiar ground. He had worked here until the day the mine closed. Only then, in a fit of anger at the way he and his fellows had been thrown aside by the mine company, had he taken the Queen's shilling. He had been mad to do so, should have known the regimented life of the soldier was not for him.

If his memory remained true this drive led to the bottom of Johnson's shaft. But there was no escape that way, for they would be waiting for him at the top. There was no sound now of pursuit; their chase below ground had ended, but guards would have been posted at the surface exits from the workings, men at the shaft tops waiting to pounce like cats on any mouse daring to leave its hole. But he was no mouse, no timid easy prey; this was his ground, his Wheal Kitty; she would keep him safe.

He took a candle from his pack and struck a lucifer. He was hungry and felt in his pack for the crust he had saved there, but water had made it soggy and tasteless; he swallowed it nonetheless. He was soaked to the skin, his uniform draggingly heavy from the damp, his head ached from the intensity of staring into the dark and a shiver convulsed him in spite of the sweltering heat.

He held the candle aloft and looked around. A stranger would think one drive no different from any other, but he recognised this one. A hundred steps or so along there was an incline — a winze — leading upwards to the three hundred level and beyond to an adit coming out to grass well beyond the mine's boundary. Sergeant Greenwood would be unlikely to have posted men there, would not know of it. No working miner would have told him. They knew the man the troops were hunting and had no reason to betray one of theirs.

He moved cautiously along the drive, stopping from time to time in case any men had remained underground, waiting for him to reveal himself. But he heard only the drip of water and the familiar rustlings that never ceased here below. He sheltered the candle flame by a hand and peered about him.

It was here the winze should be, he thought; he could not be mistaken.

He was not mistaken. The winze was there, but a fall of rock had closed the passage. There was no way out there.

He had lost sense of time. He had come down at dawn when the glint of the rising sun on a rifle barrel alerted him to the arrival of the patrol. As he ran to the shaft-head and scurried down the ladder-way he had heard a shout, a view-halloo: the hunt was on. His sympathies had always been with the fox when, on Carn Brea above his village, the red-coated gentry and fat farmers had gathered for the hunt. Now redcoats of a different sort were the hunstmen, but he was as cunning as any fox, knew the bolt-holes as well as any creature of the wild.

Time? It must be night by now, or late evening. If he could find his way to grass he could escape the hunt in the dark. He could find another, more comfortable hole than this, a place where he would be welcomed, fed and given shelter; his sister's place, Trecarrow.

He turned from the rock-fall at the entrance to the winze and retraced his steps. He would find his way to the foot of the shaft and climb the ladder-way until he reached the platform at the two-hundred level. Along there he could reach another adit, a little nearer the main surface workings, but he could evade capture even so. He knew every inch of the ground, the way out of the workings and across country to safety.

He had to move with care as he climbed the ladder-way, for, since the closing of the mine, neglect had rusted it, with staves missing. Once he almost dropped his candle and wished for his old miner's hat so that he could fix the candle to it. He heard a sound above, at the remote head of the shaft, and stopped, ready to hasten back down if the patrol were on the move again. But it was nothing save a spill of stone, falling down, bouncing from side to side. He put his hand to his head to protect it but the rocks passed, descending harmlessly into the shaft's black depths.

He reached the sollar, clambered on to it and paused to get his breath. His chest felt tight. He did not find it as easy as it had once been to climb the ladder-way; the days of running

31

and the dankness of the mine had weakened him. Now, no longer shivering, he was oppressed by the heat. He was tempted to take off his tunic and throw it down the shaft; he might feel better for getting rid of his military trappings. But he kept it on, against the expected cold of the night air above. He detested his uniform and everything that went with it; the automatic response to command, the subordination to men for whom he had no respect, like Rennie, the loss of his own will. 'There's a devil in the man,' Captain Roberts had said of him. They had tried to rid him of it, but it was a devil of pride that could not, would not, be driven out.

He moved from the platform into the drive, holding his candle aloft so that grotesque shapes ran ahead of him. He spoke softly, placatingly to them. They must be spriggans, the spirits that lived in the dark tunnels of the mine.

He was becoming light-headed and tried to harness his wandering thoughts to the task of finding his way out. The spriggans would lead him to safety; he could trust them. He had to trust someone and they were all he had. He spoke to them and they answered him until he recognised the voice as his own, echoing back to him.

They were there, nevertheless; he could feel their presence ahead of him, beckoning him on.

'I'm coming,' he said. 'Wait for me.'

3

Ada Prideaux saw a police sergeant and two constables looking speculatively at the outbuildings as if they intended to search them. And without permission, she thought angrily, going to challenge them. The sergeant seemed amused at her annoyance.

'We're here to look after you,' he said, smiling, knowing it was her brother they were seeking and taking pleasure from what he thought was her discomfiture.

'We can look after ourselves, thank you,' she snapped. They had been children together, she and Matt Penrose. She had thought him good-looking once, but ale and petty authority had coarsened him.

'Your George, 'tes, I do hear. Up to his old tricks, then.'

32

She turned away, saying over her shoulder, 'Tell those men of yours to behave themselves.'

Penrose said something to the constables and their laughter rang in her ears as she went into the house, past the servants' hall and to the drawing room.

Caroline was at the window looking out over the lawns towards the bay. She turned at her housekeeper's voice.

'The police are here, ma'am. I've warned them to keep themselves to themselves,' Mrs Prideaux said, her voice flat and expressionless, though she still felt anger at the police presence, anger at its necessity, resentment at George for giving rise to this disturbance to their lives.

'What is he like?' her mistress said, eyes wide, cheeks flushed.

'Who do you mean?' For a moment she thought Caroline was asking about the police sergeant.

'Your brother. Is he what they say he is?'

'I've not heard what they say about him.' She turned to go but Caroline went quickly on as if it was important for her to see the runaway through his sister's eyes. What interest could a woman such as Caroline have in a man like George?

'Tell me.' her mistress said. 'Is he as dangerous as they say? Have we reason to be afraid? Must we be on our guard against him? Is all that true? Is he really like that, your brother?'

Ada Prideaux looked closely at Caroline, seeing her fear, wanting to reassure her, but unable to do so. 'He does not belong to your world, ma'am,' she said. 'Nor to mine. Not any longer.'

'What will he do? Will he come to you for help, d'you think? And what will you do if he does?' Her voice rose so that Ada wanted to put her arm about her mistress to comfort her. But she said nothing in answer. What could she say? She did not know what she would do. She desperately hoped the question would never arise, hoped George would see the folly of coming to her for help.

'Is that all, ma'am?' she asked.

'No. It is not all. I want your answer. It is a very unpleasant feeling knowing a man like that may be near, may at this very moment be heading this way.'

33

'We have Sergeant Penrose and two constables to see we come to no harm. I'm quite sure there's no need to worry.'

'What will you do?' Caroline insisted.

'I shall do my duty as I see it, ma'am,' she said and, before her mistress could continue questioning her, she left the room. She understood why Caroline was uneasy at the thought of a man like George being on the loose. But it might not be for long. He might well already have been caught. Ada's feelings were in turmoil and she did not like the sensation. She did not want him caught but she did not want him here.

4

Caroline wanted to call her housekeeper back and question her further about her brother. A man of 'brutish instincts" Thomas had called him and she felt a spasm of fear at the thought and, yet, at the same time, she was curious, wished to know more − of him and that other world to which he belonged. What kind of world was it to fashion such a man?

Prideaux had said she would do her duty as she saw it. How did she see it? To obey the law or to follow a sister's instincts and protect her brother, violent though he was? Surely Mrs Prideaux would not give succour to such a man, however close the tie?

By the time Thomas returned from his smelting works at Truro, she had become increasingly uneasy. Thoughts of this man − vicious and dangerous as described by Superintendent Groves − filled her mind to the exclusion of all else, so that when Thomas came to her, she ran to him for protection.

'You mustn't worry that pretty little head of yours,' he said, putting his arm about her and holding her close, so that she nestled her head against his chest. 'There, there,' he said. 'We'll hear no more of this fellow now that the police have set a guard on the house. He'd be stupid to come near. In all probability he's still down the mine and beginning to think of giving himself up, I shouldn't wonder.

They've got him trapped down there, Groves tells me. Men have been posted at the head of every shaft to seize him the moment he shows his face. And if he doesn't come to grass they'll go below again and hunt him down.'

Caroline felt a twinge of pity for the man. 'What will happen to him?'

'The law will take its course. He'll go before a court martial. He can expect little mercy, only justice. The army doesn't treat its offenders lightly. One might almost feel sorry for him when one thinks of what fate has in store for him.'

It was no concern of hers. The man would be caught, sent back to barracks and, though Mrs Prideaux might have cause for sorrow, everyone else would sigh with relief, get back to normal, and she herself would be able to move about the grounds again without fear at every step of meeting this man of "brutish instincts". Thomas's words kept rising in her mind, sending a shudder through her at the image they evoked.

He spoke reassuringly. 'You've no cause for concern. We shall all look after you, never fear.'

It was not only fear that moved her. There was excitement too and she could not understand why.

5

He was light-headed from hunger. For a moment he wondered where he was, imagined he had wakened in his cell in the barracks; then he remembered: this was not Bodmin but Wheal Kitty, but he was not clear why. He crouched by a shaft, Johnson's shaft he believed. He could climb up the ladder-way and reach ground, "come to grass".

There was some reason why he could not do that, but for an instant he could not bring to mind what it was. Then from high above a shout came echoing down, a remote, disembodied voice, booming and fading. 'Prideaux,' it called mockingly. 'We've got you cornered. Come up like a man and face the music.' Something else followed but he could make no sense of it.

They were there, waiting for him, confident he would have

35

to come up in the end. They had had their fill of the drives and winzes of the mine. The dark had terrified them, the closeness of the rock, the sweltering atmosphere. But they could afford to wait.

He was in the dark and was afraid his candle had burnt itself out, until he recalled blowing out the flame when he reached the platform. He could not afford to be extravagant with light for without it he might never find his way out from here.

George Prideaux tried to clear his mind. Tiredness, hunger and the damp sapped his will. He saw the danger. He must keep his wits about him or he would, as Corporal Rennie hoped, rot here as many a good man had. He would not let that happen to him. He knew where he was, within a few yards, could find an adit leading out of here, if he only had energy enough to crawl the ways.

He felt in his pocket for a lucifer. At least he had managed to keep those dry. But he could not find his candle and thought he might have dropped it when he had stumbled along here earlier. He felt about for it and his hands touched the tallow by his side. He sighed with relief. He might still struggle to grass without it but the odds would be against him; with it he felt confident he would reach the open, be safe again. He reckoned there was enough — three inches of candle — to see him through, but he would need to be sparing with it.

Before lighting the candle he crept away from the shaft, then lifted it above his head and peered forward. He knew this drive. Off it were stopes long since worked out and further along a narrow passage driven at a steep angle upwards to an old drive; along there was an adit that came out on the cliff face, well away from the main workings. He had explored that adit as a boy, from the cliff end, to the horror of his sister. She had forbidden him to go near it, but he had defied her, risked his life for the sake of a dare from his friend Caleb Pascoe. Caleb was dead now, killed in a rock fall in this very mine, only days before the mine was closed for good.

His thoughts were wandering again and he saw the danger of it. He must stay alert, make sure he was moving in the right direction. When the lode had been worked out, this part of the mine had been abandoned and waste cluttered the drive and hindered his progress. Water poured down the rock face and lay in pools so that his feet were soaked, even his stout army boots giving little protection.

Then he saw ahead a dark opening at the side of the drive — the winze he had known was there. His memory had not failed him. He sat down for a moment to gather his strength for the climb.

He woke to the realisation that he was in the dark again and this time he was certain he had not blown out his candle. He had fallen asleep — or fainted, he was not sure which — and in doing so must have let the candle fall. He could see nothing. He held his hand in front of his face and brought it close to his eyes, trying to persuade himself that even here, twelve hundred feet below ground, there was light enough to see his fingers move. But it was not so. There was nothing but the feel of them. He put his hand down to search for the candle in the jumble of stone around him. Nothing.

He stretched out his arms and scoured the ground, slowly and methodically at first, and then frantically. He dislodged a stone which set others falling, but there was no danger in that. The danger was that, without light, he would take a turn along a drive or winze that would lead him away, away and away, into the far recesses of the mine. He took a deep breath to calm himself and tried to tell himself he had been in worse situations than this. If he kept his head he could survive. He would survive.

Earlier he had heard the spriggans singing, those elfin creatures that were supposed to watch over miners. He could not hear them now. He was on his own.

He remembered that, before giving way to weariness, he had seen the opening to the winze. He felt along the rock face and found the gap. And again he felt about him in hope of finding his candle but it was no good. He had one lucifer left. He could light it to look for the candle. If he did not find it he would be bereft of light until he reached the outside world or until ... He thought no further, could not think of failure.

37

He struck his last lucifer and, in its weak and flickering light, looked about him and saw the candle at his feet. As he reached for it and picked it up the match died. He searched in his pocket in the hope that another lucifer might have lodged in the lining, but the hope was in vain. Nevertheless he put the now useless candle in his pack. He could not waste it.

In the moment before the match died he had seen the opening to the winze. In spite of the intensity of the dark he was confident his way to safety was clear.

He felt a new surge of energy and a new courage. He groped his way into the passage and slowly, crawling because the space was narrow and the roof low, he made his way forward, his hands and knees scraping against rock, his head bent but hitting jutting stone from time to time. Inch by inch he went, conscious of the rock enclosing him, but recalling how, as a boy of eleven, he had done this same sort of journey as an escapade, not as a desperate venture to escape the law. Painfully he made his progress along a way which, for all he knew, might end at a rock fall. He heard a sound like thunder and felt a moment of panic. Surely not a fall now.

Then he knew the sound. It was not the tumbling of rock but the pounding of waves, the surge of sea against cliffs, a sound he knew and loved, a sound which told him he had reached the adit's opening and was safe.

Corporal Malcolm Rennie turned away from the mine grounds. He needed to escape from these depressing surroundings. He wondered how men could tolerate working so. He had faced danger often in the course of his service, but had never felt so fearful as he had in the search underground for the man Prideaux. He had been glad to get out and was eager now to get a breath of clean air, to free himself of the terror that had clutched at him there in the narrow, rough-driven channels of the mine. They were men of another sort to toil there, the hard-rock men, and hard as rock they must be, with courage to match, he reluctantly admitted.

He had to get away. Guards were posted at every shaft-head, ready to seize Prideaux when he appeared, as appear he must. No man, not even one as stubborn as Prideaux, could stay below for long. He could leave them to their task for a little while.

He walked briskly away towards the sea. He could hear its swell and surge. That was another element for which he had little liking. He had been nourished among mountains and it was the highlands of his native Scotland that he longed to see, the burns tumbling down the braes, the great sweeps of heather on the moors. There was heather here, true, on the scarred hillsides, but it was not enough. He hated Cornwall and the Cornish. He hated Prideaux too, with an intensity that gripped him like a fever; he would see the man brought to justice, come what may.

He reached the cliff top and took a deep breath of the salt air. There was a warmth to it that for a moment put him at ease with his world. He stood listening to the sound of waves breaking against the rocks in the cove below, idly watched the gulls gliding on the eddies, thought of home and forgot for the moment his enmity towards Prideaux.

He stretched his arms and raised his eyes to the sky. Soon it would be dark and he would have to return to the workings to take up watch again at the top of the shaft. Sooner or later Prideaux would come out and he wanted to be there to welcome him. Smiling at the thought he turned to retrace his steps. As he did he caught a movement below him on the cliff and wondered what sort of animal it was.

Then he knew and his heart gave a leap. He stopped himself from shouting aloud in triumph, and waited.

Chapter Five

At the tail end of the year dark came early and that was a part of winter that Caroline Trevarth heartily disliked. Perhaps Maud was right and she would feel less affected if she were to move from this house, surrounded as it was by spreading lawns and woodland, and move to Falmouth; be only a stone's throw from neighbours.

'Have you reminded everyone about the black-out?' she said to Mrs Prideaux. 'We don't want the police or the air-raid wardens coming after us again.'

Mrs Prideaux had gone slowly round the house to check that no chink of light was showing, a simple enough task for her.

Caroline was conscious that her housekeeper was not looking well, but the woman refused to admit to weakness. She had always been the same, and until the last months seemed to have energy enough to cope with the few tasks Caroline left to her. Now even those were beginning to be too much for her.

Caroline hoped the arrival of the family would not put too great a strain on Ada. Maud would make sure she did not do too much and Ada enjoyed the visits of the family almost as much as Caroline herself did. And she too spoilt Joseph. They all did. She wondered what it was about him that brought out such affection in others.

She knew what it was in her case that made him her favourite. Perhaps it was the same for Ada. Perhaps she too remembered, though she had never spoken since of that time.

Caroline sat in her chair with Samson on her lap and let

memory flood her mind. It was all so real to her that, with only the slightest of hints, she could be taken back. The visit of the village policeman the day before, for example, had reminded her of that other policeman. His name escaped her for a moment and then returned, with a picture of him clearly before her. Groves, that was it, and a big, broad-shouldered, bulky man, with great hands, always clenched in fists, his red-face thrust forward threateningly, puffed with authority; a hateful man.

She smiled, the pleasure still with her after all those years, recalling how she had outwitted him. But there had been danger, to her and the whole household. And the danger had brought out the real woman in her, changed her whole life. Only with difficulty now could she remember the emptiness of her life before that time. What a feeble creature she had been, taking fright at every sound, running to Thomas for protection.

Mrs Prideaux appeared at the door to report that the black-out was all in order and that the rooms were ready for the family. Caroline smiled, for she had seen to that herself, knowing how uncertain Ada's memory was these days.

'It can't be long now,' Mrs Prideaux said. 'I keep imagining I hear them.'

'It's not till tomorrow, Ada, you know that,' Caroline said, but her imagination too was playing tricks, hearing another voice in another time, a voice that brought a smile to her lips and warmth to her cheeks.

Chapter Six

1

George Prideaux scrambled on to the ledge outside the adit and looked down to the white-frothed angry sea lashing against the cliffs. Spray reached him where he lay exhausted, taking great gulps of air. He had surely not been as frightened as this when, as a boy, he had climbed the cliff and explored the adit. Yet he was safer here than hiding in the mine. He could have mouldered there had his memory of the drives not held firm.

He clung to the cliffside, lifting his eyes from the waves, looking up to see what path to take to the top. There were footholds and handholds in plenty, wiry bushes growing from the rock, leading to safety.

He wanted to shout for joy at his escape. He had found his fox-hole and eluded the huntsmen. Once he reached the top he knew where to hide, could find his secret way to Trecarrow and his sister. They would not catch him now.

He found his pack an encumbrance and loosed his arms from it and let it fall. He turned his head to follow its descent. It caught for a second in a cleft and then the rising sea snatched it forth and swept it down, to be lost in spume.

The sky was darkening and he knew he must reach the cliff top while the path was still visible. When he got to the top he would lie low until night was well advanced. There would be no moon, as he remembered; he would have the dark as a friend and protector now.

He climbed slowly, carefully, upwards, aware that a slip

might see him following his pack to the wild sea; but there was no real difficulty about the climb, only the fear of falling that clutched his heart every time he shifted foot or hand.

Within a few inches of the top he paused to get his breath. Something above had moved, alerting him to a danger other than the waves below. He stopped, stock still, pressed against the cliff, listening, but hearing nothing save the restless sough of the swelling sea. Yet a sixth sense had warned him of someone's presence and, in the moment's quiet, he heard a slow exhalation, as of someone catching his breath, someone waiting at the cliff top, watching.

He could not climb back down. There was no escape there. He had barely enough energy to reach the last inches to the top. The wind clutched at him and his aching hands began to lose strength. He had to move. Slowly he raised himself a few inches and a few more and, as he lifted his head above the edge, he saw a large threatening shape swinging a brutal kick at him. He twisted aside to avoid the attack and managed to keep his hold and scramble up to the grass as another kick was aimed. This time he was ready and threw up a hand to ward it off, turning himself away to get to his feet and face his attacker, but the man, unbalanced by the impetus of his own assault, stumbled, and, as George helplessly watched, fell spinning from the cliff top, clutching and calling as he went.

George Prideaux cautiously went to the edge to look down to see Rennie, for it was he, he knew. But he saw nothing, nothing save the sea's fingers clawing, curling, sinking back, rising again, and falling, dragging away living or dead, whatever came its way.

He could walk no further. Fear and hatred had exhausted him so that he knew he had no hope of getting to Trecarrow that night. He had to find shelter close at hand and gather strength and courage before he went so far. He glanced down again and watched as the waves reached their peak, slackened and retreated, sweeping rocks and shore clean.

2

Something had wakened him. He sat up, startled. But the sound which had alarmed him was nothing more than the pecking of a jackdaw at the slates in the roof of the hut. He was confused. He had been dreaming of the days long since when, as a boy, he had clambered down these cliffs seeking gull's eggs. Then memory returned, vivid and terrifying.

He was a boy no longer, but a man on the run, cowering in the shelter of a ruined hut, frightened by the mere sound of a bird.

He got awkwardly to his feet and stretched. He had been lying curled in a corner of the hut, trying, without much success, to get shelter from the wind and rain of the last night. His right arm was stiff, the wrist swollen; he must have wrenched it somehow in crawling along the mine adit or in his climb up the cliff face.

He remembered then the man who had been waiting for him at the cliff top − Rennie − remembered his fall to a certain death. No man could survive that sea. His body would be swept into the depths − and good riddance.

George Prideaux stood in the shadow and peered out of the hut over the heather that purpled the downs. The rain had ceased; the sky was a bright crisp blue, the air keen and sparkling. It was good to be alive. A rabbit scampered at the sight of him, scurrying to its hole, a magpie dipped into the wind and found a perch on a stunted, wind-shaped tree. He could hear, not far away, breakers rolling in to shore.

It was good to be alive. He was hungry and cold, his clothes sodden with damp, but he was alive, and free; free of Rennie and free of the army. He had eluded them and now he would escape them for good. His sister Ada would see to that. She had written to tell him of her place at Trecarrow. There would be a place for him there too; she would shelter him, give him food and new clothing, and money for his passage to America or Australia, anywhere away from here.

Voices came to him from a distance, men's voices. He could not tell what they were saying but they were locals, fishermen maybe, in the cove below the cliff. They held danger for him and he cowered back into the hut.

He wondered if he should stay hidden until nightfall, but knew he could not bear that; he had eaten nothing substantial for a couple of days and was faint with hunger. He doubted if he could go another twelve hours without something to eat.

44

He would have to break cover for a while, find something.

He knew this part of the coast from his childhood. Inland a mile or so, a narrow lane twisted its way past a huddle of cottages and, a little way beyond, through a farmyard. There would be dogs there and he must be wary but, in the fields, there would be turnips growing or hens running free, with the chance of an egg or two. At the thought his hunger sharpened and he knew, whatever the risk, he had to find food. He could not wait till dark.

He left the shelter of the hut and stood for a moment, alive to danger. The men were still below in the cove. He could hear them calling to each other, but up here there was no one, merely a long expanse of heather and, silhouetted against the sky to the east, the outline of an engine house, gaunt and majestic, a noble ruin.

Out of the shadow of the hut the sun struck warmly so that he was tempted to stretch himself out, lie on the ground and let the heat dry him. Such luxury was not for him. He ran across the downs, conscious that the tufts of heather hid holes — for rabbits or old men's workings. He sprang light-footedly to where a hedge — a Cornish wall, thick with foxglove and pennyroyal and thorn and gorse — divided the old mine workings from rough grassland. It led down the slope, he recalled, to the lane. Keeping his body bent he moved along under the hedge, feet stumbling at times in the coarse grass. A flight of finches rose, alarmed. Brambles caught and snagged his clothing. Blossom gave promise of rich fruit later but there were no berries to pick now.

He heard voices and crouched motionless behind the hedge. On the other side, in the lane, women passed, talking, slowly, comfortably, reminding him of his boyhood and those years when he had lived and worked here, before he had yielded to folly and joined the army. The voices moved away up the lane and he found himself wishing he could have joined the women in their morning gossip.

When he thought it safe he moved along the hedge until he found a gap, with a rusting iron bedhead serving as a gate. He stopped to listen. He could hear nothing, neither bird, nor beast, nor man nor woman. He climbed over into the lane. To his right the road rose steeply toward the farm.

To his left stood a row of three cottages; whitewashed walls with small deeply-set windows, thatched roofs, smoke drifting from the chimneys.

Here there would be dogs for sure. If he was to get into one of the cottages to steal food he would need to move quickly – in and out in a flash. For a moment he thought of going openly to a door and begging for something to eat but rejected the notion.

He crossed the lane and walked to the end of the row and back again. No sound came to disturb the rural quiet, not even the warning bark of dog. The creatures must be with their masters in the fields. The women he had heard must have left their houses to go up along to the general store he remembered at the top of the hill. They would have left their doors unsecured; in these backwaters you did not suspect your fellows of theft.

He tried the first door and it opened. Ready at a word to take flight he waited for a challenge. None came. He stepped in and stood, still expecting to be asked to explain his intrusion. But the cottage was empty, or seemed so. He walked towards the rear of the house, past the foot of the stairs. A voice above made him halt and hold his breath.

'Is that you, Amy?' The voice was a man's, thin, sick, quavering.

George Prideaux did not move.

'Are you there?' The tone was querulous as words gave way to disgruntled mumbling.

Prideaux stepped with infinite care past the stairway to the kitchen and saw a white-scrubbed table, on it a jug of milk. He could not resist and drank, savouring the rich warm taste of it. This morning's milking. By the oven was a fresh baking of bread with a heady aroma of yeast, making his mouth water. He reached out a hand to take one of the loaves when he heard footsteps shuffling on the floor above, and the voice again: 'Is that you, Amy?' George snatched the loaf and ran to the front door, across the lane, over the gate and into the field, but not before he had heard the voice call, 'I know it's you. I know it's you.'

He ran, bent double, along the hedge until he was well away from the hamlet. Then, his back against the hedge, he sat in the warmth of the sun and ate the freshly baked bread. He could not remember ever enjoying bread so. He knew he should save some of it for later but he ate every crumb and, the loaf finished, lay back, savouring the aftertaste, refreshed in body and in spirit, confident now he would reach Trecarrow and Ada and find safety there.

3

Superintendent Groves was a large, powerfully built man, threatening, by his manner and the assertion of his authority, the quiet of the household. Caroline had always disliked him. Now she felt an unwarranted fear. He was there to protect them, but she could feel no security in his presence, nor in that of the men posted to watch the house and grounds.

'There has been a further development,' Groves said, looking in her direction as if unwilling to mention it in her presence. She saw no reason for moving and remained seated.

'A development?' her husband said. 'In the matter of the fellow Prideaux, I suppose?'

'Yes. Altogether unpleasant, but perhaps to be expected from such a quarter.' He looked over to Caroline, his eyes speculating on her reaction, ready to take pleasure, she thought, from any shock she showed. 'I told you the man was violent and dangerous. But, don't worry, ma'am, we'll see you come to no harm.'

She tried to seem indifferent, but she could not help but be apprehensive.

'What has he done now?' Thomas asked.

'A body has been found in Butcher's Cove. A soldier beaten about the head and thrown into the sea. Prideaux's doing, without a doubt. It was Corporal Rennie, the one Prideaux assaulted before. Perhaps Rennie surprised or challenged him. Now Prideaux is wanted for more than just assault. It's murder, brutal murder.'

Thomas moved quickly to his wife and put his arm on her shoulder to show his concern. 'The sooner he's caught, the better for us all,' he said. 'I hope your men will remain here until the fellow's taken. Though I can't believe he would be

47

foolish enough to come here. He must know you're watching his sister.'

'I'd like to speak with her,' Groves said. 'In your presence, if you don't mind. She must be persuaded to help us catch him.'

Mrs Prideaux came at Caroline's ring. She looked from Groves to her mistress and back again to the policeman.

'Have you heard anything from your brother?' Groves demanded.

'Is it likely?' she replied.

'He has no one else to ask for help.'

She did not respond and Groves went on, 'You'd do well to consider that he's no longer a boy. He's a man, and a dangerous one at that.' His eyes narrowed as he watched the housekeeper. 'It's murder now, you know.'

'Murder!' she exclaimed.

''tes true, there's blood on his hands now. A brutal and vicious murder, what's more, so brother or not, there's no excuse for you to protect him. It's a hanging matter.' He smiled, as if enjoying telling her the news.

'Mrs Prideaux,' Caroline's husband intervened, 'I'm sorry it has come to this, but we know you will want to help the police bring him to justice. If he tries to get in touch with you, you must let me or your mistress know — or Mr Groves, of course. You do see that?'

The housekeeper's calm had been shaken but she regained control of herself and faced them impassively.

'Well?' said Groves.

'I know my duty. I shall not hesitate to do it.'

'I did not think you would do otherwise,' Thomas said.

'Can she be trusted?' Groves asked when she had gone. 'Does she mean what she says?' He turned to Caroline to answer.

'She means what she says,' Caroline stated. 'I've never known her break her word or even change her mind, once she's committed herself.'

'Nevertheless I'll have my men keep a careful watch on her, and on the house. If you see anything, hear anything, have any reason to suppose the man is around, warn us immediately. One of my officers will always be within call

48

till we take him or until we know for sure he's left the area. I regret bringing such commotion into your home. We shall spare you as much as we can.'

'God grant it will be over soon,' Thomas said.

'I dislike that man,' Caroline said to her husband when he returned from reviewing with Groves the arrangements for the watch on the house. 'He's pleased he has a murderer to bring to book, glad he has a real crime to deal with. If I had not been here he would have revealed all the gory details and taken pleasure in the tale.'

'I'm glad he spared you. It was a horrible crime.'

'You see. He did tell you, *had* to tell someone. He delights in violence.'

'I can see you're upset. I don't blame you. It's not pleasant knowing a servant of ours is sister to a murderer. I wonder if we ought not to think of asking her to go?'

Caroline looked at him in disbelief. She did not see how she could do without Ada Prideaux. They had grown used to each other, got on well enough, and, in a way, understood each other, even had a certain intimacy as far as that was possible between servant and mistress. 'It would be dreadfully unfair,' she said. 'She has done nothing.'

'I was thinking only of you,' Thomas said, and smiled. 'I'm concerned only with your safety, nothing else. And, with the men Groves has posted, none of us is in any danger. The fellow will be taken soon enough. You can sleep safe tonight and every night, I'm sure.'

4

The elegant chimney stack of Killifreth stood out starkly against the setting sun, filling his soul with wonder at the skill of the Cornish masons and engineers. This was his world, he thought, that of tin and copper and the search for it, the craft he had been taught as a boy but which he had betrayed when he shouldered a rifle and surrendered his will to that of others. Corporal Rennie belonged to that latter world. Joe Beskeen and his like to this.

He wondered for a brief moment if he should have thrown himself again on the mercy of his old comrade, but he knew that would have been to ask too much of friendship. It was to his sister he must look for help now. He could leave his hiding place with the dark and find his way across country to her.

Trecarrow — he did not know the house, knew in fact little of that part of Cornwall, but he had to head south, that he knew, make for the estuary of the Fal. Ada had described the house in one of her letters, when she had found employment there. And she had written of her mistress, in terms that surprised him. "Mrs Trevarth is so delicate and tender a creature, she sems almost too good for this world. I love her dearly." He smiled at the recollection: it was the Ada he had known, when he was a boy, loving and protective, but it was not the Ada most people saw.

He could be certain of her help. She would give him food and a change of clothing and shelter him until he could find his way to the coast to take ship.

The watch for him on Wheal Kitty would be there still, waiting for him to come to grass. He laughed aloud at the thought but the laugh turned to a cough that racked his chest with pain. And hunger tore at his belly so that he regretted he had not saved some of the bread he had stolen.

In the west the sun had finally set and the mine buildings, of Wheal Busy and Killifreth, were almost lost in the surrounding dark. It was time to move, as safe now as it was likely to be. He could crouch here no longer like an animal, hunted and afraid. Hunted he was but not afraid, he told himself.

Not to feel fear was dangerous, for fear made one alert, kept the senses keen. He must not let hunger and weariness weaken that instinct to survive which had been his salvation so far. He had enemies still, even though Rennie had gone.

He climbed to the top of the wall which had given him shelter and stood there listening but heard only the common noises of the night, an owl, the bark of a distant fox, and somewhere along the lane the whistle of a man summoning his dog to heel. George jumped down from the hedge and walked in the opposite direction. Even if he were seen he would not be recognised in the dark. People here might be curious about the presence of a stranger, but he did not suppose they would be concerned about him, a mere army deserter. Those were not so unusual.

50

He turned east and then south. He was not sure how far away Trecarrow might be, maybe two or three hours' walk. He was glad to have a purpose, to know that before long he would be with Ada, glad to think he could leave his problem to her for the night at least. She had always been there when he needed her, when he got into trouble, scolding him maybe but wrapping him up warmly and feeding him and putting him to bed. His mind took refuge in thinking himself a young boy once more, dependent on his sister for everything, love, comfort and security.

He stumbled and was brought back to the present. The lane wound narrowly between high hedges of blackthorn and bramble, the overhanging branches clutching at him as he passed. It was so quiet he thought the whole world would hear him. Ahead a glimmer of light showed him a wider road and not far along it an inn. He was briefly tempted to venture into its warmth and companionship but crept past; it was no place for him, however welcoming the sounds coming from the open door, a song, a shout, a loud guffaw.

Around the inn lay a straggle of cottages. He walked on. A dog barked but no one paid any attention. As he left the village dark enclosed him again and once again his mind wandered so that he lost account of time.

He became aware that the blackthorn hedge had given way to a high stone wall, the boundary of some estate. Trecarrow would it be, his goal, his refuge? He hardly dared to hope. He followed the wall, supposing that if he walked its length he would come at last to an entrance to the grounds.

Caution made him pause; fear had returned and with it the knowledge that his connection with Ada must be known. The police — if they were interested enough in an army deserter to be concerned — would expect him to turn to her for help, might be waiting for him to step into a trap. Yet he had to get to her, for she was his only hope.

His mind filled with the problem, he walked slowly along the estate wall. When he came to a narrow wooden door he stopped, stood still, ears pricked for a sound on the other side. All was silent.

There was a metal latch to the door. He lifted it and the door gave inwards. He waited, senses now alert, nerves ready

51

to stir him to flight at the first alarm. There was nothing to warn him of danger so he stepped through the door on to a narrow path running beside the wall and followed it as it turned into the grounds, under a grove of trees and out on to grass. He could feel and smell lush pasture.

His eyes were attuned to the dark and beyond the field of pasture he could see a large building set on higher ground, a more imposing house than he had imagined from Ada's letter. Perhaps he had stumbled on another country mansion. He climbed over a fence from the pasture and circled the place warily and came to the front of the house, with a pillared portico, just as Ada had described it. This was Trecarrow he was sure and here he would find somewhere to hide until he could make contact with his sister. He moved slowly, with infinite caution to the rear of the house, over a cobbled courtyard, where a cluster of outbuildings straggled, darkly shadowed, and saw a man, uniformed and helmeted, standing in the light issuing from a door into the house.

George Prideaux drew back. The police were here as he had half expected. But he was not beaten yet. The man's attention was elsewhere, on the young woman handing him a mug of steaming liquid.

Prideaux crept along the wall, in the deepest of the shadow, until he came to a door and smelt the warm sweet smell of horses and heard the shifting of their hooves. The stables would give him cover. He could hide there, confident in the knowledge that he was within reach of Ada, who had never failed him in the past and would not fail him now.

5

Caroline tried to ignore the movement of police through the gardens and turned away to watch her cat cross the room. It could not be long before Claudia had her kittens. Perhaps this time she could be persuaded to have them in the house and not in secret somewhere in the stables.

'I shall watch you,' Caroline said to her. She always had beautiful kittens but what happened to them Caroline never knew. She presumed they were taken by the estate workers or found good homes elsewhere.

It became impossible to ignore the presence of the police for she could hear Superintendent Groves's voice raised in argument with the housekeeper. There was a knock at the door and Mrs Prideaux came in, her face white, dark eyes for once revealing emotion. 'It's the police, ma'am. They insist on searching the house.'

Caroline caught her breath in alarm. 'They've seen him? He's here?' She looked about her as if for a way of escape.

Groves came from behind Mrs Prideaux into the room, his burly presence as always holding a threat. His face was red with indignation. He was not used to being thwarted and it seemed the housekeeper was unwilling to let him pass.

'Have they seen him?' Caroline whispered.

'There's been a sighting of the man certainly,' Groves announced. 'Over to Perranwell last night, slinking along the side roads, making his way here likely as not.' He glared at Mrs Prideaux then turned to Caroline. 'Your husband promised every co-operation.'

'Of course.' But the idea of heavy-footed policemen tramping about the house offended her.

'We must catch him before he kills someone else,' Groves said. There was a relish in his voice, as if he were thinking, "just let him try".

Caroline, eyes wide with alarm, looked from Mrs Prideaux to Groves. 'Yes, yes, of course. I do see. But tell your men to be careful. Let them go where they want, Mrs Prideaux. He must be found. You see that?' She recoiled at the idea of these clumsy men bustling about the house but how much more horrid it was to think of that man, hands stained with the blood of his victim, hiding somewhere within reach. 'Do you think he could be in the house?' she asked and sat down, appalled at the thought.

Groves shook his head. 'No. I don't think so, but we need to be sure. Your husband expects us to do all we can to protect you. You'll tell your household to give us every assistance?' He looked pointedly at Mrs Prideaux.

'Show them whatever they need to see, Mrs Prideaux.'

The houskeeper frowned as she led the superintendent from the room. Caroline heard Groves instructing his men on their

53

duties, followed by the sound of their footsteps moving about the house, on the stairs and the floors above. She could not reconcile herself to the intrusion, needful though it was, and left the house to go into the gardens. She walked round to the rear of the house and was glad to see there were no policemen there though she assumed they would take up their guard again when they had finished searching the house. She supposed they had already made search of the outbuildings.

She prayed they would find Prideaux, but elsewhere. She wanted him caught — so dangerous a man should be locked away — but she did not want her house sullied by his capture here.

Earlier, thinking of the danger the man represented, she had been excited, but now it had come too close to home and she was afraid. She had told herself she wanted to know something of him, but in truth that was madness. He belonged to another, different world, a violent, destructive world; hers was a settled and secure place where order ruled, where all turned out as expected, where no unpleasant surprises interfered with routine.

She saw Claudia, her dear plump little tortoise-shell cat, crossing the cobbled yard towards the stables and was about to follow her to see where she was going, perhaps to have her kittens, when she heard Groves at the rear entrance. Again his voice was raised, blustering angrily. When he saw Caroline he came over to her. 'I am not getting the co-operation I should,' he complained. 'I can make things very uncomfortable if I so choose.'

Caroline controlled her resentment at his manner. She must try to placate him. It was true he could make things unpleasant and Thomas would not like it if they obstructed Groves in any way. And the man Prideaux must be caught.

'What is it?' she asked. 'I'm sure we can clear up any misunderstanding.'

'I'm wondering if your housekeeper has something to hide. Maybe it's her brother.'

Mrs Prideaux, standing in the shadow behind the superintendent, protested, 'They're behaving like animals, ma'am, going wherever they want as they think fit, turning things

54

over without a care of how things were. It will take days to put everything in order again.' She was quivering with indignation, rising in defence it seemed, not of her brother, but of her domestic arrangements.

'I understand,' Caroline said, 'but the easier we make it for them, the sooner they'll be gone.' She went into the house, through the domestic quarters to her drawing room. Perhaps she would be free of them all there, but she could still hear footsteps and voices as the police moved along the corridors, opening closets, calling to each other.

They found nothing but when he reported the fact Groves seemed pleased with himself. He had succeeded in humiliating Mrs Prideaux. 'We'll keep a sharp eye on the house and grounds,' he said, and with a significant look towards the housekeeper he added, 'and on your staff. We'll get him sooner or later, either here or elsewhere. You can sleep safely in your bed, Mrs Trevarth ma'am, knowing we're on the look-out. He won't slip through our fingers, I assure you.'

She was relieved when the house became quiet again. She wanted to ask Mrs Prideaux about her brother but the housekeeper was not in the sort of mood to respond to questions, angry as she still was at her confrontation with Groves and the disturbance to the household. How could she be concerned with that when her brother was the object of a hue and cry? Where was he, if he was not in the house or grounds?

Ada Prideaux was not given to shows of anger. She had long learned to control her feelings, but it went against the grain for her to take orders from Superintendent Groves. She followed his men about the house, watching their every move, ready to note and report anything they did which was beyond the call of duty. Mr Trevarth would not condone any abuse of authority, however close his friendship with the superintendent.

At the end, she had no real cause for complaint. The man's manner was offensive, but he had kept a tight hold on his officers. And, she supposed, their search was justified. Her brother might come here. She hoped not, prayed he would look elsewhere for help. She had none to give him, wanted nothing of him now. He had forfeited her respect once and for all.

She could not bear the thought of his coming to Trecarrow for sanctuary. Her mistress was terrified enough at the mere idea of his being in the neighbourhood. Ada Prideaux could not have her threatened further. She must go and assure her that she cared nothing for George, would even yield him up to the police if he arrived on their doorstep, rather than have Caroline upset.

She went to find her. The drawing room door was open and Caroline was standing gazing out of the window. Ada stood unnoticed, quietly observing her mistress. There was something insubstantial about her, as if a puff of wind might blow her away. She was a delicate thing, fragile and lovely. It was understandable that Mr Trevarth should treat her with care, shielding her from the world. And Ada, for her part, would do the same, as long as she was privileged to serve her.

The marriage had not been blessed with children and Ada Prideaux was not surprised. Caroline was surely not robust enough for child-bearing. It was a pity nevertheless, for she would have made a good mother and Ada would have liked to share in the joy a child might bring.

She remembered, with a sudden feeling of guilt, the pleasure she had got from George when he was a child and she had had the responsibility of bringing him up. She tried to dismiss it from her mind but it would not go. She could not forget how full of charm he had been, his quick intelligence, his lively smile. What had happened to change him to the point where he was now accused of murder?

'What is it?' Her mistress had seen her and turned anxiously.

'Nothing, ma'am. I hoped you were not upset. I'm sure we shall come to no harm. I don't like having the police about the place, but it's for our own good.'

Her mistress seemed surprised. 'Your brother? Aren't you concerned for him?'

'He won't come here, ma'am. And if he does, I know my duty.' She wondered, for a moment, if she was so sure she would give him up to the police. Yet, what else could she do, if his presence threatened her mistress's safety and happiness?

6

The small semi-circular window of the stable-loft looked out to the cobbled yard and the kitchen court. George Prideaux watched from it as the household went about their tasks. He saw a garden lad bringing vegetables to the house, and caught a glimpse of a kitchen maid at the door taking them. There was a moment's passage of arms between the two which ended with a playful slap across the boy's face. The young people hurried to their tasks when a woman appeared. It was his sister. She had not changed, still the stern-faced, rigid-backed martinet in appearance; still, he hoped, the woman who had loved and cherished him. She looked about her anxiously and he wished he could do something to reassure her, but he dare not reveal his presence for only a few yards away a police constable stood, sharp-eyed watchful.

He had been prepared for the police when they searched the stables, had feared discovery when one of them climbed the ladder to peer into the little room. He had hidden behind a pile of straw and a clutter of old harness, holding his breath, while the policeman, from the top of the ladder and without climbing into the loft, gave a cursory glance around and then, satisfied, called to his companions that the place was clear and departed down the ladder again.

George waited, thinking the man might be setting a trap, but he heard him and his companions moving off and breathed relief.

They would be back. The man below in the yard was proof of that. They would be suspicious of Ada.

He watched his sister go back into the house. He must let her know somehow that he was here. He needed her help, to give him food, find him new clothes. He felt unclean, wanted to rid himself of his uniform and his past, to wash away that and the dust of the mine. He wondered if anyone ever came up here; a stable boy might, he supposed, but he dare trust no one save his sister.

From his spyhole he had watched movement in the yard

since morning: a horse led out for the master of the house, a groom brushng the yard, a scullery maid emptying kitchen waste into a bin, normal domestic activities until the police posse arrived. They had gone methodically from shed to shed, from one outbuilding to another before moving into the house. They had missed him on their first search. They would not be so casual the next time. He was cornered.

He saw a woman – not a servant, that was obvious from her bearing – come from the front of the house. He studied her, as she lingered for a moment below him. She was tall and slender, with fair hair hanging loose about her shoulders. From his high vantage point he could not see her face clearly but she glanced up and, before he drew away from the window, he caught a glimpse of a pale face, high cheek-bones, well-spaced eyes. He crept near to the window again and raised his head slowly to look out, afraid she might have seen him, but she had not; she was still standing on the cobbles, gazing about her, interested in a heavily pregnant cat which was walking across the yard towards the stable block. She seemed about to follow the creature when a policeman came from the house towards her.

Prideaux drew back, not daring to stay near the window to look out. He heard voices but could make no sense of them. Then silence fell and he cautiously peered out again. The woman had gone, and the policeman. He relaxed.

A sound came from behind him at the top of the ladder and he turned sharply, ready to defend himself or take flight, but it was only the cat he had seen in the yard below. She struggled up the ladder, peered over at him, clawed her way up, gave a little mew, and settled down into the corner of the loft in the straw which had hidden him earlier.

'Hello,' he whispered. 'Welcome.' He put his hand out to touch her and she began to purr.

Chapter Seven

Up-country, snow had brought chaos, with tales on the wireless of railway passengers stranded in unheated carriages, of doctors unable to get to patients in isolated farmhouses. Here there had been rain to add to the miseries of the black-out, but no blizzards, nothing but a long spell of wet weather and chill winds. Here there was still plenty of wood from the estate to heat the few rooms they used.

Caroline Trevarth got slowly up from her chair and went to make sure that the bedrooms set apart for the family were warm, the beds aired in readiness. A visit from Maud and her children was always something to look forward to, however much work it brought, and this Christmas might well be the last in Trecarrow, for she could not hope to keep the house going much longer. Maybe too, she supposed, it might be the last Christmas for her, for she had passed well beyond the normal span of three score years and ten.

She heard a car in the drive and the laughter of young voices. Her heart leapt at the sound. Maud had hesitated to bring the family this year, thinking it might be too much for her mother, but Caroline had been so upset at the thought of not seeing the children that her daughter had given way.

'Mother,' Maud said as she came through the door. 'What are you doing? Give those to me.'

Caroline handed the hot water bottles to her daughter. 'I'm quite capable,' she protested.

Maud ignored her mother's protests. 'Go and say hello to the children,' she said in a voice that brooked no argument.

Caroline smiled. It was good for once to have someone take responsibility.

The young voices had ceased. Sarah and Simon would have gone down to the river, as they always did first when they came to Trecarrow. But Joseph would come to see her. She waited for him in the hall, listening for his footsteps on the tiled porch, longing to hear that warm deep voice, to feel his arms about her and his lips upon her cheek.

She closed her eyes. She had been seeing, not Joseph, but another, a vision so sharp and fresh and real that she turned, expecting to see him standing there, holding his arms out to her. But it was Joseph, Joseph coming towards her.

'Grandmama,' he said and bent to kiss her. She held him from her to examine him. He had grown another inch in height since last summer and he had filled out. His dark eyes and curling lips reminded her of someone and as he spoke the vision returned. She tried to shut her mind and memory to it but it would not go. She closed her eyes, listening to him, and imagined so easily that time had slipped away.

Other voices broke into her reverie. Simon and Sarah had come into the house. 'Grandmama, let Joseph go,' Sarah said. 'Come and say hello to us.' The twins knew her fondness for Joseph and did not seem to mind. They indulged him too; he exercised his charm even over his own brother and sister. But it was not just his charm that made him Caroline's favourite, or only part of it; it was his dark look, his quick smile, his soft voice, echo of another's.

'Are you all right, Grandmama?' she heard Sarah say.

'Why?' she asked.

'You looked miles away.'

Not miles away, but years. Caroline put a hand up to her cheek. For a moment she had felt young again. Now she was aware of the wrinkles that furrowed her face. She had been proud of her smooth roses-and-cream complexion then.

'I'm just a silly old woman,' she said.

Joseph laughed and again she caught her breath at the memory it called up. 'There's nothing silly about you,' he said. 'And nothing old either. You're beautiful and I love you.'

'Get on with you,' she said, dismissing the flattery, but she was pleased. Does he mean it? she wondered. She had wondered that then.

The black-out had to be in place by half-past four to be safe. Caroline could not understand the fuss. No one could possibly be interested in bombing Trecarrow, she argued.

'You'll have the air-raid wardens after you,' her daughter said.

'We've had them already, Maud,' she told them. 'Anyone would think we were German spies. Can you imagine? Poor Mrs Prideaux took it quite to heart. She thought they'd come to arrest her, poor old thing.'

'Poor old thing indeed! She's a couple of years younger than you,' Maud reminded her, laughing.

'Which makes her eighty-four and every right to be talked of as a poor old thing.'

'And you?' said Maud.

'Prideaux has always been old. I've stayed young.' And it was true; she was still young at heart, had the passions of youth, felt love and longing as strongly now as then.

'Where's Joseph?' she asked.

'I expect he's gone to see Prideaux,' Maud said. 'He always likes to gossip with her. He's fond of her.'

'And she of him,' said Caroline. But she thought Joseph had probably gone to see the young maid Rachel. Earlier she had caught a glimpse of them together, Joseph with his arm round the girl, bending down to whisper in her ear. She hoped the girl would be sensible and not allow herself to be swept off her feet by his sweet talk. She must have a word with him.

'Is there any news of his call-up?' she asked, dreading the answer.

'He'll finish his year at college and then go,' Maud said. 'I wonder what sort of soldier he will make?'

Caroline wondered too. There was a wild streak in him. He did not often show it but she recognised the signs. She could not imagine his taking kindly to the discipline of training.

61

'I expect he'll find his niche,' she said but she feared for him.

He came in, a secret smile on his face, his cheeks slightly flushed, his eyes sparkling. Poor Rachel, Caroline thought.

Chapter Eight

1

There was a drowsy hum of insects in the rose bed. Bees were busy in the lavender hedge and the walls of the house still held the sun's warmth. Caroline hoped nothing would happen to disturb the peace and comfort of the day, hoped the man Prideaux was miles away, disturbing someone else's routine, rather than hers.

Superintendent Groves came in to report that he had detailed men to patrol the outside of the house from time to time. 'He's not here, ma'am,' he told her. 'We've been over every inch of the house and stables and every outbuilding. There's no sign of him now, but I reckon he's not far away. He'll look to that sister of his for help. Where else can he turn? We'll catch up with him. I've had posters with his description printed and pasted about the whole district. Everyone will be on the look out for him, every man's hand against him now he's known to be a murderer.'

'I hope it won't be long before you take him if he's as dangerous as you say.' How dreadful to think the man might be lurking near the house at this very moment. There were times when she felt sick at the thought and she had even found herself looking at Mrs Prideaux with a feeling not far from fear.

Groves turned to go but added, 'You will need to be careful, Mrs Trevarth. He's a desperate man. I don't suppose he'll get through our cordon, but ...' He left the idea hanging in the air to worry her so that in every sound she heard the approach of George Prideaux, murderer. When she heard footsteps at the door of the drawing room she drew in her breath in fear. It opened to show her husband and she threw herself into his arms in thankfulness.

'It frightens me so,' she said, 'thinking he might be somewhere in the grounds, waiting for a chance to slip into the house to see his sister.'

'Perhaps it would be sensible for you to go to visit some friend until they catch him,' Thomas said, but Caroline, anxious though she was, would not admit to such weakness. 'I want to stay here,' she said. 'I shall feel safer with you.'

'Then I shall not leave you until we're satisfied the danger is past. I'll conduct my business from home, have my agents come here to see me. I'll protect you, my precious. I'll see nothing happens to you.'

He had acquired a new piece of Dresden, a pretty shepherdess. 'It reminds me of you,' he said, as he placed it in the cabinet with the other figures. He stood back to admire it, and then carefully closed and locked the cabinet door. He would lock her up in the same way if he could, she thought, to keep her safe and sound, and wondered why she should feel ungrateful for such concern. 'My precious,' he had called her as if she too were a piece of porcelain, valued for her fragility, a thing of beauty to be admired but not to be endangered by use.

Before nightfall, as the heat of the day changed to the soft warmth of twilight, she went to the rear of the house in the hope of seing Claudia. She had not seen her since morning, when the cat seemed to be making its way to the stables. She must have found the hidey-hole where she could have her kittens in private. Caroline thought of going into the stables to look but she could hear the horses restless in their stalls. She was slightly afraid of the creatures, since an accident riding some two years back. They were such large and powerful animals. She decided to wait till the morning when they would be out of their stalls and running in the meadow.

She turned to go round to the front of the house and saw Mrs Prideaux standing at the door leading to her own quarters. She was looking out, almost as if expecting someone, but when she saw her mistress she went inside and closed the door.

A dark figure emerged from the shadows and Caroline started until she recognised one of the constables who had earlier been with the police posse.

'All right, ma'am?' he said and touched his helmet in salute.

'All right,' she answered, using the local greeting.

2

The cat did not seem to mind his presence, showed no fear of him. She had made a bed for herself in the straw and, washing herself carefully, turned around several times then settled down, purring as if content to have him near. As the light from the little window faded he was aware of her only from the rustling in her bed and the low murmur of her purr.

He sat by the window looking out on to the yard and, as his eyes adjusted to the dark, watched the movements of the policeman set to patrol the rear of the house; once his sister came from the house and stood for a moment before going back inside; and briefly there appeared the tall slender pale woman he had seen earlier. She would be the mistress Ada had mentioned when she first took service there; she had described her as a 'sweet young thing, but delicate'. There was about the woman, as she stood below, that indefinable manner deriving from generations of privilege, from wealth bequeathed not earned. A flash of resentment rose at the notion, but he dismissed it: it was of no interest to him what her manner signified; his thoughts were dominated by the need for food, and for help to get away. The woman had nothing to offer of that. It was Ada and Ada alone he had to rely on.

Somehow he must get in touch with her. How, he could not yet see, but the opportunity would arise and he must be alert to take advantage of it. In the dead of night, he would find a way of letting her know where he was hiding. He would stay awake till then.

But he slept, only waking when there was a stirring in the straw in the corner and the cat emerged from it. The pale light of dawn showed the cat to be no longer heavy with kitten. She came to him, mewed as if she wanted something from him, then turned back to her corner. He crawled quietly after her and saw her kittens, four tiny creatures. He watched as their mother curled to them, licking them. He slowly put out his hand to stroke her and she purred, proud and confident. He felt rewarded by her trust in him and sat by her as she suckled her litter.

He was light-headed, he supposed from hunger, and found it difficult to recall all the events of the last days. Then, when he looked from the window to the yard below and saw a policeman, it came sharply back. He was a fugitive, hunted as a deserter, a man without friends, save his sister. She was near, so near, but there was no way he could get to her.

The cat left her corner and walked to the loft ladder, mewed and climbed down to the stable floor. She had more freedom than he. He watched from the window to see where she was going. She crossed the yard and the policeman bent to stroke her. She ignored the man and made her way to the kitchen door, scratched at it till it was opened to allow her to go inside.

Food, that was what she was seeking, and his own hunger gnawed anew at the thought, so that his mind began to wander. He could not go much longer without something to eat; he dared not leave his hole here, but he had to find food, had to reach Ada.

He watched from his window in the hope of seeing her and somehow catching her attention, but she did not appear. Below, in the stables, he heard horses shifting, the voice of a stable boy, and then the clip-clop of horses' hooves on the cobbles. The policeman had gone to the kitchen door and was chatting to a woman there. She handed him something and he put it to his mouth. Food. George's mouth watered as he watched, envious, angry when a crumb dropped to the floor and the man let it lie.

The cat reappeared, crossed the yard and climbed up into the loft; he sat by her and watched as she tended her kittens. How sleek and satisfied she was and how he envied her. He spoke softly to her and she purred. He was glad of her company and she seemed to welcome his.

He woke from another short uneasy sleep, disturbed by sounds in the yard below. He crept to the window and saw his sister. She seemed to be looking towards his window and he raised his hand to attract her attention. If she saw him, she gave no sign but turned to talk to a new policeman, a man with sergeant's stripes, who appeared from the side of the house.

George drew back. He thought of himself as a man of courage but now he felt fear. He was cornered.

Here under the low roof of the stable loft the heat was stifling and he sweated grossly. He needed Ada, as he so often had as a child. She had always comforted and loved him. It was that love he needed now as much as food. He would go to her, ignore the presence of the police, and ask her to help him. She would not deny him.

He realised hunger was clouding his judgement. He must continue to lie low until the police had gone. Only then could he go to her, ask her to save him.

3

Ada Prideaux had slept uneasily, aware of the likelihood that her brother would come to her for help. She had wakened once, got up, left her room and walked through the corridors, past her mistress's room, reassuring herself that he had not come to disturb their lives. Rooms that had been well-searched by Superintendent Groves's men she visited again to make certain they had missed nothing. She went even to the nursery wing, that part of the house where children had been provided for but which was unused, clean and, like Caroline herself, sterile.

Holding a taper aloft, Ada moved through the rooms, making sure they were empty. George was a cunning man, might have watched the police, slipped into the house when they had finished their search and taken refuge here. But the rooms were as always — without a breath of life. If only, she thought as she turned to go, if only the mistress had been blessed with child. But it was not to be. She would have liked to have a young Caroline about the house. They would see then, all these people who thought her cold and loveless, what she was truly like.

She shrugged her shoulders at such foolish thoughts. There was no child here and was never likely to be. She must find contentment, as indeed she did, in watching over her mistress, guarding her from the perils of the world, keeping her safe from the threats an army deserter, a murderer such as brother George, might hold.

She would not hesitate to give him up if his coming brought danger to the household. Yet it would not be easy to behave so, however clear her duty was.

She retraced her steps to her room. The house was still. All was secure. Her mistress could sleep soundly.

4

There had been no alarm in the night and no sighting of the murderer. The whole household had been in a state of unease the day before, but with the start of a fresh day — a beautiful summer's day — everyone seemed to believe the danger was over. Caroline thought Mrs Prideaux might show signs of anxiety, or even of knowledge, but she was her usual impassive self, going about her work with cold authority.

'I expect he's left the county by now and is somewhere up-country,' Thomas said. 'But I want to be quite sure of your safety so I'll stay with you till we have news of him.'

Caroline was more concerned this morning for news of Claudia. She had missed her company the previous evening. Sometimes the cat wandered from the house into the fields or woodlands. Caroline hoped she had not gone so far, fearing she might be in danger from foxes. She went to look for her and asked Mrs Prideaux if she had seen the cat. She, who had no love for animals, said she would ask in the kitchen and returned to say the cat had come for food early in the morning and had disappeared again. 'It seems she's had her kittens somewhere,' she added. She had no interest in the creature's whereabouts.

Caroline left the house, intending to look for Claudia, but the warm morning air and the clear blue sky led her to walk over the lawns towards the river. Here a welcome breeze refreshed her. She loved this outlook; whenever she felt restless and dissatisfied with her own place in things, this view brought fresh heart; she could relax, dream she was mistress of her fate. But she was not. Something was missing from her life. She only half understood why she felt unfulfilled. It was not entirely due to her failure to have a child; that was part of it, but not all. There was somehow a void at the very centre of her being.

She thrust her self-analysis away; she had come out to look for Claudia and her kittens. She turned back over the grass, went round to the stables at the back of the house and spoke to the policeman lounging there.

'Still no news?' she said.

He shook his head. 'He'll be over to St Ives or somewhere by now,' he responded. ''tes a waste of time if you do want my opinion.' Then, realising he was speaking to Mrs Trevarth herself, he straightened up, shuffling with embarrassment. 'Ma'am,' he added and touched his helmet in salute.

Will he have got away? she wondered. She hoped so, then they would be spared the attention of the police. Their presence was a constant reminder of the ugliness of the world outside.

She went to the stables and peered in the stalls for a sign of Claudia. A stable boy came in with bucket and brush and she asked him if he had seen the cat but he had not. She called 'Claudia, Claudia,' and gave the soft whistle which usually brought her, but there was no response. She went to the ladder leading up to the loft but thought it unlikely Claudia would have climbed it in her pregnant state, so walked away. The cat would appear when she was hungry. She would follow her then. She went into the house and through the kitchen and asked Mrs Batten, the Cook, to make sure to let her know the moment Claudia came to be fed.

'I shall see where she goes, find where she's had her kittens,' she explained.

'Poor thing,' Mrs Batten said and, for a moment, Caroline thought the servant was referring not to the cat but to her. Maybe that is how they think of me, she thought. Maybe they think of me as I was when I came here fifteen years ago, a young bride.

5

George Prideaux lay on the straw not far from the cat and her kittens. From time to time, as a sort of comfort to himself, he put out a hand to touch the cat and stroke her. By now he was familiar with the sounds of the stable, had identified from their voices that there were a couple of lads and an older man – a coachman, he supposed. He had heard them gossiping and had come alert to the sound of his own name. 'Poor bugger,' the older man had said. 'He'll swing for it if they catch him.'

'I hope he gets away,' said a younger voice.

'There's not much risk of that with a murder charge against him. They'll hunt him down.' Their voices drifted off as they led the horses into the yard.

Murder? They must have found Rennie's body. And of course they would accuse him of the man's death. He would have no defence, for what evidence could he produce in his favour? They would not listen. He was already condemned.

He must get rid of his army uniform, get out of the country. There were Cornishmen who sailed to the Newfoundland fishing grounds; if only he could get as far as Newlyn or St Ives he might persuade them to let him join them and sail to the New World.

He had been stupid to come here; he should have known a watch would be set on the house where Ada worked. He had played into their hands and now he was no mere army deserter but a man wanted for murder, an outlaw.

He needed food and fresh clothing. He could find both in the house. He need not make contact with Ada – he did not want to compromise her, now he was thought to be guilty of murder – but could choose his moment, break in sometime during the night. It would be dangerous but it would be better than cowering here. He had seen where the police were posted, and there was only one man kept regularly on watch, though he had the impression there were others within call. He would move tonight, the sooner the better.

He was hollow with hunger but, more than food, he wanted new clothes; his uniform, briefly worn with pride once, was an offence to him now. He felt unclean wearing it. He *was* unclean; the hours spent crawling along mine workings, sleeping under hedgerows, scrambling through scrub, had left him filthy, and the close heat of this cramped space made him sweat. He stank, his clothing and himself, and, almost more than he needed to eat, he needed to get clean.

He had heard water being drawn from a tap in the stables. When it was safe he would strip to his waist and go down and wash.

There was no one there now. He took off his flannel shirt, threw it beside his tunic and went to the top of the ladder. He put his foot on it and hastily drew back into the loft, holding his breath, when he heard sounds below. A woman was talking to one of the lads he had heard earlier; then in a clear sweet voice she called 'Claudia!' followed by a soft, enticing whistle. The cat pricked up its ears but settled back comfortably to its suckling kittens. Light footsteps drew near the ladder and he crouched, tense, in the dark. A moment and the steps moved away and, shortly after, the heavier-footed stable boy left too and there was quiet in the stable once more.

He crept to the window and lay beside it, peering out to the cobbled yard; he decided morning was not the time to risk going below. There was too much activity, garden produce being brought to the house, maids moving in and out, emptying buckets, a laundry maid with a basketful of dirty linen going to the washhouse, a man carting coals. He would wait till the afternoon; it would be quieter, with the somnolence of summer heat to make everyone less vigilant. He could, must, risk it then.

He dozed from time to time, waiting for an opportunity to move. He heard a rustling in the straw and saw the cat — that was Claudia, he supposed — stirring. She got up, stretched, gave her kittens a roughly maternal lick, went to the ladder and climbed down. He watched as she made her way over the yard to the open door of the kitchen.

He followed her down the ladder, pausing every now and again to listen, but there was no one else on the move. It was as if a spell had been cast over the house and its surroundings, the torrid spell of the sun, making the whole world indolent.

There was a wooden bucket under the tap at the other end of the stable. He went cautiously over, for he had to pass the open door, and filled the bucket, though fearful the running tap might alert anyone near. But no one was near, it seemed. He saw a bar of carbolic soap on a ledge over the tap and took it, with the bucket, back to his hiding place. There, in the centre of the little room, he was just able to stand upright. He took off his trousers and stood, naked, stretching his arms out to let the air get at his body. Then plunging his hands into the cold water he began to wash, humming with pleasure at the chill feel of it.

<h1 style="text-align: center">6</h1>

Caroline looked up to see one of the housemaids at the door of her drawing room.

'Mrs Batten says to tell you Claudia is in the kitchen, ma'am.'

Caroline got up quickly and followed the girl into the domestic quarters, past Mrs Prideaux's room, to the kitchen. There Mrs Batten pointed to Claudia, lapping thirstily at a saucer of milk. 'She's had her kittens, ma'am. You can see that.' The cat looked up, conscious they were talking about her. When she had finished her milk she washed herself and strode to the door to be let out.

'I'll see where she goes,' Caroline said. 'I'd like to know what she's had.' Mrs Batten opened the door for them both and, with Claudia leading the way, the cat and her mistress crossed the yard to the stables, Claudia looking round from time to time as if to make sure Caroline was following.

Knowing the kittens must be near and not wishing to startle them, Caroline walked on tip-toe after Claudia and stood at the foot of the ladder watching the cat as she climbed nimbly from step to step to disappear at the top into the loft. So that was where she had had her kittens! Caroline put her foot on the ladder and slowly, expectantly, went up, thrilled to think she would see the litter, glad Claudia had let her come with her. Birth was so lovely a thing; the thought struck her with sudden hurt, so that she paused for a moment before going further.

She reached the top of the ladder, looked into the loft and caught her breath in horror. A man, muscled and lean, stood, his naked back to her, droplets of water dripping from his flanks as he rubbed himself with soap. She gasped with shame and he half-turned at the sound. She covered her eyes with her hands and stumbled back down the steps, almost falling in her haste to get away, and ran out of the stables into the house, up the stairs to her bedroom and sat before the mirror of her dressing table looking at herself in disbelief. Her cheeks were red, her eyes wide with shock and she clutched her arms about her shoulders as if so she could protect herself from what she had seen.

What had she seen? It had been only for a moment but that moment had revealed more to her than fifteen years of married life. Never before had she seen a man naked; not even Thomas had been so shameless as to show himself like that. She continued to gaze into the mirror to see if the shame of the sight was revealed in her face. How could she tell Thomas? But of course she wouldn't, could not tell him. Such a thing must be private to her, and she must put it from her.

It would not leave her. She could see, as she closed her eyes, the brown firm limbs, the tight, neat buttocks, the sudden turn of the body and the half-glimpse of the secret of the man. She hid her face again at the memory.

Who was he? She did not think he was one of the stable hands, but he must be. No one else would be there.

No one else?

There could be someone else, there could be. In that moment she knew the man she had seen was the murderer — the man Prideaux. Fear struck her as she realised how near she had been to him. She could have reached out and touched him. What if she had? The thought both frightened and fascinated her.

She must come to her senses, must tell Thomas. She need not reveal what she had seen, only that she thought a man was hiding in the stable loft. The police could come then and take him.

She got up and went to the door, put out her hand to open it, but could not.

She did not want him taken. She did not know why the idea disturbed her, but she could say nothing, not yet. Perhaps the man was not Prideaux, merely one of the gardeners trying to cool himself from the heat of the day. She would look foolish if that were so.

She knew it was not so, knew the man she had seen, the man she could have touched — who could have touched her — was

Prideaux. She must tell them. Yet she could not, could not give him away, Mrs Prideaux would never forgive her if she did; but she did not care what Mrs Prideaux thought.

Nevertheless she could tell no one. Shame, guilt, and curiosity combined to make it a secret she could not share.

7

The sight of the woman set George Prideaux trembling with fear. He turned to go after her, catch her before she alerted the house to his presence, but she fled before he could stop her. He hurried to the window and saw her disappearing into the house. He thought it was the woman he had seen earlier but his glimpse of her was too brief for him to be sure.

Quickly he rubbed himself dry with his flannel shirt, put on his breeches and sat, head in hands, shivering. He had felt a moment of pleasure when he had dowsed himself with cold water, pleasure so intense that he had failed to be warned of the woman's approach.

The alarm would be raised, for she would know who he was. He would be caught, but he would sell himself dear. Nor was he going to wait here to be cornered by the police; he would make a run for it. He sat down and put on his stockings and boots, and his shirt, damp though it was, threw his tunic aside and took another look through the window to see where the police guard was positioned. The yard was as lazily quiet as before, except for the appearance of the coachman and a groom. They came over to the stable and he heard their voices below, though he could not make out what they were saying.

He hesitated. Perhaps he could rush past before they stopped him, but the coachman was a powerful man and he himself was weak with hunger. Like it or not, he was trapped.

He was surprised the alarm had not been raised immediately. There was no sign of the policeman, no sign of the return of the posse. For a moment he began to feel he would be safer staying where he was. Perhaps for some reason the woman had decided not to give him away, though he could not imagine why.

Then the fear returned, fear of being cornered like a rat. He would not let that happen. He went over to where the cat was lying with her kittens, leaned down and stroked her gently to say goodbye. The gesture comforted him; she at least did not shrink from him, but purred and rubbed her head affectionately against his hand.

The voices below drifted away and when he went to the window to look out he saw the two men walking away towards the fields. Now was the time. He took a last look to reassure himself the yard was empty when he heard more voices and saw a group of seven or eight policemen come round the corner of the building to draw themselves up in line in front of the stables.

So — the woman had given him away and he had left it too late. Desperately he looked around for a place to hide, but there was none. He could either be caught here, trapped and helpless or he could go down into the stable and give himself up, walking to his fate like a free man. There was no hope now of escape.

He was trembling uncontrollably again, from fear and indecision, and he buried his head in his heads, ready to weep for despair, but was spared that weakness by the sound of commands barked from outside.

It was time to move, time to go down and offer himself for capture, either that or a bid for freedom, taking the posse by surprise and darting through their ranks towards the fields. He put a foot to the ladder.

8

A knock came at Caroline's bedroom door, Thomas's knock, she recognised. 'What is it?' she called, hoping he would not come in, fearful her face might reveal her shock and shame.

He opened the door. 'The police are here again, in force this time, my dear. They seem convinced Prideaux must be in the house or one of the outbuildings. They've asked my permission to make a thorough search.' He looked at his wife with concern. 'I shan't let them disturb you, my love. There's no need to be afraid. When they find him they'll take him quietly away. You're not likely to be troubled.'

She *was* troubled. She opened her mouth, intending to tell him what she knew, but the words would not come.

'What is it?' he asked and came over and took her hand. 'Stay here in your room and I'll warn Superintendent Groves that you're not well. I'll tell him to keep his men quiet. Take a sleeping draught. That way it will all be over without your knowing a thing.'

She did know, could not hide that knowledge from herself. She could keep quiet and they would find the man with no help from her. They would capture him and she need not feel responsible.

She could see him, half turning towards her, handsome as a god carved by some Greek of old. But he was not sculpted in marble, he was made of flesh and blood; she had seen the flesh, knew him to be alive and vibrant. The thought rushed into her mind and she felt herself reddening.

She turned to Thomas. 'I shall speak to Mrs Prideaux and the staff. It is my duty.'

'There's no need for you to bother yourself. I shall do that.'

'It is my duty,' she repeated emphatically, glad to have something to occupy her, something which might dispel the image of the man Prideaux.

She went to the servant's hall where the indoor staff were gathered. Groves had already seen to that and, to her annoyance, was addressing them as if they were dependent on him for their orders. He did not even acknowledge her arrival and she angrily went past him and out into the yard at the rear. Groves's men were drawn up, awaiting their instructions. She resented their presence, bridled at the way Groves took it for granted they had the right to pry into every corner.

She glanced at the curved window of the loft and thought she caught a flash of movement. He must be terrified. Poor, poor man, she found herself repeating, and pity for him overwhelmed her. Nothing could save him now, no one.

No one save her.

She did not know how or why the idea came to her, but she knew she could, she must, save him. She and no one else knew where he was hiding. She and no one else was in a position either to condemn or reprieve him. She saw him in her mind again, a young virile animal, startled faunlike by her gasp of

76

shock, and knew she could not think of so beautiful a creature being manacled and led away, betrayed by her, to languish in some dank gaol.

She did not question the impulse which led her past the policeman into the stables. She was aware that one of them, a sergeant, had followed her.

'My cat is up in the loft,' she said. 'She's just had kittens. I want to see she's not frightened by all this hullabaloo.' She spoke as haughtily as she knew how, making it plain she was not to be challenged.

'That's all right, ma'am,' the sergeant said deferentially. 'We're only anxious about your safety. You'll be safe, we'll see to that.'

'I don't think my cat is likely to do me any harm,' she said.

He smiled. 'No, ma'am,' I suppose not.' He went back to his men and she heard him yelling orders to them. She went to the ladder and put her foot on the bottom step, then called softly, 'Claudia, Claudia, I'm coming up.'

He was there, crouched beside the window, dressed now, so that she was not afraid to look at him. She put her finger to her lips to warn him to silence and sat on the floor of the loft at the head of the ladder, reaching out her hand to her cat, while keeping her eyes on the man.

'George Prideaux?' she whispered.

He nodded. His eyes were wary. There was a dark stubble of beard and his hair was curled about his ears. He flushed under her examination and she too reddened, aware how she had last seen him and how she was staring now. He did not look like a murderer or a violent man or − how had Thomas spoken of him? − a man of "brutish instincts".

Boots clattered on the floor of the stable below and the sergeant's voice called, 'Are you all right, ma'am?' Caroline gathered Claudia in her arms and held her up to show the sergeant. 'She's fine, sergeant, provided you don't make too much noise.' The cat wriggled out of her grasp and went back to her kittens.

'I'll tell the men to keep away then. There's no one else up there, I suppose?' he said jokingly.

She laughed brightly.

Chapter Nine

Snow had reached Cornwall, only a light sprinkling but enough to lend a touch of wintry verisimilitude to Christmas. The twins, Simon and Sarah, were young enough to be excited by it, but to everyone else, after the first thrill of surprise, it became a nuisance, turning quickly to slush as the sun rose higher in the sky.

Christmas had always been a very special occasion for Caroline, for her birthday fell on Christmas Eve. Now she looked round at her family, Maud and the children, gathered to do her honour on her eighty-sixth birthday. She found it difficult to believe she was really so old. She supposed she looked old and, in some ways, her body told her she was old, but she could not think of herself as old. Her thoughts were those of a young woman. Age should bring wisdom but she knew, if she were faced with the situation she had met those many years ago, she would do the same again without thinking twice about it.

'What is it, Mother?' her daughter Maud asked. 'Are you tired? Should I see you to your room?'

'Of course not,' Caroline answered firmly. She had eaten sparingly, too full of memories to want more than a little of the meal Mrs Batten had provided. No, it was not Mrs Batten now, of course. She had gone long since.

'You should think of giving this place up. It is really too much. We could find you a small house or apartment near us.' Maud knew better than to suggest she should go and live with them.

'I wouldn't be happy anywhere else.'

'And where would we go for our holidays?' Sarah said.

'This is home, Mother,' Joseph said. 'You know Grandmama would never leave here.'

Caroline patted his hand in approval. She had insisted on Joseph sitting next to her. It was the privilege of age to be able to do such things. She had treated fairly with them all in her Will but while she was still here she could indulge herself by favouring him. The others did not resent it, put it down now to the fact that he would soon be going to war.

Caroline wondered what Maud would say if she knew the reason for her fondness for the boy, in the way he revived her memories of the old days, more than ever now that he was almost twenty-one, almost ... She let her thoughts wander until she heard her daughter speak again. 'I think it's time we let Grandmother have a rest.'

Maud was as solicitous as Thomas had been, always anxious about her well-being, worrying about her doing too much. Caroline remembered in particular how concerned he had been when she told him she was with child, how he wanted to treat her as an invalid, urging her to rest when she was in fact full of energy. He had always been considerate but with her pregnancy his own longing for a child filled him with never-ending concern, until she felt hemmed in by his watchfulness and almost resentful of his attention.

'Grandmama.' It was Joseph, bringing her back to the present, instead, as so often, of taking her back to the past. He held out a small package. 'Happy Birthday,' he said and kissed her on the lips, as he had done as a small boy, and as ... She had to concentrate to prevent her thoughts wandering again.

'Open it, then,' he said, his eyes shining in anticipation of her delight at his gift.

'What is it?' She wanted to draw out the pleasure to make it last.

'Open it and see.'

Slowly she untied the ribbon and removed the wrapping to reveal a small silver brooch, of a bugle-horn, beneath it the one word, 'Cornwall'. She stared unbelievingly. How could he have known? Her eyes slowly filled with tears and she dared not look up at him in case she revealed more than she should.

He stooped down to pin the brooch to her shawl. She felt his hand touch her neck and the moment's contact was almost too much for her to bear.

'Why?' she whispered. 'Why?'

'It's my unit, or will be,' he said. 'I wanted to give a brooch to the woman I love. Don't you like it? It's the regimental badge of the Duke of Cornwall's Light Infantry, you see.'

'I know. I know.' How could he take it so lightly?

Maud was standing by, ready to see her mother to her room, careful she should not over-tire herself, and Caroline was grateful, for she felt suddenly weary and in need of solitude. Memory was dragging her back, away from this cold blacked-out winter of 1939, to the sunlit days of that long past summer. With Maud at her side she went upstairs to her bedroom.

'Why did you let him do it? Couldn't he have deferred his call-up till he's finished his degree?'

'You know what he's like. He's so headstrong. I don't know where he gets it from.'

Caroline smiled. Maud had had a wilful streak as a child too. She was like her father in that.

Chapter Ten

1

She could hear the police calling to each other as they went from building to building, even down to the washhouse, the ice-house in the woodland, and the glasshouses, searching every inch of the property outside.

She reached out to stroke Claudia. The man moved and she turned round sharply.

'Don't come near me,' she said.

'It's all right,' he said quickly. 'I shan't. But why?' He could no more understand her impulse than she could herself. Why had she deceived the police? It had nothing to do with the fact that he was Ada Prideaux' brother.

'Why?' he repeated.

'I can't say.' They kept their voices low for, not more than a few yards away the men were coming back towards the house, still in search of him.

She pretended to be concerned for Claudia and bent down to watch the kittens suckling at their mother. Claudia was purring with contentment and, for a moment, in her own pleasure, Caroline forgot the presence of the murderer. Then, hearing him shift his position, she again looked up in alarm, conscious of the folly of her behaviour. How had she come to act so, in defiance of all good sense? True, he did not look like a murderer; as he looked at her now, his eyes held no threat, only misgiving as if he wished to trust her but dare not. Some instinct made her want to reach out a hand to comfort him and she made a half-movement before prudence intervened and she sat back, away from him, watching him, ready to call out to the police if he should make a move towards her. Curiosity drove her to ask, 'Why? Why did you do it?'

'Do what? Desert?'

She conquered her fear of the words she needed to speak. 'Murder. Why did you kill him, that man?'

'Corporal Rennie, I suppose you mean?' He turned his head in sudden fright and Caroline heard someone in the stable below. She called out, 'Who's there? Who's that?'

'It's all right, ma'am. It's only me.' It was the sergeant she had seen earlier. She leaned out and saw him standing below and wondered what had brought him back.

'Are you all right, ma'am? I thought I heard voices.'

'My cat likes to have me speak to her. She's nervous with all this going on.'

'She'll be all right now. We're calling off the search. There's no sign of the man. Mr Groves said to tell you we'll be leaving a constable on patrol. Not to worry, ma'am. We'll not let that fellow near you. You need have no fear of that.'

She watched him leave the stable and listened to the sound of the police squad parading in the cobbled yard and marching off. They went, leaving her alone with a man accused of murder. She should call them back and have him taken, but she could not. For the first time in her life she had done something unexpected and she was excited by it, but a shiver of fear stirred her nevertheless.

He had moved closer to the window to look out. 'They've gone,' he said. 'There's just one man, at the corner.' He stood up, his head almost touching the rafters. She recoiled thinking he was going to approach her. He realised her fear of him and shook his head. 'I'll not touch you.' His voice was deep and gentle, so that she knew he would do nothing to harm her.

'What will you do?' she asked.

'I'd better go. I don't want to bring trouble to you or my sister. I'll take my chance.'

It would be better so, better that the household should not be involved with him in any way.

'I'll go now,' he said.

'Wait till dark,' she urged. 'It will be safer then.' She again wanted to put out a hand to him in friendship; he was so

82

young and vulnerable, a mere boy in spite of the growth of beard darkening his chin, barely into manhood.

'I didn't kill him,' he said. 'He came at me and fell over the cliff.' She did not want to know the details but he seemed to want to tell her. He turned his back to her to kneel by the window and, with his eyes averted, began to talk. 'I know I hated him. Good riddance, I thought, when he went over, but I didn't do it. I think I would have saved him if I could, but there was no chance.' He turned his head to look at her but his face was in shadow so that she could not read what was in his eyes; his words held truth, and more. She wanted him to carry on talking. The depth and resonance in his voice sent a shiver down her spine so that, though the words he spoke had little meaning for her, the sounds vibrated and sang, bewitching her.

She came to her senses. He was still talking, as if he needed expiation. She wished she could give him that but there was nothing she could say, nothing more she could do; she had done enough; she should leave him to follow his own devices, to escape if he could, to be caught if the dice should so fall.

He stopped talking and put his head in his hands as if in despair. Pity moved her and she went to him and reached out. This time she did not withdraw her hand but touched his head in a gesture of concern.

'You are ill,' she said, feeling his brow hot and wet under her fingers. 'You have a fever.'

'It's nothing,' he said, looking up and directly at her, only inches away. His eyes were dark, almost black. 'It's nothing,' he repeated. 'I'm hungry, that's all. I don't know when I ate last.'

'I'll bring you something. Wait here.' She stood up and looked down on him. Helpless and in need as he was, he seemed a mere boy. But she remembered how she had first seen him, lean and strong and manly, and she blushed at the recollection.

As she left the stable she was surprised to see how late it was, for in the darkening sky there shone a lone star. The heat of the day had given way to a mild evening breeze. She felt an unusual exhilaration as if, for the first time in her life, there was purpose to it. She wondered how she could take food to her protégé, for she rarely visited the kitchen and had never, save for the begging of a titbit for Claudia, asked for food from it.

Perhaps it would be wise to take Mrs Prideaux into her confidence, but Caroline did not feel easy about that. The housekeeper talked of knowing her duty. What if duty bade her betray her own brother? That was not beyond belief. Caroline, moreover, had no wish to share responsibility for the young man. He was hers to care for, no one else's.

As she opened the door into the house she glanced back at the loft window. She could see nothing, only the reflection of the evening sky, but he was there, the young man she had helped save, whom she would still help. He depended on her, her alone, and she was glad of it.

'Is Claudia all right, ma'am?' Mrs Batten asked.

'Yes. But I don't want anyone to disturb her. I'll look after her myself. I'll see she gets enough to eat. Show me where I can find something for her, something tempting.'

'There are always bits and pieces left over. I'll put some on one side for you to take to her.'

She had to be satisfied with that, must be careful not to arouse suspicion, and when Mrs Batten said, 'The master was looking for you, ma'am,' she hurried to her room to dress for dinner. Hearing her moving, Thomas came to her.

'I was concerned for you until I heard you were fussing over your precious Claudia.' He spoke kindly, indulgently, but with none of the suppressed fire she sensed behind the words of the young man in the stable. She felt guilty at her treachery, for in thinking of Prideaux she was betraying her husband, and he was dear to her. She put her face up to be kissed and, surprised at her gesture, he bent to her and brushed her forehead with his lips, as a father might, not a lover. She blushed, unable to understand why such thoughts cluttered her mind. She closed her eyes and could see the young man, slender, lissom – and naked. The image lingered until, through the haze, she heard Thomas speak.

'It's been a strain for all of us, but it's over now. The hunt has moved its ground, I'm glad to say.' He thought she was still anxious about the man; so she was, but not in the way he imagined. He went on, 'There's been a sighting of him in

84

Camborne, they say. He'll be seen here, there and everywhere, you may be sure. But the police will catch up with him.' He patted her shoulder comfortingly. 'You can clear your mind of him now.'

But she could not. Whenever she closed her eyes he was there, turning at her gasp of shock.

She excused herself immediately after dinner, when she knew the servants would be gathered in the servants' hall over their meal. She went into the dairy and saw the bits and pieces put aside for Claudia and took them, but she also took a loaf and a baked ham she saw in the meat safe. She hurried to the stables and, seeing no sign of the police guard, climbed up the ladder to the loft.

'It's me,' she whispered. 'I've brought some food. I'll leave it here. I'll go and get you a drink of milk. I couldn't bring it all at once.' She pushed the ham and bread towards him, put Claudia's titbits near the cat and went back down the ladder and out of the stables, to be met by a constable.

'Good night, ma'am,' he said and went on his patrol.

She returned to the kitchen but was dismayed to find the kitchen maids busy about their work. They looked at her in surprise and even eyed her with suspicion as they curtseyed. She saw a pitcher of milk but thought it wiser to give up any idea of going to the loft again. He would be all right now till morning.

She had a moment's fear that he might do as he had said and leave during the night to avoid embarrassment to her and his sister. She wanted to go to him and persuade him to stay, but she could do nothing; she would endanger him if she drew attention to the stable loft. She wondered if she could somehow bring him into the house but saw how foolish a notion that was. He was better where he was until the coast was clear and he could leave in safety.

She was aware Thomas was watching her and wondered what she had given away.

'It's been a trying time,' he said. 'I'm glad it's over. I think you have behaved with dignity and decorum through it all. I'm very proud of you. I know how very afraid you must have been.'

She smiled to herself. Of course she had been afraid, but

85

there had been no cause to be. The young man held no threat for her, she knew that.

As she rang for the housekeeper, she said, 'We should let Mrs Prideaux know that the hunt for her brother has moved away. She must have felt very uneasy with the police at her elbow.'

'They still have their eyes on her. Groves is sure her brother will have to turn to her. He has no one else to help him.'

Mrs Prideaux showed no reaction to the news that the police thought her brother was in Camborne. When she had gone Thomas frowned. 'Do you think she knows where he is? She doesn't seem concerned. Perhaps she knows he has got away and is safe.'

He is not safe, Caroline thought, not yet, and when she retired to her room she lay thinking of him, concerned for him. And, when Thomas came to her later she closed her eyes and it was the grace of a young man she saw and his firm body she felt as she took her husband to her. Thomas was surprised and moved at her unusually urgent response and when she began to weep, for no reason that he could see, he gently stroked her head, saying, 'You need have no fear now. It is over.'

It has only just begun, she thought.

2

Every sound startled him to wakefulness: the shifting of the horses in their stalls, the rustling of the cat in her corner, the whispered conversations of a maid and a boy in the shadows of the yard outside. Then he would fall into an uneasy doze, less of a sleep than a moment or two's semi-consciousness.

He should get away from here; it had been folly to come to ask his sister's help; he had not even seen her.

Or had he? Someone had come to help him and in his fever he thought it must be Ada. But it had not been her. Ada was dark, this one fair. But, like Ada, she had been kind to him, had protected him from the boys who chased him. In his dreams he was a boy again, coming home from a fight in the Red River with Abram Sparnon, muddied and scratched and submitting to Ada's stripping and washing him. He had

86

wriggled and twisted to get away from her but she had held him firm.

As she did now, pinning him down, binding him. He woke fully, believing the police had discovered his hiding place and had handcuffed him and were about to drag him to trial. The dream, vivid and frightening, was with him still. He tried to get up to thrust his captors away, but there was no one there. The loft was in total darkness and the weight he felt at his chest came from inside him.

He tried to get to his feet but could do no more than crouch on all fours. His legs would not support him and his arms felt weak but he crawled towards the opening, intending, as far as his delirium could hold any intention, to get away. But it was no use; pain in his chest and at his back made it difficult to breathe and he lay on the floor, face forward, incapable of movement or thought.

Dreams still troubled him, images racing in and out of his inner vision, first of his sister, then of an army corporal, then of a young girl who changed in a moment to a woman with wide eyes, a soft mouth, reaching towards him to plant a kiss on his cheek. The touch was so real that he came wide awake expecting to see the woman who had helped him, who had promised to bring him food, but it was her cat, not her. She was licking him with her rasping tongue, washing him as she had earlier washed her kittens. He raised himself enough to stroke her and hold her for a moment before she twisted away and returned to her litter.

His thoughts were briefly clear but he knew that fever and its delirium would soon take hold once more. He had no hope of getting away while he was so weak. She had said he was ill, he remembered. She? He found it difficult to recall the detail of her appearance. It did not matter; she had kept him from being caught, promised to bring him something to eat. She had come back, keeping her promise, or had that too been a dream?

Dream and reality mingled so that he felt he was falling into a sleep that was a kind of death. He tried to fight it off but it was no use. Though he knew he must keep quiet he opened his mouth to shout for help. He did not know if he uttered any sound but nobody came, for the next time his mind cleared he was still lying in the loft with enough weak light coming from the window to tell him a new day had dawned.

3

Caroline had slept heavily. Usually she was awake at daylight, alive to the movement of servants about the house. This morning her eyelids were unwilling to open. She was haunted by a fleeting vision, the fragment of a dream, of which there only remained an unexplained feeling of joy. Something, but she could not tell what, had filled her with contentment.

'Good morning,' she heard and reluctantly opened her eyes to see Thomas, dressed, standing at the end of the bed, smiling down at her. He looked as if his dreams had been pleasant too.

She remembered then they had made love the night before impulsively and with her, to her shame, taking the initiative. She could not meet his gaze and closed her eyes and, as she did, the image of the young man stood before her. She made to get out of bed.

'I thought you would want to stay in bed a little,' Thomas said. 'I have already breakfasted and thought you would want to have your breakfast here.'

She could not lie there, not knowing what was happening to him. He might have left during the night and, in leaving, have been caught.

'Is there any news?' she asked, unable to stem her need to know.

'Of Prideaux, you mean? I've heard nothing. But I'm sure we can feel safe. He can't be hereabouts or the police would have found him when they searched the house and grounds. No thought of him need enter your head. And I think I may return to my normal routine now. You don't need my protection against him. I have contracts to sort out at the works and I should go back today.' He waited for her comment, but her mind was elsewhere.'

'Do you agree?' he asked.

She tried to recall what he had been saying.

'You will feel quite happy if I return to work today?'

'Of course,' she hastened to assure him. It would be so much easier if he were not at home, so much easier for her to help that poor young man. If he were still there.

'What is it?' Thomas sensed her concern and misinterpreted it. 'I'll stay if you think it necessary.'

She got out of bed and reached for her robe. She must be quick to go to him. 'Of course it's not necessary. I'm sure he must be miles away by now.' Please God, he's not, she thought, for he will be in grave danger once he leaves here.

'Off you go,' she said, pretending a cheerfulness she did not feel. 'And let me get on with my duties.'

'And what duties might those be?' he asked indulgently before he turned to go.

'I have a thousand and one things to see to,' she said, knowing she had only one thing to do, one duty to fulfil.

4

'I'm concerned for your mistress, Mrs Prideaux,' Thomas Trevarth said. 'This business over your brother has upset her more than she is willing to admit.' He looked at the housekeeper as if unsure whether to confide in her or not.

'I am sorry,' Mrs Prideaux said. 'Sorry it should be my brother who is responsible for her anxiety.'

'I want to make it clear you must not think of helping him. He can bring nothing but trouble. I do not want Mrs Trevarth disturbed in any way whatsoever. In any case she's highly strung and, with the news about your brother, she has become increasingly nervous. I am anxious to protect her from anything untoward.'

'I would do nothing to harm her, I can assure you. You cannot doubt that?' She felt angry that he should feel it necessary to speak to her so. Surely he knew where her loyalties lay. 'I am devoted to her,' she said firmly.

Trevarth looked surprised at her vehemence, then smiled. 'Of course you are, Mrs Prideaux. I never questioned it.'

'Has there been any news?'

'Of your brother? No. But Superintendent Groves seems to think he is still somewhere in the district and will try to make his way here. That's if he's not here already, hiding somewhere in the house.' He looked closely at her and she knew she was not yet entirely free of suspicion.

'I shall do nothing to help him,' she re-asserted. 'I know my duty. He will get short shrift if he turns to me. The mistress's peace of mind is of much more concern to me than my brother's freedom.'

She turned away at his gesture of dismissal. She must go to her mistress and give her the same reassurance. It distressed her to think that Caroline was uneasy, though it was not surprising. The whole household had been shaken by the presence of the police and their search of the house and grounds. Routine had been set on its head. Even the gardeners had lost their calm, protested that it was not safe, with a murderer on the loose, to work too far from the house. The housemaids had been excited, hysterically so, pretending more alarm than they felt, and, she knew, taking pleasure from her own discomfiture. They gossiped behind her back and she had had to assert her authority even more strongly than usual.

She could not have her mistress alarmed by what was going on. She would go to her and see what she could do to help her over these trying days. No doubt George would be taken soon and, if not, he would have more sense than to try to come to her. He would know the police were guarding the house and would give it a wide berth.

She hoped he would get away – as far away as he could be; she hoped he had already left the area, and found someone else to give him shelter. There was a woman in Redruth who had been fond of him, Molly Sullivan she recalled; she would hide him.

She wondered if she ought to tell the police about the woman, but could not bring herself to do that to George. If he could escape so much the better. Only if he brought danger to Trecarrow and her mistress would she think of betraying him. Otherwise let him take his chance. And Molly Sullivan was the right sort of woman for him. Ada remembered the slattern, comely enough once, but coarsened by experience. George would go to her; they would suit each other.

She felt a little easier in her mind and went to find her mistress to get her orders for the day. It was a pleasant fiction that Ada Prideaux maintained, that Caroline was in control. They both knew it was she, Ada Prideaux, who determined the order and routine of the house.

She could not find her mistress and was puzzled until she learnt that she had been seen going over to the stables. Of course — that cat Claudia, on which Caroline lavished such affection.

5

Caroline was impatient for Thomas to leave for the works. She needed to find out if the boy was still in the stables. If he had gone — as she half-hoped — she would be free of the responsibility she had assumed for him. Yet, if he had gone, she would somehow be disappointed. And without her help he would be in great danger. She was not sure what she could do for him apart from giving him food and keeping him hidden until the hue and cry died down. Then she would be willing to let him go; then, and only then, he would be safe.

Would he be safe, ever? He was accused of murder and though he was innocent — she believed his protestations — every man's hand would be against him. She shuddered at the thought.

She collected some scraps for Claudia from the kitchen, told Mrs Batten that she would see to the cat herself and that no one else must disturb her, and went to the stables. A groom was saddling Thomas's mare. He touched his brow. 'I'll keep an eye on your cat, Mrs Trevarth, if you do want me to,' he offered.

'She's a nervous little thing. She's better left to me. I don't want her running away,' she said. She hoped the man would be convinced; she dared not think what would happen if he were to peer into the loft and see the boy and know she was harbouring a criminal.

She waited until the groom had taken the mare round to the front of the house before she went to the ladder and slowly climbed up, feeling an excitement she could neither control nor comprehend.

He was there, under the window, but the food she had brought the night before had not been moved. Claudia or some other creature had nibbled at the ham but the loaf was untouched.

She softly called his name. 'Mr Prideaux.' He gave no sign that he had heard. His breathing was shallow and rapid and she became anxious at the sound. She clambered into the loft and went towards him, ignoring Claudia's mew of greeting. 'Mr Prideaux,' she said again. 'Mr Prideaux,' more urgently. He made no answer. She put her hand to his forehead and felt the fever. His dark hair was wet, his face pale, his lips blue. She knelt beside him and lifted his head to her lap as if she could comfort him so. She spoke his name again and he opened his eyes briefly to look out at her but without recognition. 'Please speak to me,' she said and stroked his head with the cuff of her sleeve to remove the beads of sweat. Again he opened his eyes and this time they remained open for a long moment as he looked at her, smiling weakly and then, sighing, closed them.

'Oh, God,' she said. 'How can I help him?' She sat cradling his head in her lap, wiping his forehead from time to time, listening with dismay to his breathing, knowing he was ill, desperately so, and that she on her own was unable to do anything for him.

She could not leave him here in this bare room, in these damp clothes. He needed nursing – she had seen pneumonia before, had watched her sister die of it years ago – and this she knew was the same, could tell from the cough which racked him now. She held him close, telling herself he was too young to die. She would not let it happen.

How could she prevent it? To call for help would bring about his capture and what good would that do? She was near tears from helplessness and pity but refused to give way to weakness.

She looked out of the window to the yard outside. There was the usual traffic between the outbuildings and the house, the bustle of household chores, the chatter of servants, a brief moment of quiet as Mrs Prideaux appeared, glanced over to the stables, then returned inside.

She turned back to the boy. He was stirring restlessly on his bed of straw. She must, somehow, get him into the house where she could look after him. For the moment she brushed aside the problems that would bring. He must be moved, and quickly. But for that she needed help, help that could come only from Ada Prideaux. Surely, when the housekeeper saw her brother, knew his condition, she would not think of betraying him? Perhaps she never had thought of betraying him. Perhaps when she assured Thomas and Groves that 'she knew her duty', she had seen that duty as loyalty to her brother rather than obedience to the law.

She wished she knew her housekeeper better; the woman kept her thoughts hidden, allowed no one to intrude upon her privacy. Caroline had never thought of her as anything other than a coldly competent servant. Whatever she was, she had to be trusted now; there was no one else to turn to.

She stroked his head and, without knowing why, bent to him and kissed him on the brow, and held him against her breast. She had never seemed so close to anyone, not even Thomas, was filled with an overpowering affection. There was something about his weakness and his dependence upon her that held her fast to him. He was defenceless and she was there to guard him, sick and she was there to make him well.

She hated leaving him but knew she must. She lowered his head gently to the floor and looked for something to cover him. There was nothing save his army tunic. She picked it up and put it over him, bent again to stroke his head, then turned away and hurried back to the house.

At her mistress's summons Ada Prideaux went to the drawing room. Caroline looked flushed and for a moment the house-keeper wondered if the excitement and fear of the last days had brought on a fever. Her words seemed to confirm the suspicion.

'Come with me to the nursery,' she said.

Mrs Prideaux opened her eyes wide in surprise. The nursery rooms had been empty and unused in the whole of her time here. They were kept clean, ready for the use which to everyone's disappointment never came. She looked closely at her mistress, examining her for signs that she was sure could not be there. Had she missed something? 'The nursery?' she said, unable to hide her surprise.

'Come with me. I shall explain.' She led the way upstairs.

The housemaids were busy on the stairs and landings. They bustled out of the way when the housekeeper frowned and gestured to them to go.

There were three rooms set aside for the non-existent children: a day nursery, a night nursery, and, in the tower at the corner of the building, a bedroom for the nurse. Adjoining the nurse's rooms was a bathroom and a small scullery. There had been a use for these in the last Trevarth generation. What use could there be for them now?

'We keep them in such a state that they can be brought into use at any time they're needed,' Ada Prideaux said and again looked at her mistress for signs of pregnancy. There were no such signs.

'Who comes up here? And how often?' Caroline asked.

'Agnes or one of the other housemaids. And as often as I think necessary. At least once a week, though of course they need very little doing to them since there are no children to make them untidy.' As soon as she had spoken she regretted it. She had not meant to sound accusing, but her mistress seemed not to have noticed.

'I want you to let no one else have anything more to do with these rooms,' Caroline said.

The housekeeper felt a moment's irritation. It was not for her to keep rooms clean and tidy. She was about to protest when Caroline led the way into the nurse's room, where there was a bed, stripped to the mattress. 'We shall have to provide bedding,' she said, seeming suddenly uneasy.

Poor woman, thought Ada Prideaux. What does she imagine we want with bedding here? There is no need for a nurse, for there are no children to tend, nor ever will be. Poor, poor woman. She wanted to reach out and take hold of her mistress and comfort her, but that was not her place.

'Bedding?' she asked.

'Immediately, but without involving anyone else. You see ...' she hesitated.

'Ma'am,' began Mrs Prideaux, 'let me take you to your room. It has been a very trying time. Perhaps you should rest.'

Caroline smiled at her. 'You think me sick — or mad. Maybe I am but not in the way you imagine.'

94

'There are no children, ma'am.' The housekeeper could not hide her distress at her mistress's delusion. 'Come with me, please.'

'There are no children, of course there aren't! I know that. But there is someone who needs care and attention. Yours and mine.'

'Who?' Mrs Prideaux knew before Caroline answered.

'Your brother.'

6

Spencer Groves, police superintendent, reviewed the events of the past week without pleasure. So many times he had felt on the verge of taking hold of the man Prideaux. It would be a feather in his cap to seize so dangerous a criminal, to deal rapidly with a crime that had so caught the attention of the local community. It was not often that a murder held such interest, and not often that a household of such importance as the Trevarths was involved.

He pretended respect for Thomas Trevarth, but he would not be sorry if the man was brought down a peg or two, and that would surely happen if the housekeeper, Mrs Prideaux were found to have helped her brother.

He would have her watched, followed wherever she went. She must know where her brother was hiding. Her pretended indifference to his whereabouts was plainly a lie. The woman was full of deceit. He would make sure she was brought to justice as an accessory to murder.

He pitied Mrs Trevarth, to have the woman Prideaux as her housekeeper. He was surprised she allowed the woman to remain in her employment but he imagined she had had little to do with that. She was a sorry thing, with no authority in her own house, no children to occupy her time. No wonder she had been driven almost to distraction by the thought of murder so close at hand. She showed fear at his every visit. He wished he could spare her that but if duty involved her being alarmed, then he would not balk at it.

Groves was angry at the failure of his men to flush out the fugitive. The army of course had complicated matters when Prideaux was hiding underground. Left to him and his men they would have taken him. But he could not understand why they had not caught him near Trecarrow. He was sure the man had been making for the house when he had been seen near Perranwell. He must have hidden out in the woods. Or, perhaps he had some one else to turn to. He called Sergeant Penrose to him.

'You knew the Prideaux family of old, I understand,' he said.

Penrose nodded.

'Had George any close friends in those days? Anyone who might give him a helping hand?'

Penrose thought. 'He was a miner for a time. He made friends there. But we've questioned his old mates. They know nothing.'

'Women?'

'Ah!' said Penrose. 'He was a lad, he was. There were a few girls sorry for his going when he joined up, though some husbands gave thanks for it.'

'Anyone willing to risk their neck for him?'

'That's a big thing. They'd risk something else, maybe, but not their neck. There was Molly, though. Molly Sullivan, over to Redruth. Maybe she would give him shelter. I reckon we should have a look at her?'

'Do that. And keep a sharp eye on his sister.'

It would be a waste of time watching Molly Sullivan, Groves thought, but he could not afford to ignore any possibility. His reputation was at stake.

7

They had caught him and, though he struggled, they held him firm. He had no strength to resist, not even these women. He cried out but one of them told him firmly to be quiet.

He ceased to fight them and became briefly lucid, calmed by the voice, a voice he knew. What was Ada doing seizing him like this? He realised then she was trying to help him. Someone else was with her, another woman, someone he knew from the past. He felt safe with her and tried to thank her.

'Don't talk,' his sister said. 'Don't make a sound and listen carefully. We're taking you into the house.' He tried to show he understood but he did not; what house and why? Reason drifted from him again and he made an effort to escape, but it was no use.

'You have to help us,' the other woman said and her voice had a calming effect on him. 'You must keep quiet and do what you can, try to walk.'

'I'll try,' he said and got to his feet but would have fallen had not his sister and the other woman supported him. He felt safe between them and strong enough to take a step forward. He had known he could rely on Ada. He wanted to tell her so but his mouth was dry and he needed to concentrate on staying upright. They helped him down the ladder, his sister moving slowly in front of him, the other woman coming after. When he got to the foot of the ladder he lay down, unable to get his breath, happy to stay on the straw-strewn floor.

'No,' said the other woman. 'You must get up. We have no time to lose.'

His sister urged him to his feet and with one arm round her shoulder and one round that of the other woman he stumbled, haltingly, across the courtyard to a door into the house. He heard a voice, a high-pitched giggle and then a deep roar of laughter, at first remote and then close enough for him to think the laughter was directed at him. But he was alone with the two women, in a narrow corridor lit by a gas flare on the wall. Its light cast crippled shadows and he shied away from them in mindless terror, so that the women almost let him fall. They pulled him upright and he tried to help them, putting one foot in front of the other in a pretence of walking.

The effort was too much for him. Why could they not just let him go, let him sink into a corner and die? Why had they forced him to come here with them? He tried to twist out of their grasp but was too weak to get free.

They took him into a room at the end of the corridor and sat him in a chair. They said something but it made no sense. Nothing made sense any longer. Walls pressed in upon him, walls of rock, with water pouring down them until he was in danger of drowning. He fought for breath against the torrent but it rushed upon him and swept him under.

'George,' he heard his sister say and knew she had rescued him. He saw her leaning over him, gripping his shoulders.

Behind her stood the other woman and he recognised her as the one who had found him and lied to the police for him.

'George,' Ada said again. 'Can you understand?' He nodded. It was too much of an effort to talk. 'Then listen. This is my room. No one comes here save at my invitation. You'll be safe for the time being but there's a better place for you, a room upstairs where I can nurse you till you are well enough to get away.'

He looked from his sister to the other woman in enquiry.

'My mistress, Mrs Trevarth,' Ada explained. 'It was her idea to bring you into the house, but that's all. From now on you are my responsibility. I'll look after you, get you better, tell you when to go.'

He was not listening. He was looking at the woman called Mrs Trevarth, wondering what had led her to risk helping him. He tried to look his thank and she smiled as if she knew what he wanted to say.

Reality and reason slipped away again. When he came to himself it was to feel a cloth at his brow, cooling his fever. He opened his eyes and saw Mrs Trevarth bending over him.

'Your sister is making sure all the servants are occupied elsewhere.' He did not understand but he felt at ease with her, knew he could trust her, wanted her to wipe his forehead cool again.

He began to cough, a harsh racking cough that made him close his eyes against the pain. A hand reached to him and held him with a gentleness that even Ada had never shown. Slowly the cough eased. He opened his eyes and saw the concern in hers. 'Keep still,' she said. 'We shall soon have you in bed where we can look after you properly.'

His mind was wonderfully free from delirium now so that he saw her clearly: a squarish face, with full lips to a curling mouth, a slightly turned up nose and widely-spaced deep blue, almost purple eyes. She was aware of his scrutiny but did not seem to take offence.

'Well?' she said, as if she wished to know his judgement of her. But he could not say, did not know the words. All he knew was that he would never cease to be grateful to her. He tried to tell her so but before he could speak the door opened and Ada came in. She looked from him to her mistress as if wanting to

98

know what they had been saying to each other. Then she said, 'It's safe to move but we'll need to be quick.'

Mrs Trevarth and Ada helped him to his feet and together they supported him to the foot of a narrow curving staircase. He looked up in dismay but, with Mrs Trevarth in front leading him and Ada behind, he slowly made his way up. When he reached the top step he sat down, unable to go further. The effort had done for him. He would stay here. It was as good as anywhere to sleep, but they would not let him. He tried to protest but they would not listen. He refused to help them and let his weight sag as they tried to lift him. 'George,' Ada said angrily, 'you have to help us.' He groaned. Could she not see he did not care what happened to him? Why did she not leave him to die? He shook his head in weak defiance.

He felt a hand take hold of his chin and lift his drooping head. He opened his eyes and saw the woman Trevarth. 'Try,' she said. 'For our sakes, for my sake, try.' She took his hand and he let her lead him from the stairs. He felt carpet under his feet. With slow shambling steps he managed to go where the woman took him. He felt himself slipping again into faintness and tried to resist it. He fell, to land softly on a bed, where at last he was able to lie in peace. Voices faded in and out of his hearing; hands touched him, removing his shirt and trousers until he felt the coolness of fresh sheets enfolding him. For a moment, before a fevered sleep took him, he felt close to paradise.

8

Caroline stood in the background watching Ada Prideaux attending to her brother. He looked, in his defencelessness, a mere boy. She could not tear herself away, needed to be sure she had done all she could to help.

'There's nothing more you can do,' the housekeeper said. 'You'd better leave him to me. I'll look after him from now on. It's not safe for you to have anything further to do with him.'

'He needs a doctor. He's ill, you can see.'

'A doctor? What good would that do? Where would we

find a doctor willing to risk his neck for a murderer? Bringing a doctor would be the same as bringing the police. Do you want that?'

'God forbid!'

'Then leave him to me. I know pneumonia when I see it. It will just have to take its course.' She turned her attention to her brother. She had propped him against a nest of pillows. He was sleeping, but restlessly, muttering incoherently from time to time.

Mrs Prideaux turned back to her. 'You must go, ma'am. It's not your place to be here. You've done enough.'

She did not want to leave, still felt responsible for the young man, but she could see the housekeeper was uneasy at her presence.

'I'm going to bathe him,' Mrs Prideaux said. 'You cannot stay.'

'I'll bring you a bowl of water and whatever you need.'

'I have them all ready in the bathroom. Now please go, ma'am. It isn't proper for you to stay. I can do all that's needed.'

'Take care of him,' Caroline said. The housekeeper raised her eyebrows and for some reason Caroline felt a qualm of guilt and could not understand why.

She left the room but lingered in the nursery quarters. She had never imagined they would be put to such use, or indeed any use, for she had abandoned hope of having children. She was still young enough at thirty-six but fortune had not smiled on her so far and there was no likelihood her luck would change now. She was barren and must reconcile herself to that.

She wondered how long they could keep the boy (for so she had begun to think of him) hidden; might not the servants become suspicious at being forbidden to approach the nursery rooms? What excuse could they think of for that?

Mrs Prideaux would have the answer and the housemaids would not object to being spared the need to clean rooms which were patently never going to be used. They would accept as natural a decision to close them off.

She heard her husband's voice downstairs and hurried away. He must not see where she had been. She went to her own room and was at her door to meet him when he arrived. He was cheerful and relaxed. One of the mines in which he had an interest had declared better than expected figures for its tin production, and he had heard good news of his mining affairs in South Africa. The hunt for the murderer had slipped his mind until, on his return home, he had seen the policeman still on guard.

'I shall ask Groves if he thinks it necessary to keep a man here. The fellow must be miles away by now. I don't think you're in any danger, my dear.'

She smiled.

'Do you think Mrs Prideaux knows anything about that brother of hers?' he went on. 'Perhaps I should question her before I speak to Groves.'

'I'm sure she has nothing to tell us. You're quite right, dear, we're in no danger and it would be better if the police were to leave. Their presence about the place upsets the servants.' It would be safer without the guard. Surely Groves must be convinced the fugitive had left the area? She had a sharp picture in her mind of the young man, upstairs, lying desperately ill, in need of the best attention, and she could do so little for him.

'You look anxious, my love,' Thomas said. 'It has been a worrying time for you.'

She wanted to tell him her worries were not of the kind he imagined, and wished she could confide in him, but he would not understand. He would think her mad. Nor could she herself comprehend why she had behaved as she had or why it was so important to her to reassure herself the boy was all right.

She could not resist the urge to see him and, when Thomas went to change for dinner, she hurried to the nursery wing. Mrs Prideaux had gone. Caroline listened outside the room where George was lying. She put her hand to the door handle and turned but the door was locked. She looked around for the key but of course Mrs Prideaux, wisely no doubt, would have put it on her chatelaine with the other household keys.

Yet the boy might need her; someone should be with him at all times. She must get the key from the housekeeper so that she could go to him, as often as possible.

101

She went to find the housekeeper and met her coming up the women servants' stairs, the stairs up which they had smuggled George to the nursery.

'These are the servants' stairs,' Mrs Prideaux told her. 'You should not be here, ma'am.'

'I shall go where I wish,' Caroline said with sudden anger. The woman treated her as if she were in the house only on sufferance. She needed reminding who was mistress. 'I want the key to the nurses's room.'

The housekeeper looked at her as if she did not understand, or did not wish to understand.

'You cannot always be at hand to help your brother. I can do my share.'

'It wouldn't be right, ma'am. And he has no need of anyone's help but mine. I wish he had never come, but now that he's here, he's my responsibility. I cannot have you putting yourself at risk for him.'

'Who is to know?'

'It would not be wise for you to be seen there.'

'I can say I have a perfectly good reason for being in the nursery.'

'What reason? After all this time?'

'Is that what they all think, Mrs Prideaux?' She felt humiliated at the thought, natural enough she supposed, that the household had written her off as barren, a childless, weak, delicate nonentity.

'I'm sorry, ma'am,' Mrs Prideaux said. 'I'm thinking only of your safety. Don't blame me for that.'

Caroline was not appeased. 'Find another key. It's obvious you can't take the whole burden of nursing him on yourself. You have other duties. You cannot be seen to be neglecting those. And what duties have I to distract me?' she added bitterly.

'Very well, ma'am. I shall do as you say, but I do not think it wise for you to be involved.'

She resents my interest, Caroline thought.

'I shall take the key now,' she said. 'When I listened at the door he sounded distressed.'

'Then I shall go to him,' Mrs Prideaux said. 'It is my place to do so, not yours. Please, ma'am.'

Caroline did not answer but led the way to the nursery rooms and waited for the housekeeper to open the door to the nurse's room.

'He is worse,' she exclaimed at the sight of the young man. 'We must fetch a doctor, don't you see?'

'And condemn him to death in that way?'

'He did not do it. He is not a murderer. He told me.'

'You may believe him, but no one else will.'

Caroline looked at Ada Prideaux distrustfully. She had condemned her brother without hearing him. Perhaps she was not to be trusted.

'I shall take my turn at nursing him,' she said.

Mrs Prideaux shook her head. 'You have no experience of nursing, ma'am. Leave him to me, I beg you. I can manage without your help.'

'You may not need me, but he does. Someone should be with him night and day.'

The young man gave a sudden cry and burst into a fit of coughing that brought the women to his side. He opened his eyes and, seeing Caroline, put out a hand to her. She grasped it and, without thinking, put it to her lips to kiss it, in reassurance, to comfort him only.

'You must go,' the housekeeper said angrily. 'Leave him to me. He is nothing to you, cannot be.'

He is everything to me, she wanted to say as she looked at him, his face pale, his forehead bathed with sweat. She wanted to hold his head to her breast, to mother him, to make him whole again.

She heard Mrs Prideaux say again, 'Leave him to me,' and felt the woman's hand at her elbow urging her to go. She must go before she gave herself away, but she would return. She could not abandon the boy. He needed her still, perhaps even needed protection from his own sister, though Caroline could not understand why she thought that might be.

'Let me have a key,' she said and put out her hand for it. 'I have a right.' She knew now she had the best of rights. As she left him she turned to look at him. He was watching her from across the room but she was not sure that he recognised her, for his eyes glazed and he relapsed again into unconsciousness.

103

Chapter Eleven

Snow had given way to rain, then that too had changed as winds from the south west brought unseasonably warm weather. The Christmas tree looked out of place, Maud thought, but she knew her mother would let nothing of Christmas be removed until Twelfth Night. Caroline had followed tradition as long as she could remember, had crept in to the nursery to fill her daughter's stocking with fruit and sweetmeats long after Maud had guessed all about Santa Claus.

She looked across the room to her mother, apparently asleep in her chair by the window, and moved to gather up Samson as he was about to jump on to her mother's lap.

'That's all right, dear,' Caroline said. 'I like him resting with me. We both enjoy it, though he gets too heavy after a while.'

'I didn't want him to disturb you. I thought you were asleep.'

'Dreaming, but not sleeping,' her mother said, and Maud wondered what memories filled her dreams. She had lived so settled a life here in Trecarrow that Maud could not imagine there was anything of excitement to be relived. She had always been so self-contained, so content, there could be few secrets of any moment in her past. Her life was an open book.

'What were you dreaming about?' Maud asked.

Her mother looked up and smiled. 'I know you find it difficult to believe I have any memories you're not aware of.'

'And have you?'

Her mother did not answer and Maud drew her chair up to sit beside her and took Samson on her own lap, stroking him firmly. He purred under her attention. As long as she could remember they had had cats, once a seal-pointed Siamese, once a great ginger tom, and once, long ago when she was very little, they had had a pretty tortoise-shell cat. 'What was the name of that little cat we had?' she asked.

'Which one? We've had so many.'

'The old one.'

'They all became old. Creatures do, even cats.' She sighed. 'There's no escaping that.'

'When I was little. The pretty little tortoise-shell.'

Her mother opened her eyes wide. 'How strange! I was thinking of her too. Claudia we called her.' She sighed again and closed her eyes.

'Dreaming again?' her daughter asked.

'I can see her so clearly, Maud.' She opened her eyes and looked directly at her daughter. 'And your father,' she said. 'What a long time ago it all was and yet it seems like yesterday, or even today.'

'Happy memories, Mother?'

'For the most part.'

Yes, it had been a happy childhood, Maud remembered. She had been indulged by everyone and especially by her father. She had come to them late in their marriage, when, it seemed, they had abandoned hope of children. She had wanted for nothing, always well provided with dolls, toys, puzzles. The nursery held a special magic for her and still did so. And Joseph seemed to feel the same, for he insisted on sleeping there whenever he visited. That would not be for much longer, she thought with a sharp sense of apprehension, for he would soon be away at the war.

'You are dreaming now,' her mother said. 'I can tell.'

Maud did not want to remind her of Joseph's enlistment. 'I was thinking back to times here,' she said, 'when I was little. Was I a handful?'

Her mother raised her eyes to the ceiling in mock horror. 'Indeed you were, but lovely with it,' she said. 'A joy, but always determined on your own way, and Thomas was always there to make sure you got it. He spoilt you.'

105

'As much as you spoil Joseph?'

'A grandmother must be allowed some indulgence. And he reminds me . . .' She stopped, looked at Maud, brushed her hand across her brow and was silent.

'Yes, Mother?' she prompted.

'No, it's gone.'

It had not gone, Maud could tell, for there was a look in her mother's eyes that had been there often of late. She supposed there must be some comfort to old people in thinking back to the past, the days of their youth. She wished she could share those memories but so much must have happened before she was born. Perhaps there were secrets to her mother's life before then? Maud could not believe there were many, and yet − as she herself had had suitors before Robert − maybe other young men had courted her mother before Thomas Trevarth came along. It was not so difficult to imagine, for old photographs showed how beautiful she had been, indeed still was, with a beauty all her own − eyes so wide and blue, square face, pert nose − and now, with the years, to that beauty had been added serenity. She hoped she would match that when she reached her own eighty-sixth birthday.

'What is it?' Her mother had been aware of the scrutiny.

'I was wondering,' Maud said, 'were you a handful when you were a child too? Or when you were a girl, before you married father, did lots of young men come courting?'

Her mother laughed. 'I was never aware of them. Those were the days of chaperones, my dear, when young girls with fat fortunes were watched over and guarded like the valuable properties they were. No, there were no young men in my life before I met Thomas.'

And after? Maud wondered, but was too discreet to ask. Nor could she imagine such a thing.

Maud enjoyed bringing her children to Trecarrow and they enjoyed coming but she did not think there would be many more visits. War inevitably brought change, but there were other reasons why they would cease to come here. For her age her mother was wonderfully well, but the house was far too large for her. Barely one-fifth of the rooms were used now and those mostly only when she and the children came to stay. She must persuade her mother to sell the house and

106

what remained of the estate before it became a total ruin. With what the property brought, her mother could buy a pleasant house in Falmouth, or near them in Surrey, and have enough to allow her and Mrs Prideaux to live in comfort, looked after by a younger companion.

Maud would be sorry when it came to that, for she too had pleasant memories, but, whatever happened to the house, the memories would remain. Nothing could destroy those.

Her mother was dozing again and Maud, holding Samson in her arms, crept from the room. She put the cat down and he followed her along the corridor and up the stairs to the nursery wing. She heard someone there and saw Mrs Prideaux, a duster in hand, bent over as if in sudden pain.

'Mrs Prideaux! What is it?' she asked, alarmed by the woman's appearance. 'Sit down.' She pushed a chair over and the old housekeeper slumped into it.

'You shouldn't be bothering yourself with cleaning up here. Others can do that.' She took the duster from her.

'I like to keep it nice for Master Joseph.'

They're all the same, Maud thought, all besotted with that son of mine, and he doesn't deserve it. But she understood the appeal of his dark looks, his devil-may-care manner and his swift smile.

'I'll see to it. You go along to your room and have a lie down.'

'You won't tell Madam? I don't want her worrying about me.'

'Not if you don't want me to.'

'I do my work.'

'Of course you do, Mrs Prideaux. We all know that.'

But she no longer ruled the household as in the old days. Maud remembered how the servants used to dread her cold reprimands. No one had been free from censure if they deserved it. She had given herself wholly to the needs of the house and the family, had no other interests. Had Trecarrow and the Trevarths been the whole of her life? It seemed so and Maud was grateful for it, though there had been times when she resented her protectiveness. If her mother had had chaperones to guard her, she had had Mrs Prideaux; though it was no part of a housekeeper's duties to watch over the

107

daughter of the house, that had not deterred Prideaux.

'Come along, Mrs Prideaux, let me see you to your room. You must learn to take things easy at your age.'

'I do my work,' the old woman repeated. 'No one can say I don't. I look after my mistress and always have, more than she knows.' She allowed Maud to take her by the arm, and lead her to her bedroom and was persuaded to lie down.

'Can I get you anything?' Maud asked. 'A hot-water bottle? A hot drink?'

'Where is George?'

'George?'

'What did you say?' Mrs Prideaux seemed confused. 'Is he there?'

She must mean Joseph, Maud thought. 'I expect he's gone down to the river.'

'No. He mustn't. He mustn't!' She made as if to get up, but Maud gently urged her back.

'I'll see he's all right. He'll come to no harm.'

'They'll find him.'

Maud looked at the old woman with concern. She seemed to think Joseph was in some sort of danger, but, when Maud said, 'I'll bring him to see you to show you he's all right,' she was reassured and slept.

Maud returned to the nursery. Its magic still held, especially the view from the window to the lawns sweeping down to the water. She had been right; Joseph had gone down to the river; she could see between the trees to his silhouette framed against the shimmering water. She could understand why her mother and Mrs Prideaux made him their favourite. There was something so young and vulnerable about such beauty. She felt a touch at her shoulder and heard a sigh. She turned to see her mother. She too was staring out to watch Joseph. There were tears in her eyes but Maud did not ask why. She thought she knew.

Chapter Twelve

1

Superintendent Groves was not going to let George Prideaux slip through his hands. A case like this had not fallen to his lot before. He would make the most of it.

He was puzzled that there had been no sightings of the man since he had been seen skulking near Perranwell, only a mile or two from the Trecarrow estate. Groves's instinct told him the man was not far away.

His men had been to Redruth and questioned the woman Sullivan, who was known to have been very close to Prideaux in the years when he was a miner, but they had brought him no news. She had denied any knowledge of the man. 'Not seen hide nor hair of him, I've not,' she told Sergeant Penrose. 'Sure I'd tell you if I had, now.' Penrose thought she was telling the truth but had agreed to keep his eyes open. 'If there's anything to be got from her, I'll get it.' Groves did not question how his sergeant would 'get it'. All he wanted was to know.

His hunt for the man Prideaux had become an obsession, something of a personal vendetta. He had never met the fellow but he had begun to nurse a hatred for him and to let the same feelings extend to those misguided enough to be sheltering the man. He hoped Prideaux would be found at Trecarrow, but, when Trevarth asked him to withdraw the police guard on the house, he pretended to accede to the request. Trevarth was not a man whose wishes could be ignored. But Groves made certain that he kept his lines of information open. One of the grooms at Trecarrow, young Bert Glasson, had a police record. It had been easy to persuade him to keep an eye on the goings and comings in the house and report them to the police.

So far, Glasson had had nothing to tell. 'Everyone do think he's up and away,' he said. 'And I do reckon so myself. There's nought happening there, nought that matters.'

'I want to know everything that goes on,' Groves said. 'Leave it to me to decide what matters.'

Patience was a policeman's most important attribute, that and tenacity. He would not let Prideaux escape. He had sworn that. He even, when he attended the Sunday meeting at the Centenary Chapel in Camborne, silently prayed that justice might prevail and the man be delivered into his hands.

2

Caroline was pleased to think the hue and cry for George Prideaux had died down and that to outside observers, life at Trecarrow could return to normal. Even the police guard on the house had been withdrawn.

'I don't suppose they'll catch him now,' Thomas said. 'If he's any sense, he'll have left the country.'

'How could he get away? Who would help him?' Caroline asked, thinking of the 'wanted' posters that had appeared everywhere.

'There are plenty of rogues and vagabonds of the same ilk as Prideaux. He'll have no difficulty hiding with them until they find a fisherman willing to take him overseas somewhere.'

'But they would surely want money to help him?'

'You seem very interested, my love.'

She wondered if she had given herself away. 'No,' she said. 'Not really.'

'One can't help feeling sorry for the man, harried and hunted as he is. I almost hope he gets away. At least then our Mrs Prideaux would be able to concentrate on her work. Have a word with her, my dear. I've noticed all sorts of ways

110

in which she's neglecting her duties. The staff will be quick to take advantage of any failing in her.'

Caroline was dismayed. She was aware how distracted the housekeeper had become since assuming responsibility for her brother, but was surprised Thomas had seen it.

'I shall speak with her,' she said.

She knew where she would find her, in the nursery wing where her brother lay, still fevered and restless and only occasionally lucid enough to recognise his sister. Ada Prideaux came in answer to her knock and peered suspiciously through the narrowly opened door.

'Let me in,' Caroline said. 'How is he?' She slipped through the door and stood inside, staring at the man in the bed.

She turned accusingly on Mrs Prideaux. 'He looks worse,' she said. 'What are you doing for him?'

'All I can. There's no need for you to be concerned.'

'I am concerned, whether you want me to be or not.' She went to the bedside and put her hand to the boy's brow. 'You need my help. You cannot do everything.'

'He is my responsibility. What can you do for him that I can't?'

'My husband has commented on your neglect of your duties in the house. You will draw attention to yourself, give yourself away. And make yourself ill.'

'What do you suggest I do? Leave him to fend for himself? I wish he'd never come near.'

Her mistress was shocked. 'How could you say a thing like that? What would have happened to him if I hadn't found him? Well, I did, and he's my responsibility as much as yours. It was I who saved him. Now I must do my share in bringing him back to health. I can stay with him during the day, do as much for him as you do. Then you can get some rest and give some mind to your household duties. At least pretend to do so. We shall both suffer if suspicion falls on you and your brother will suffer most of all. You cannot be blind to that.'

Mrs Prideaux had spent three nights with him and weariness was evident in her dark-rimmed eyes and drawn face.

'You cannot deny it' Caroline said. 'It will do him no good if you fall ill as well. I'm competent enough, I assure you. I

111

know you don't think so, but tell me what to do for him and I
shall do it, never fear.' She desperately wanted Mrs Prideaux
to agree.

The housekeeper looked at her mistress and shook her head,
but said, 'Very well. For some of the daytime. But I shall stay
with him at night. You cannot do that. And pray God he will
soon be well enough to leave us to ourselves once more.'

3

She was alone with him, the door locked against intruders.
No one would ask where she was, not until Thomas returned.
No one ever needed to consult her, save Mrs Prideaux herself
and that was a formality. Life would proceed at Trecarrow
without change or interruption in her absence.

She sat by his bed, from time to time bringing him
something to drink or wiping his forehead. She held him
up while she made his pillows more comfortable, stroked
his black hair, letting her fingers play with the wet curls,
and prayed to God for his recovery.

He was restless so the sheets became twisted and she
straightened them. He opened his eyes and, seeing her,
reached out a hand to hers and weakly held it a moment.
He recognised her, she thought, and wanted to thank her,
but his hold loosened and he closed his eyes. He began to
talk, jumbled broken sentences, making no sense at first,
and then beginning to have some thread of reason to them,
names, questions. She thought he wanted to know why his
sister was not there and who she was. She explained she
was a friend and would care for him, but he did not seem
to understand and fell into an uneasy sleep. His hand was
outside the covers and she held it, putting it to her lips from
time to time.

'You must get well,' she said. 'You must.'

Mrs Prideaux had left some phenacetin tablets to help
bring his temperature down and she had filled a jug with
milk, with instructions it should be warmed and given to
him. 'You can do all that?' she had asked, and Caroline
smiled at being talked to like some new and incompetent
maid. She understood the woman's anxiety. 'I shall care for

him as if he were my own,' she said. And, in a way, he was her own. He belonged to her; she had been the one to save him, and she would not let him go, would keep him there for ever, in her house, to love and cherish. She smiled at her fancy, knowing that when he was well again he would leave, would have to, to escape the law.

He was hardly breathing and for a terrifying moment she thought he had slipped away, but he opened his eyes and smiled at her, and said, 'Who are you?'

'Caroline,' she answered and was moved when he repeated her name. 'Caroline,' he whispered and looked about the room as if seeking his sister.

'I am looking after you for the moment,' she explained. 'Your sister will come back later. We are taking it in turns to care for you.' He seemed satisfied.

She warmed the milk in the nursery kitchen and he took it gratefully. She held him up against her to drink it and the touch of him made her tremble so, she could hardly hold the cup still against his lips. When he had finished she sat there, his head against her breast, her hand to his brow gently caressing it, as she might have done a sick child, if she had had a child. That is all he is to me, she tried to tell herself, but there was more, much more.

4

Memories flooded through the chaos of his mind, some painful, some pleasant. He felt the touch of a woman's hand and thought it might be Molly. He called her name but she either did not hear him or refused to answer. She had always been unpredictable. Like Janet too and he called her, thought she might come, but instead he saw Rennie going into her cottage and he felt a sudden rage. He tried to strike out at the man but he disappeared before he could make contact. Janet disappeared too and he tried to tell himself he was not sorry. There were plenty of others to comfort him. But he could not hold them; they rushed past, jeering and taunting him. He shook his fist at them but they laughed at his impotence.

He turned over restlessly and felt a hand reach to him; no

113

illusion this time, but a hand of flesh and blood. Not his sister's hand, for Ada's touch was firm, full of authority. This hand was hesitant as if the woman were unsure of her right to hold him so. He opened his eyes; she was bending close to him as she drew his sheets up and, when she saw his eyes looking into hers, she blushed.

He saw her clearly, the haze of his delirium gone. He knew her now; she had been in and out of his dreams; it was she who had found him in the stable-loft. He remembered her name, Caroline, and said it to himself, and then aloud.

'What is it?' she asked.

He wanted only to repeat the name, to hear it spoken, to convey his understanding and his thanks. 'Caroline,' he said again and relapsed into sleep.

When he next woke it was his sister by his bed, not the woman Caroline. When Ada saw he was awake she brought him food, calves-foot jelly. He took it meekly; whenever he had been ill as a boy he had surrendered to her care without complaint, enjoying being fussed over.

When he had eaten and she had bathed him he lay exhausted by the effort of co-operating with her. There was a candle alight by the bed, throwing shadows over his sister's face, deepening the hollows about her eyes. She should take more care of herself and he tried to tell her so but before he could summon strength to speak her head fell forward and she slept.

There was no longer any need for her to remain watchful over him; he had got over the worst. He had lost some days of his life, that was all, and there were plenty more days to come. He only half-remembered what had been happening to him recently, but the hunt for him, his sojourn in Wheal Kitty and his escape from there, came sharply back. And, suddenly, he saw a vision of Rennie and felt a surge of hatred, a hatred that vanished as another picture appeared, of Rennie falling, falling, falling.

No, he had not wished that on the man. He buried his head in his hands to dispel the memory, but it stayed with him until he fell into a desperately uneasy sleep.

He woke and felt his head was clear at last, as if in his delirium the corners of his mind had been swept clean, so

114

that what remained were positive, pleasant images of the past and hopeful prospects of the future. He recalled his childhood when he and Ada had been alone together. He could remember nothing of his parents, did not know how old he was when they had died. His earliest memories were all of the sister who had cared for him, kept him from harm. Without her he would have gone into some orphanage, he supposed. With her, though life had been hard, he had known love. He had never managed to tell Ada how grateful he was; perhaps it was only now that he knew it.

He looked over to where she was sitting, in the chair by his bed, arms on her lap, head drooped and jerking from time to time in an effort to stay alert. He wanted to tell her there was no longer any need for her to remain with him, but he was glad she was there, glad to be assured someone cared enough to put herself at risk for him.

And that other woman, she too had taken risks. Why? What had led her to save him, to lie to the police and bring him food? Caroline, he remembered, Caroline Trevarth, Ada's mistress. She too had fed him, had sat by him in Ada's absence. In lucid intervals between his delirium, he had observed her. She was a beautiful woman: at least she had the attributes of beauty, but passive and cold, a perfection of colour and form as might have been created by a skilled portrait painter, but without the passion and the breath of life. Yet, once, when she helped to raise him on his pillows, there had been a touch of warmth and, thinking back to that brief moment of contact, he wondered if he might have misjudged her.

Where is she now? he wondered. Will she come back or, now I am so much better, will she want me to leave? Wherever he went now danger went with him. He was a wanted man, and, as soon as he could, he should go. If he were discovered here his sister and the woman Caroline would be bound to suffer. The thought brought him out in a cold sweat. He must get up, dress, and get away. Without delay. He pushed the sheets back and tried to get out of bed, but fell weakly back.

Ada had heard him and sat upright. 'What are you doing?' she said sharply. 'Lie back.'

'I can't stay here. It's dangerous for you,' he said. And for

115

Caroline, he wanted to add, and did not know what made him keep her name to himself.

'You wouldn't get five yards in your present condition,' Ada said dismissively. 'When you're well you can talk of leaving. The sooner that comes the better for us all but it's not yet. You're safe enough here provided you do as I tell you.' She got up from her chair, plumped up his pillows and straightened the sheets. 'You're on the mend, I can see, over the crisis, and there won't be any need for my mistress to bother her head about you any more. She's done enough, too much to my way of thinking.'

'Why?' he began, wanting to know why the woman Caroline had done so much for him.

Ada turned away.

'Why?' he repeated. 'What made her risk her neck for me?'

'You're a child, the child she never had. She was sorry for you. You were sick and she tended you. That's all.'

He lay back, still tired at having to think and speak, but wanting to know more.

'It was kind of her,' he said at last.

He could hear Ada moving about in one of the rooms nearby. She returned with some broth she had prepared.

'What are these rooms?' he asked.

'The nursery wing. There's a scullery, with a gas ring, a bathroom — you should be able to get there now — and two other rooms.'

'And no children.'

'No children, nor ever will be after all this time.'

She stood over him while he took the broth and watched until he had finished every drop. 'I'll come back to see you later, bring you something more filling.'

'Caroline?' he asked.

His sister raised her eyebrows. 'I told you there's no longer any need for Mrs Trevarth to help. You don't need watching any more. I'll tell her how much better you are. She'll be glad to know, but she won't come again.'

He was disappointed. He wanted to satisfy his curiosity about the woman, to see whether his fever had created the vision of her beauty or whether it was real. And he needed

116

to know why she had taken the risk of helping him. He must thank her for it. But for her he would be languishing in some gaol, awaiting trial for murder.

'I must see her to thank her,' he said.

'Time enough for that when you're ready to leave. Then, if it's safe to do so, you can see her.' She put a glass of water on the table beside his bed. 'You will have to be careful. Though no one is likely to visit this part of the house, you must be quiet. We mustn't rouse suspicion. Think of Mrs Trevarth. Her safety and reputation are in your hands. An incautious move — to the window, say — and the whole household will be overrun by police. You understand?'

'I'll be careful.'

'I'll lock the rooms when I leave. You'll be all right now on your own. But I thought I'd lost you.' She left him and he heard the key turn in the door. He was alone, in silence, still a prisoner, however kind his gaolers.

5

When Ada Prideaux presented herself to her mistress for the usual pretence of discussing the arrangements for the day, Caroline was interested in nothing but the welfare of their patient. 'How is he?' she said, brushing aside any reference to household problems.

'He's over the crisis, I'm glad to say. You need not concern yourself with him any longer. As soon as he's well enough, he'll be leaving us.'

'Leaving? Where for? Where can he go? He'll need help to see him safely away.'

'You need do nothing more, ma'am. You must not be involved. I'll see to everything. Believe me, that's better. I'm sorry he ever thought of coming here. I can't forgive myself.'

Caroline looked in surprise at the woman. 'He's your brother. Where else could he turn?'

'He's my brother, yes, and my responsibility whether I like it or not. But he's nothing to you. You must forget all about him, forget you ever met him. That way will be safer for you, for everyone.'

117

Caroline let the woman go, but knew she could not accept her dismissal so lightly. How could she forget about him? How could she ignore his presence in the house? He was there, her responsibility, more so than his sister's. She had saved him, lied for him, given him shelter. She could not let him go from her like that, could not imagine turning away from him when he might still need her.

She needed him: every moment of the past days had been a torment; when away from him she pictured him fevered and in pain and was anxious for him, and when she was with him she was tormented by the need to touch him, knowing that he was unaware of her, knowing that he spoke of other women, knowing that when he became aware he would have no interest in her. He was not of her class, nor even of her generation; compared with her he was a child. Indeed she was old enough, almost, to be his mother.

She had no claim on him, must let him go, leave it to his sister to see to him now. The right and sensible thing was to forget she had ever seen him.

She tried. She busied herself with the tedious futilities of the day, pretending an interest in the garden, returning to her drawing room and picking up her embroidery, putting it on one side to read a copy of *Punch* Thomas had brought the day before. That held her interest for a few minutes, then she took Meredith's new novel, *Diana of the Crossways,* from her shelves, but was unable to concentrate, turning page after page before she realised she had not taken in a word.

It was no use. She could not resist the lure; she went to the nursery wing, took out the spare key that Mrs Prideaux had given her and put it to the lock, but did not turn it. She put her ear to the door but heard nothing until she became aware, to her horror, of a footstep on the back stairs. She withdrew the key and sped away, ashamed of the compulsion she felt to visit him. She must set her mind free of him; he meant nothing to her, would be gone from her life in a week or so, gone for ever.

At that she knew she had to see him once more, − only once more − could not deny herself that small reward. She would wish him well, let him know she had no regrets at having helped him and would do whatever she could to help him again. Her decision made, she waited till the late afternoon when she knew the housekeeper would be engaged on her normal duties, and went then.

She approached the nursery guiltily, aware of the pleasure stirring in her at the thought of seeing him. She stood at the nursery door a moment before turning the key, then slipped in softly, closing the door behind her, clicking the catch to lock it from within, and went to the room occupied by the boy.

He was asleep, his pale face framed by his dark hair, his chin firm, his nose proudly aquiline, his lips parted slightly in the beginnings of a smile as if his dreams were pleasing. She remembered how Superintendent Groves had described him. 'How shall we know him?' she had asked. And Groves had replied, 'By his hunted look. He was handsome enough as a lad, gypsy-like, with a gypsy's insolence.'

In sleep he was handsome still but there was a boyish quality about him that belied any suggestion of insolence. She recalled how she had first seen him, in the loft, strong, lean, powerful and frightening; now the threat had gone and he lay, helpless and disarmed.

She stood in silence, not wishing to disturb him yet unwilling to leave without his knowing she had visited him. She turned, intending to go, but as she did she heard him speak. 'Caroline,' he whispered and she looked round, wondering if she had imagined it. But he was awake and looking at her and saying again, 'Caroline.'

She went over to the side of the bed and looked down at him, hoping he could not read in her eyes the thoughts that troubled her. She was ashamed of them but could not hide them from herself, only seek to hide them from him.

'Are you feeling better?' she asked.

'Weak,' he said. 'But in my right mind, I think.'

She was not sure she was, but she forced herself to say, 'I came to say goodbye. Your sister doesn't think it wise for me to visit you.'

He raised himself to sit up and she leaned over to adjust his pillows. As she did her hands touched his shoulder. She withdrew them immediately but the feel of his flesh moved her. She must suppress such feelings; they held a danger far

119

greater than that of being accused of harbouring a criminal.

'You will be all right on your own?' she said.

'No,' he said, shaking his head. 'I shall not be all right. I shall be left to think and to wonder what will become of me.'

'We shall let nothing happen to you. We shall make sure you are safe.' She took his hand between hers and held it close to reassure him all would be well.

He looked around the room. 'It will be like a prison — just as bad — if no one comes to see me.'

'Your sister will come.'

'When she can.'

'I shall try to make it easy for her.'

He sighed. 'Can you not come yourself from time to time?' He seemed to be tiring. It would be many, many days, perhaps weeks, before he was strong enough to leave. How could she deny him the company he asked for?

'I'll do what I can,' she said.

He smiled, lay back, closed his eyes and went to sleep.

How vulnerable he is, she thought as she left him, and had a sudden vision of a posse of police hunting him, seizing him, dragging him off. She could not let that happen. With every man's hand against him, he still needed her. She could not fail him.

6

Caroline feared Thomas might sense the torrent of emotion flooding through her, but he did not seem to notice. He was too full of his own concerns to be aware of hers. Reports had been coming in from his agents in South Africa of the bitter feeling mounting among the Afrikaaners against British mining companies.

'I know I should not bring my business worries home to you but it weighs heavily on me,' he said in apology for revealing his anxieties. 'You can have no interest in things of that sort.'

She pretended to give him her attention but, throughout the evening, her mind returned constantly to the young man lying in the nursery. She wished she could find some excuse to leave Thomas and make her way to the nursery wing.

The opportunity did not arise. Thomas wanted to talk, but he finished with his complaints against the Afrikaaners. In spite of them his businesses interests flourished. He was proud of his success and told her so. 'I only wish,' he began, and broke off.

She knew. He had spoken before of the family business, of what the name Trevarth meant in the world of mining and had meant for generations past. She had failed him.

'What is it, my love?' he asked, full of solicitude, keen to notice her sorrow.

'Do you mind so much our not having children?' she said. They rarely spoke of this now, having long since abandoned hope.

He took a long time to answer and she could see he felt, as she did, a sadness almost too great for expression. 'No, no longer, except as now, wondering what will happen to the business when I've gone. It would have given me great satisfaction to think of the name carrying on. But there's nothing to be done and there's no point in regretting what can never be. I'm happy to share my life with you, my love, want nothing more. And you?'

She bent her head to hide her tears. She had thought she was content, had got over the hurt of barrenness, but it was not so; something had revived the longing for a child and she could not hide it. 'I wish,' she said, and then shook her head. 'No, it's no use wishing. We must be grateful for what we have, our lives together. We are very fortunate, are we not, Thomas? But it's sad to think ...' He interrupted her by getting up from his chair, taking her face between his hands and bending to kiss her. 'Don't think so,' he said. 'We are happy together, could not be happier, I believe. I have no complaints, my dear, do not imagine that. I do not blame you for it.'

Nevertheless, she blamed herself, accepting without question that their childlessness was due to some fault in her, a fault which no amount of love on Thomas's part could cancel.

'It is not to be, my love, and I have long since accepted it. If God had wished us to have a family He would have

121

worked to that end. We must accept His will with good heart.'
She hated Thomas in this sanctimonious mood; it only arose
when they discussed children, never when he talked of affairs
of business. His success in that was the consequence of his
own skill and foresight apparently; only failures were to be
excused by the intervention of the Almighty.

She felt ashamed at these unspoken criticisms of her
husband, could not understand why they should spring to
mind; she had never before had such disloyal thoughts,
accepted as gospel all that Thomas, her natural lord and
master, said or did.

'You look anxious, my love,' he said. 'I hope you're not
still worrying about that man Prideaux.'

'Of course not,' she hastened to say.

'I'll have a word with Groves tomorrow, ask him what
news there is. I'm certain he'll be able to reassure you.'

'I'm not anxious about the man, not at all,' she told
Thomas, but it was a lie, and, as she lay in bed, with her
husband only inches away, it was of the young man she
thought, closing her eyes and letting her imagination play
tricks with her. She was deeply ashamed that she could think
so of a stranger, in the very presence of her husband, and
feared that her visions of the young man were so real and
her response to them so tender as to wake Thomas, to make
him wonder what she was about. She lay motionless, trying
to conjure up other images to repel those of him which flowed
through her. But always, it was her first sight of him that
returned to haunt her. She became restless with longing,
a sensation foreign to her, frightening in its intensity. She
wanted to get up and go to him but knew she could not, was
struck with horror that an idea could have such command
over her.

He could mean nothing to her; she was thinking like a
young and foolish girl, like that girl Jessica who had been
dismissed for the sort of behaviour she was now imagining.
She was a woman of thirty-six, married – and content in
her marriage – a respected and respectable matron, yet
she was thinking like a wanton. Tomorrow she would
find something to occupy her time and her mind. She
would resume her charitable visits to families in need, rid

122

herself of this foolishness, give herself to good works, not sinful thoughts. She would leave the boy to his sister. That was best.

For two days her resolution did not fail her. She visited homes in the backlets and alley-ways of Redruth, where poverty and need overcame pride and made the women accept her offerings with gratitude. It was no comfort to her, nor did it rid her mind of thoughts of him. Wherever she went she saw him, in the young boy playing on the doorstep, in the youth at the street corner, in the gypsy hawker leading his donkey and cart out of town towards Carn Brea. They all had something of him in them, though none his comeliness.

She returned home from the third day of her visits, knowing she could no longer turn her back on him. Not seeing him had intensified her longing, not lessened it. She had to go to him, would be content merely to reassure herself he was getting better, needed no more of him than that. But it was now the week-end and Thomas spent more time at home, so that it was not easy to find an opportunity to go to the nursery. Moreover, he had asked Superintendent Groves to come to see them, to get a report on how the hue and cry was going.

Groves was his usual arrogant self, though he tempered his manner in front of Thomas, deferring to the influence of the Trevarths.

'We've certainly not given up hope of catching him,' Groves announced. 'I have my own suspicions as to what has been going on.' He seemed to look directly at Caroline as he spoke so that she was alarmed. She concealed her fear and said, 'What are those?'

Groves tapped his finger to his nose in a vulgar gesture of secrecy. 'Information. We're collecting plenty of that. He's had help from somewhere. Not from his old miner friends, I'm bound to say. Maybe from the gypsy folk living under Carn Brea, but we've been watching them and seen nothing. Maybe from a woman friend of his over to Redruth. A trollop, just the sort of woman who would go for George Prideaux.' He glanced over to Thomas who had coughed in rebuke at the mention of such women before his wife.

123

'No use being mealy-mouthed about it,' Groves went on. 'We need to know the sort of people we're dealing with, the sort of folk who would give succour to a man like that. But I don't think the answer lies there either. We've not forgotten his sister, are keeping a discreet eye on her, have her followed whenever she leaves the house. But, if she does know where he's hiding, she's not led us to him so far. We'll catch up with him just the same, have no doubt of that.'

'So,' said Thomas, 'you're of the opinion he's still in the area? That's not what I hoped to hear.'

Groves sat back and folded his arms over his massive chest. He spoke slowly, weightily. 'We shall find him, and deal with him and with whoever is hiding him, whoever they may be.' His voice held a certainty that again alarmed Caroline, making her wonder if he knew more, much more, than he said. She tried to relax but her mind was considering the possibility that one of the servants might be in the pay of the police, watching her movements, waiting to trap her into indiscretion. She had no reason for thinking any of the servants might be disloyal enough to betray her, but did not know them well enough to feel safe.

'Surely,' Thomas said, 'no one would go out of their way to protect a murderer?'

'He's a plausible rogue from all accounts. It would not surprise me if some woman has fallen for his charm and is giving him shelter. If that's the case, I'm sorry for her. She'll find out to her cost — and probably too late — that men of his kind don't stay true to one woman.'

Thomas frowned again, evidently thinking such talk indelicate in front of his wife. She tried to dismiss Groves's judgment of the young man. What was he likely to know? But the thought lingered. How could a man such as George Prideaux not be attractive to women? She brought her mind back to hear Thomas saying, 'Bring him to book, Groves, and quickly. It's unthinkable that a man like that may still be roaming the neighbourhood.'

Groves was complacent. 'He won't escape me. I mean to get him if it's the last thing I do.'

He knows something, Caroline thought. But he cannot know. If he was certain we were harbouring him here he would have come back to search even more thoroughly than the last time. Maybe he's playing cat and mouse with us, she thought, looking at his self-satisfied smirk. He was enjoying the cruelty of the game.

Perhaps she was reading too much into his manner. Of course he suspected everyone; it was one of the tricks of his trade to make people uneasy. Well, he had succeeded with her, but she would not let him change her plans, or frighten her into refusing the boy shelter.

She had to warn Mrs Prideaux she was being watched and must alert her to the possibility that one of the servants might be helping the police. She excused herself and went to find the housekeeper. She met her at the foot of the stairs leading to the nursery wing. She had just come from seeing her brother.

'How is he?' Caroline asked.

'Making progress. I hope it won't be long before he's fit to leave.'

'Superintendent Groves is here. I'm sure he suspects something.'

'He can't know anything, ma'am, and you must be careful he never does.'

'They're watching you, having you followed.'

'I have done nothing to make them suspect me.'

'You are his sister, that's reason enough for them. And I wonder if one of the staff is helping them. Groves hinted at it.'

'I do not believe it.' Then she was silent, as if reviewing the servants in her mind's eye. 'No, I can't think of anyone who would be so deceitful. Jessica might have, but I got rid of her. I can't believe it, but I shall keep my eyes open.'

'Be careful, I beg you,' Caroline said.

'It is you who must be careful, ma'am. You must keep away. I would never forgive myself if you were to suffer on account of that brother of mine. I'm glad you have been sensible and left him to himself.'

The housekeeper was talking to her as if she were a young girl and Caroline resented it, even if the woman's concern was well-meant. 'I shall do what I think best,' Caroline said firmly. 'I want his safety, just as you do. I shall do nothing to put that at risk.'

125

But she would not be able to keep away, however dangerous it might be. She watched the housekeeper go towards the domestic quarters and immediately turned to the nursery. Everyone was occupied elsewhere and it would be safe to go, just for a moment, just to make sure he was improving, as his sister claimed, just to let him know she cared. Only for a moment.

She hurried up the side stairs and unlocked the nursery door and went into the room where he should be. But he was not there. She called softly, 'Where are you, Mr Prideaux?'

The clothes on the bed were stripped back, but the pillow still bore the marks of his head. She heard him moving in the bathroom next to the night nursery. He had not heard her and she stood waiting for him, in silence, full of expectation and longing.

He came back into the room and stood framed in the doorway. He was wearing a nightgown that barely reached to his knees. It must be one of his sister's and was too small, clinging closely to his firm body. She turned away hurriedly. He walked slowly to the bed and climbed on to it then lay exhausted, unable to find energy enough to draw the covers over him. She went to him and pulled sheets and blankets up around him. He smiled weakly.

'You're still poorly,' she said, unable to hide her concern.

'Just weak, nothing more than that.'

'It takes time,' she said.

He nodded. 'Where have you been?' he said. 'I thought you would come to see me. You promised.'

'Did I?' She moved away from the bed and sat on a chair a foot away. She did not dare to stay near him, afraid of what her instincts might draw her to do. She could control herself if she remained at a distance.

'The days are very long with no one to talk to,' he said.

'Your sister comes.'

'When she can. But you said you would come.' He sounded like a small boy complaining of neglect.

'I shall. I promise, but I cannot stay now. My husband will be curious. We have had a police superintendent to see us. Don't be alarmed,' she quickly added. 'Whatever happens we'll keep you hidden.'

'Be careful,' he said as she went and she wondered if he was thinking of her safety or his own. 'And come back soon.'

7

Spencer Groves smiled to himself as he left Trevarth. He had given the man something to think about, planting suspicion of his housekeeper in his and in his lady's mind.

Mrs Trevarth interested him. She had not reacted quite as he thought she would. She had been alarmed, as anyone would be at a murderer being on the loose. But the woman was exercising some sort of self-control which he had not expected from her. He admired her for it. He had always thought her a vapid creature, spoilt and empty, but under the threat that the nearness of Prideaux had brought, she had developed a sparkle, almost as if the danger had touched some core within her that demanded excitement.

And she was a beautiful woman with it. She had seemed pretty enough before but, for himself, he liked a woman with zest and liveliness, something to challenge him, someone worth beating into submission. Before this he could not have imagined Caroline Trevarth offering any such interest. He wondered what had happened to trigger the change. The excitement of the hue and cry, perhaps.

He dismissed thoughts of the woman Trevarth from his mind. He was not satisfied that his men had got as much information from the groom, Bert Glasson, as they could. Glasson was a slippery customer, but a weak one; he would respond to fear.

Groves went to the rear of the house to find the lad. He was just preparing to leave. He had a bright, perky face, but it fell when he saw the figure of the policeman looming at the stable door. He tried to go round him but Groves put out a hand and held him back, drawing him into the shadow of the stable for a talk.

Groves said nothing for a long while, staring accusingly at the lad.

'How old are you?'

'Twenty,' Glasson surlily replied.

'Happy at your work?'

''tes better'n bein' down the mine. 'Tes all right.'

'You want to keep your job?'

Glasson did not answer.

'Did you tell Mr Trevarth you'd been in trouble with the law?'

''twas nothing, sir.'

''twas the law, lad,' Groves said mockingly. 'Don't let me catch you thinking 'tes nothing breaking the law.'

'No, sir,' Glasson meekly replied but scowled rebelliously.

'You're going to help us now, aren't you? Catch that villain Prideaux?'

'I know nothing, honest to God.'

'Then find out something. There's something to be found out, I'm sure of that. Keep your eyes peeled, boy. Report anything unusual, anything that woman Prideaux or anyone else in the house gets up to. He's hiding somewhere, maybe nearer than you think, maybe near enough to lay his hands on you. He's a murderer, boy, don't forget that, killed one man already and not likely to stop at killing another. So watch out for him and let us know the moment you've anything to tell us.'

Glasson shuffled uncomfortably and looked around as if imagining the murderer might be hiding there, in the stable. He looked towards the ladder which led to the loft.

'What's up there?' Groves said sharply.

'Nothing but old tackle and straw and the mistress's cat and kittens,' the groom answered.

Groves went towards the ladder and began to climb.

'The mistress don't want her cat disturbed,' Glasson said.

'She doesn't, eh? We'll see about that.' His nose was sharp for something out of place, a hint of the unusual. He stood at the head of the ladder looking into the gloom of the loft. He heard a cat and put out his hand to reach to it. The creature snarled angrily and he snatched his hand away, putting it to his mouth sucking at the scratch she had given him.

'You brute!' he exclaimed.

'I warned you,' said Glasson with a smugness that angered Groves. He climbed down the ladder and took hold of the groom by the shoulders and shook him.

128

'Keep nothing from me, understand, boy, or it'll be the worse for you. Look about you, tell us everything and maybe we'll stop bothering you. Everything, mind.' He threw the man away from him. He would leave Glasson to his subordinates in future. He had softened him up for them now.

He looked back at the house. It was a fine house from every aspect and especially so from the front, with its handsome porticoed entrance and the gracious sweep of its lawns to the river. Out in the bay there was a fishing boat, and another, returning to harbour. He must have them watched too. Prideaux might well escape from the country that way.

But he felt he was still here, and very near. His instinct told him so.

8

She could not keep away and when Mrs Prideaux begged her not to visit her brother, saying it was not proper for her to be involved, Caroline said with more firmness than she had ever shown that she would go where she wanted in her own house. 'The boy needs company. He will get better more quickly for it and you haven't time to give him all the attention he needs.'

'I beg you,' the housekeeper said, 'don't take such risks. You may be noticed. Your husband . . .'

'Leave that to me. I know what I'm doing. Do you think I would risk the boy's life?'

But she did not know what she was doing, only that she had to go to see him.

The housekeeper slowly shook her head, as if she knew there was no point in arguing. 'Remember you warned me there might be someone among the servants who is reporting to the police. You may even now have given yourself away. Be careful.'

Caroline thought she understood the woman's anxiety. 'I shall do nothing to hurt him. I care for the boy too.'

'I was thinking of you, ma'am, not of him. He will soon be able to look after himself.'

'When he is, then will be time enough to let him go. In the meantime I shall go on seeing him. He needs me.'

Mrs Prideaux looked so closely at her that Caroline became uneasy. 'He's just a boy,' she said, trying to justify her interest in him. 'Your brother, and innocent.'

'Yes, ma'am,' the housekeeper said, but Caroline saw disbelief in her eyes, a strangely intense look, controlling some covert emotion − anger, maybe? Jealousy? Caroline could not tell but, disturbed though she was, she chose to ignore the woman.

'I shall take care,' she said, and she turned on her heel, conscious that Mrs Prideaux remained watching her as she went towards the nursery wing.

I only want a moment with him, she told herself, only to see him for a second, reassure myself that he is improving. He is a boy, a mere boy, and in trouble.

He seemed pleased she had come and sat up in bed to greet her. She remained at a distance, holding herself back, denying the instinct that drew her to him.

'You look so much better,' she said. His pallor had gone and what had been stubble had grown to become a tight black beard, giving him the look of a pirate, a boy no longer. He was no less beautiful but to that beauty had come a hint of danger, and, she saw, that touch of insolence mentioned by Groves. She was reminded of another thing Groves had said: 'That sort of man doesn't stay true to one woman.'

'What are you thinking of?' he asked.

'That I must bring you something to read,' she said hurriedly. 'Something to occupy your time.'

'I would rather you read to me. That would help. Lying here, with nothing to do but think, I get so bored.'

'And what do you think about?'

'Tomorrow and the next day and the day after that. What I shall do when I get away from here. Where I shall go.'

She had not foreseen the emptiness that came at the mention of his going. 'And where might you go?' she asked.

'How can I tell? I have to get out of the country first. Then America, Australia, South Africa − who knows? There's a world waiting for me. No one out there will want to trap and manacle me, no one there will accuse me of murder. I shall be free.' He did not seem to be talking to her so much as to himself. 'Men have a choice in those places to be whatever they can make of themselves, no lords and ladies, no longer master and servant.'

She hoped for his sake it was true but did not think it could ever be so. She wanted him to keep talking; the resonance of his voice made her close her eyes for the pleasure of hearing it and feeling the shiver it sent through her. What he said mattered nothing, the sound alone moved her. But he had stopped.

She opened her eyes to see him gazing at her, smiling as if perhaps he knew the effect his voice was having.

'Go on,' she said.

'What else can I say? I have no idea what's waiting for me round the corner — a posse of policemen maybe, ready to snatch me, haul me off to gaol.'

'No, no,' she protested. 'It won't happen so. I shan't let it.'

'You have done enough for me. But for you I would already have been caught, already been tried and condemned.'

The mere idea of it upset her and she got up from her chair and walked about the room, trying to hide her distress.

'You must not speak so,' she urged.

'Sometimes when I'm lying here I feel afraid. It gets so lonely I want to scream, to call for someone, anyone, to come.'

'You mustn't. No one must know you're here.'

'I know. I don't make a sound, only feel like shouting my innocence, but I don't. I'm safe here, I know, but I hate the loneliness. It unmans me.'

'I shall come as often as I can, I promise.'

'You promised before, but you left me for days.'

'Your sister comes.'

'My sister is not you.'

A note in his voice made her wary, a note she wanted to hear but which she did not trust. She had pretended to think of him as a boy, but it was the voice of a man she heard, a man of experience, a man of the sort who did not stay true to one woman — the 'plausible rogue' Groves had depicted. She laughed, pretending to treat his remark lightly, but when he repeated 'My sister is not you,' she looked him full in the eye.

'She still treats me like a child,' he said. 'And there are times when I'm glad of it, when I'm ill. But I'm not a child. You — I can talk to you, tell you what I hope from life. You don't think of me as a child, do you?' He seemed to be serious in his enquiry.

'No,' she said. 'I do not think that.' She could not trust herself to say more, could not say that when she had first seen him she had seen the man in him, and could think of nothing else. She went towards the door, afraid that, if she stayed, she would give herself away.

'Don't go,' he pleaded.

'I must.'

'Come back soon.'

'I'll bring something to read, for me to read to you.' That would help to keep a distance between them.

She locked the nursery door behind her and went to her bedroom, wanting to be alone, to give herself time to let her thoughts calm. How could a voice, the look of dark eyes, affect her so? And how many others had responded as she did? She would not let herself think of those others; they were of no consequence. He needed her now, someone who understood him; she could not deny him that. But she must hide her own feelings, keep a space between them, physical and emotional, think of him not as the naked god she had first seen and saw still whenever she closed her eyes, but as a poor sick young fellow, brother to her housekeeper, a man of different class, for whom she had no more feeling than she might have for a wounded animal.

That was all he was, a wounded creature to whom she could freely give her sympathy and care — but nothing more. That was all he meant.

Chapter Thirteen

Winter, as always in Cornwall, Maud thought, was treacherous, giving days of springlike warmth only to return with a sudden sharp and vengeful frost. She bustled about the house making sure the pipes were kept from freezing, but there were so many in this great house that she knew she was bound to fail. It was altogether too large to keep warm and, as fuel rationing bit, it would become intolerable. She must persuade her mother to sell up and move. And now poor Prideaux had taken to her bed. It was too much for her even to make a pretence of work. She should have been pensioned off at least ten years ago.

Maud went to her mother to tell her she had insisted on Mrs Prideaux going to bed. 'I promised her not to tell you. She is afraid you'll find an excuse to pension her off.'

'I've had no such notion,' Caroline said.

'Well, perhaps you should have had, years since,' Maud asserted. 'She's far too old to carry on.'

'I don't expect much of her — nothing really. it's just a fiction that she runs the house. But it would be the end of her if I told her I had no further need of her. She has always imagined I couldn't manage without her.'

'She's not at all well,' Maud said.

'Do you think I'm blind to that? She would be much worse if I took away her sole purpose in life.'

'Is that all she's ever had? Has there never been anything in her life but looking after us?'

Her mother did not reply at once but at length said, 'She had a brother.'

'She's never mentioned him.'

'No. No one's mentioned him for years.'

'Why? What happened to him? Did he do something to be ashamed of?

Again Caroline was silent for a long moment, until Maud said, 'I'm sorry. Perhaps I shouldn't pry.'

'There's no harm now. I expect he's long since dead. There's been no news of him for fifty years.' She sighed. 'It's all so long ago.'

'Did you know him?' Maud asked. She was bustling round the room picking up papers and magazines which the children had left scattered about.

'Sit down,' her mother said impatiently. 'Why are you so restless?'

'Did you know him?' Maud repeated.

'Yes. I knew him.'

'Was he like her, like Mrs Prideaux?' She was only idly curious, had no real interest in a man who had not been heard of since before she was born.

'No,' her mother said emphatically. 'He was like nobody I've ever known.'

Maud looked at her in surprise and thought she ought to ask no more, but it seemed her mother wished to speak of him.

'He was younger than her by ten years or more, handsome, like a Greek god I always thought. He stayed here for a time once, when he was ill. I got to know him then.'

'And then?'

'He went. We lost sight of him. Heard no more.'

'What do you think happened?'

Her mother got up from her chair, walked to the window and looked out to the bare trees and the frozen grass, turning her back on her daughter.

'I wish I knew,' she said. 'I wish I knew.'

Chapter Fourteen

1

Caroline was certain no one but she and the housekeeper knew of the presence of George Prideaux in the nursery wing. The household had settled to its normal routine. At times Caroline felt she was bound to give herself away, from the inner excitement which filled her to overflowing. Even Thomas commented on how vivacious she had become. 'It's the weather,' she explained, and indeed the long hot days of summer seemed to bring a fullness of hope.

She visited the nursery at least twice each day, however briefly. Mrs Prideaux had come to accept this, even to rely on her for help in reconciling George to his confinement to his room. He was recovering, slowly at first, but beginning to be impatient to get out.

'It is not safe,' Caroline said, putting aside the book of Browning's poems she had been reading to him. 'You must be quite well before you leave.'

'I need fresh air,' he said. 'I'm not the sort of man to languish indoors. I might as well be in Bodmin gaol for all the freedom I'm allowed.'

She laughed at the notion and he laughed with her, but said, 'I shall have to leave soon, you know. I shall be well enough in a week or so.'

She dropped her head, not wanting him to see the distress the idea caused her.

'I shall need some other clothes. I can't be seen in my Army uniform.'

'We'll find something.' Thomas's clothes would not fit. He was shorter by three inches or more, and was much more thick-set. Mrs Prideaux would have to buy something in town.

George Prideaux always stayed in bed when Caroline visited. She would knock on the door to let him know she was there and by the time she went in he was lying down, the bedclothes covering him. She was somehow aware that he was often naked beneath the covers, for his shoulders, brown and solid, were bare. Sometimes she saw a disturbing look in his eyes, a glance from under his dark eyelashes hinting at the insolence Groves had mentioned, but no sooner did she think she had recognised it than he opened his eyes wide to look openly and frankly at her, as a friend might.

What an odd friendship, she thought, between a young man on the run and a thirty-six-year-old woman from the best ranks of Cornish society. The differences counted for nothing; there was something between them which seemed to Caroline unique, a trust that had come from her instinctive defence of him.

It was friendship, she told herself, true friendship, nothing more. She was glad she had been able to persuade herself of that, to suppress those other feelings which had threatened to betray her into unforgivable folly. There were still moments when her imagination escaped the shackles she imposed on it and she saw him rising from his bed in his nakedness and coming to her; she repelled the image almost as soon as it appeared, refusing to let such appalling notions take hold. But they were there, like yeast waiting only warmth to set the ferment working.

Each day was a joy. Even as she woke her first thought was of the visit she would pay him, so that the whole day took on a glow of expectation. She wondered if this was how it might have been if she had had children, this longing to see the loved one, to nurse and tend him. This was love, she admitted, but not, she told herself, the love that bonded man to woman; it held a tenderness and affection of a kind unknown to her till now, an immediacy of understanding and sympathy. She thought − at times − that he felt the same; certainly he found it easy to talk, telling her about himself and, gradually, as they came to feel at ease with each other, speaking of his hopes for the future.

'I was a fool when I joined the Army,' he said once. 'I had no notion what it meant. I never imagined I would have no right to think for myself. I hated every moment.'

She wanted to ask what led to his court-martial. Thomas had told her the man had got into a quarrel over some woman. She could not ask him about that, but curiosity rankled. What woman?

He was talking about his sister. 'She always looked after me, never wanted me to go away, wouldn't let me out of her sight if she could help it.'

'She's concerned for you,' Caroline said. 'I know how she feels.'

'So do I, but I don't belong to her, nor to anyone, only to myself. But now she wants me to go, I feel it.'

'She's thinking only of you.'

'And of course I will have to go, leave not just Cornwall but the country. There's no hiding place for me here in England. The law has a very long reach, but it won't stretch as far as America or Australia.'

'You must not think of leaving yet. You are not fit.'

'Not yet, but soon.'

She wondered how he could talk so calmly of leaving when the thought was so painful to her. She got up to go, not wanting him to see her dismay, but he seemed to be aware of it from that understanding that had come to them both; he knew how she felt — or part of it.

'I'm sorry,' he said. 'It has to come. There's no help for it.'

There was no help for it, but it was not yet. He was still not strong enough and she and his sister needed to prepare for his leaving, buy him clothes, see what they could find out about voyages to the New World, somehow get him a new identity.

'In time,' she said.

2

George Prideaux watched Caroline leave. As soon as he heard her lock the door he got out of bed and flexed his muscles. The

137

exercises he practised each day saw him fitter, stronger, more and more anxious to leave. He had not been exaggerating when he said the nursery rooms were as confining as a prison cell; that was how they felt to him. It was wise to stay until he had fully recovered, but he was determined to bring that day nearer. His body had been supple and powerful before; it would be so again. Each day he felt a renewal of strength, the beginning of the return of his old self, so that he bridled at his enforced idleness.

As his health improved his mind felt free to think of his circumstances. He recognised an urge for comradeship, the satisfaction of some emotional need. He had been harried and hunted, set apart as an outcast, and had felt alone, rejected, but here he was welcomed by the woman Caroline and admitted to her friendship. She cared for him, expected nothing from him but his company and he was grateful for it. No other woman had ever dealt with him so.

When, in his delirium she had come into his dreams, he had imagined her to be beautiful. Now he could see imperfection in her, but the flaws — her upturned nose, her too-high brow, her awkward, almost graceless, posture — somehow made her more endearing, more human and more attainable. The woman he had created in his imagination had been beyond reach.

His thoughts about her began to take on a more intimate shape and he felt himself stirring with desire, but he told himself that had no part in his relationship with this woman; he could not think of her like that; she was a friend, a companion, not the sort of woman to allow such thoughts to enter her mind but a woman to be respected, his sister's employer, a woman of standing. The women he had known around the army camps and in the town bars were of a different breed.

He said her name aloud and the sound pleased him. 'Caroline,' he repeated.

He must get well and leave before resolution failed him and he let his instincts take command. He was too fond of her to deal so with her. He cherished her friendship too much to risk offending her. He would keep his distance however difficult that might be.

138

3

Thomas Trevarth dismounted and handed the reins to the young man. 'Glasson, is it?' he said.

The man touched his cap and said, 'Yes, sir, Bert Glasson, sir.'

Thomas could see the fellow was anxious to please. 'Are you settling in here well? Get on with everybody, do you?'

The young man smiled and nodded and led the horse away. Thomas Trevarth liked a personal touch, here at home, in Truro at his smelting works and even in the various mines in which he had some interest. He thought of himself as a good employer, and he believed his employees thought so too and repaid him by giving the loyalty he thought characteristic of the Cornish working man.

It was not so everywhere, he knew. Elsewhere in the world there were men willing to betray their masters. But not here.

There were difficulties now in South Africa and he was beginning to regret having invested so much in that troubled colony. He would have to go out there and see if he could straighten things out, though he feared the quarrel with the Boer farmers might be beyond his powers to resolve. Why could these Afrikaaners not see that their interests overlapped with his, in the exploitation of the vast mineral resources of the veldt?

He hated the thought of having to tell Caroline he was leaving her for as much as six months. He wished he could take her with him but the voyage and the heat of the Cape would be too much for one of her delicate frame.

He saw she was dismayed at his news. 'Can't you send one of your partners?' she asked. 'Must you go yourself?'

'I'm afraid it has to be me. I wish it could be otherwise, but there's nothing for it.'

She did not reply and he took her hands. They were hot and her face was flushed.

'Are you well?' he asked.

'Of course.'

As always he felt ciumsy beside her slender fragility, fearing almost when he touched her that she might shatter, as once when he had let fall one of his Dresden figures and it had broken into irreparable fragments. There was something unworldly about her; beauty such as hers did not belong here in this brutal world.

'What is it?' she asked. 'Are you worried at leaving me?'

'Of course. I hate the thought of your staying here on your own. Is there no one you could invite to keep you company?'

'I have no one, no one but you, my love. But you must not be concerned about me. Mrs Prideaux is a tower of strength. She will take good care of me.'

'I am not sure.'

Caroline looked sharply up at him.

'She is still under suspicion. More so. Groves saw me earlier and brought me up-to-date. Our Mrs Prideaux has been behaving strangely. She's been followed.' He paused, noticing Caroline had paled, drawing in her breath.

'There's no need for you to be disturbed, my love. You'll be in no danger. Groves and his men will see to that. But if Mrs Prideaux is indeed helping her brother, the police will know and will show her no mercy. I've assured Groves we will do nothing to protect the woman.'

'What has she done? What have they seen? Do they know where he is?'

'My dear Caroline,' he laughed, then became serious again. 'No, they don't know where he is. But Mrs Prideaux has been seen buying men's clothes and there can only be one reason for that. She must be hiding her brother somewhere. The police don't know where, but it's only a matter of time before she leads them to him. The man will have to break cover sometime anyway and then they'll have him.'

Her eyes opened wide and for a moment she looked terrified and he wanted to apologise for bringing such raw unpleasantness into their home.

'No,' she said. 'No, you don't understand. The police are wrong. They've misjudged Mrs Prideaux. I asked her to do that for me, get some clothes. I know of a family in Redruth in desperate need. It was for them Mrs Prideaux

140

was buying things. The man of the house had no clothes to go to work.'

'A common enough thing, unhappily,' he said and smiled at his dear wife's concern. 'You are an angel,' he said. 'An angel of mercy. I shall tell Groves. Reassure him about our Mrs Prideaux.' He bent down and kissed Caroline lightly on the forehead. 'You have my blessing,' he said. 'I'm so proud of you.'

4

She wanted to tell him, everything, even of the young man in the nursery. Guilt at her deceit of him oppressed her, so that she felt physically sick. But how could she reveal it? Would he understand what had made her behave so? How could he when she did not understand it herself? And with each day, the secret had become more private, the guilt greater. She loved Thomas dearly, knew him to be a good and loving husband and would do anything to avoid hurting him; but in this she was not free. Another's life depended on her keeping the secret to herself. She could not betray that other, though in so doing she was betraying her husband.

Yet, how could she not be honest with him? She opened her mouth to speak when Thomas said, 'The fellow deserves all that's coming to him. He's a bad lot if all that Groves tells me is to be believed.'

Her short-lived impulse to confess her knowledge vanished. She could never tell him. The secret was not hers alone. However burdensome it was, she had to bear it and she was suddenly glad. It was this, and this alone, that gave purpose to her life.

When she could get away she found Mrs Prideaux and told her of the excuse she had made for the buying of men's clothes. 'I shall visit Redruth again,' she said. 'There are families only too glad of such help. You must see to buying some more, from second-hand stores, say. That will seem natural enough.'

She was surprised at her ingenuity. 'And you must be careful − we must both be careful. The police must be given no cause to think George is hidden here in Trecarrow.'

141

His impending departure for the Cape made Thomas even more solicitous and attentive to Caroline. She was more than ever conscious of his affection for her. In a thousand little ways he showed how deeply fond of her he was, making her acutely conscious of her guilt in the way she was deceiving him. But she could not change things; she had assumed responsibility for George Prideaux and must see it through to the end.

When she was able to snatch a moment she went to the nursery wing. In the morning she had been driven to Redruth to dispense charity, and avert suspicion from Mrs Prideaux. In the afternoon, depressed still by the poverty she had witnessed, she went to see the young man.

When she went into his room he was asleep but, though she trod lightly, he woke immediately. Startled as if ready to take flight, he sat up, half out of bed, showing his naked torso to the hips. She turned away to give him time to cover himself. He could not know how disturbing it was to see him like that.

'You surprised me,' he said. She turned back to him. He was still sitting up but had drawn the sheet up. 'Where have you been?' he asked, accusing her of neglect. 'I missed you. What have you been doing?'

'You seem to think I have nothing to do but visit you.'

He smiled and she saw again why Groves had spoken of his insolence. She should be annoyed at it but instead was moved by it, quite unable to take offence.

'I am selfish, I know, but when you don't come my whole day darkens.' She wanted to believe him but told herself it meant nothing.

'Your sister will have told you the police know she has been buying men's clothes.'

'They are over there,' he said, nodding to a chair. 'They'll do.'

She took hold of them, a rough fustian jacket and trousers and a flannel shirt, working men's clothes, good enough. Wearing them and the beard he had grown, he might not be recognised, but she thought that even with everyday clothing he would still be a man set apart from the rest for his bearing and his looks. How could beauty such as his be disguised?

142

'What is it?' he asked and she was afraid she had let the thought reach her eyes. She turned away to hide her feelings. They crept upon her treacherously when she was least prepared to resist them. She picked up his army tunic. 'We must get rid of this and everything to do with your past,' she said.

'If it were only as easy as that,' he said.

She fingered the bronze bugle-horn badge, emblem of the Duke of Cornwall's Light Infantry. 'I'll keep this,' she said casually. It was little enough, but it would be a reminder of a man met, a man for whom she had risked her safety, a man who would soon be gone from her life. She moved towards the door.

'Must you go already?'

'I'll come tomorrow and spend more time with you if I can.' She would come prepared to read to him, so that she could sit at a distance, head buried in a book.

'You promise?'

'Does it mean so much to you?' She spoke lightly, but she knew what answer she wanted.

'Everything,' he said. 'It means everything.'

She opened the door and left him without looking to see how serious he was. She did not believe him, but was pleased he had spoken so.

5

George Prideaux watched her go with regret. While she was with him he was almost reconciled it his idleness. When she went his restlessness returned. He knew he was not ready yet to leave, still felt weak. The severity of his illness had surprised him. Previously he had suffered no more than a childish ailment or two and then had enjoyed being fussed over. Now, to be as helpless and dependent as a child made him uncomfortable. As strength slowly returned he found it frustrating to be so confined.

He continued to follow a routine of exercises to try to regain that vigour – muscular power combined with speed of movement and suppleness of limb – which had once made him a formidable wrestler in the Cornish style. He

143

was very conscious of his weakness when he first rose from his bed and saw his naked body in the bathroom mirror, its flaccid muscles reflecting the enervation fever had brought. He was ashamed of his feebleness and was determined to overcome it.

He had been used to a physically hard life from as far back as he could remember and had taken pride in his hardiness. Yet here he was, imprisoned by debility and the temptations of fresh cool sheets, the attentions of his sister and the visits of the lady of the house, Caroline.

He thought of her always as Caroline, never as the Mrs Trevarth his sister spoke of. They were two separate women, Caroline and Mrs Trevarth. The visitor to his room was Caroline, came as such, was happy to be known as such, but when she was absent and his sister spoke of her she became a creature of another world, one distant from his in every way.

As soon as she came, in her hesitant fashion, into the room, that changed. Her world became his or his became hers. He was at ease with her as with no other woman, save his sister. He saw no sexual challenge in her; he did not define it in this way, merely felt she made no demands of him, took him as he was, a young man, sick and in need of company and comfort. There were times when, lying in bed and thinking of her, he found his body stirring but he refused to let the feeling take hold, telling himself his regard for her — and hers for him — was passionless.

Nevertheless, as vigour returned, he found it increasingly difficult to keep those thoughts and that stirring of the blood under control. She had a sort of beauty, a calm serious look in her eyes when he could hold her gaze, a soft blush when he held that gaze too long; her voice was quiet, gentle, warming, and once, when she bent to straighten the covers and touched, by accident, his naked shoulder, he felt a shiver of desire and was not sure if it was his or hers. She had moved quickly away and left him so that he was fearful he had revealed a secret that he wanted to keep hidden even from himself.

He let his thougts drift to other women he had known — Janet who had been the cause of the quarrel with Rennie: lively, lustful and with no sense of loyalty to one man rather

144

than another. He had known that at the time but it had not seemed to matter till he discovered Rennie was the other.

And Molly, Irish Molly, the red haired, green-eyed maid he had known those many years before. He had been fifteen when she, a woman already four years older than him, had seduced him. He had no complaints. They had loved each other in a way and he felt affection for her still, thought if he ever needed her help, she would give it as readily as she had given herself to him before.

There had been others, but none evoked the feelings he had for Caroline. Those other women — the camp followers who paraded the streets around the barracks or jostled in the bars and taprooms — had left him ill-prepared for a woman like her. He could not, in his wildest dreams, imagine her the object of a street brawl, like Janet, or taking the initiative in love, like Molly. She was of another kind; her instincts were pure, her nature delicate and refined, her tastes discriminating, fastidious even; there was no place in her thoughts for a man like him — a common soldier, a fugitive — save from that generosity of spirit which had led her to keep him from capture. He would be for ever grateful to her for that.

That was all there was to their relationship, he told himself, gratitude on his part, protectiveness on hers; no more.

6

She had promised to go back. He had told her how much her visits meant and she wanted to believe him. She had ample opportunity to go to him for Thomas now felt it necessary to spend time at the works in Truro and his other enterprises before he had to leave for South Africa. Nevertheless she held back from going to see the boy, trying to find small tasks to occupy her mind, pretending to herself that it did not matter whether she went to him or not.

She found working in the garden helped her, not to forget him, that seemed out of the question, but the simple tasks of dead-heading the roses and geraniums enabled her to think of him with more calm and serenity. She could not help looking up from time to time to the window above which gave on

145

to his room. She thought she caught a glimpse of him in the shadows of the room. She must tell him to be careful. If others saw someone there in the nursery wing, the game might be up.

Brought up sharp at the thought, she decided to go to see him immediately. Mrs Prideaux was in town, diverting suspicion by buying more second-hand clothes for the needy of Redruth. No one else would see her. She went into the house and hastened upstairs, the urge to see him occupying her mind to the exclusion of all else. She let herself quietly into the nursery without the usual knock to warn him of her approach. She could hear him moving and, alarmed at the sound of heavy breathing coming from him, she hurriedly opened the door to his bedroom.

She froze on the threshold, rigid with shame. He stood facing her, legs apart, thighs braced, arms raised high above his head, stretching to his full height, firm, muscled, lithe and beautiful, and naked, so that the whole secret of his manhood was revealed. She tried to close her eyes against the sight but could not, for there was a magic to it that held her spellbound.

It seemed he had not seen her, for his eyes were closed. But he knew she was there, she could tell by the way he held his breath. Then she raised her eyes and saw him gazing at her. She could only stare back, pretend there was nothing amiss – and wanted to laugh at the thought. She wanted to speak, to apologise for breaking in on him, but her mouth was dry and the words would not come. She wanted to turn and fly but her legs trembled so that she was powerless to move. She closed her eyes and, unable to contain the pressure of emotion that welled up in her, let a great sigh escape.

She knew he had moved – away from her – and opened her eyes to see him reaching for a blanket to cover himself and break the spell which held her to him.

'I'm sorry,' she said. 'I should not have come in without knocking.'

'My exercises,' he explained, but she hardly heard what he said from the hoarseness of his voice. He is annoyed that I have seen him so, she thought.

'I am sorry,' she said again. 'I should not have come.'

146

'You said you would.' His voice held a plea. He had got into bed, under the covers, and was sitting up against the pillows, so that she could see the upper part of his torso, his shoulders and chest. She was surprised to see him reddening under her glance and she blushed, thinking of the shamelessness with which she had gazed on him before.

'You are beautiful,' she was astonished to hear herself say. The words were uttered before she was aware. 'Your body,' she began to explain, and broke off in confusion. She walked to the door intending to leave before she caused more difficulties between them. He wanted to hear nothing like that from her and she had no right to say such things.

'Stay,' he urged. 'There is no need for you to go.'

'I think there is. I have caused us enough shame.'

'There was no shame.'

'I meant none.'

'Then stay.'

How could she make him see that the shame was still there, in her holding in her mind's eye a clear image of his naked grace and strength? How could there not be shame in that?

'I have things to see to.'

'You will come back?'

'If you want me to.'

'I need you,' he said.

Chapter Fifteen

Caroline Trevarth looked from the drawing-room window out to the frost-glistening grass. The sky was clear crystal blue. To young bones the air was invigorating and she could see Joseph chasing Simon and Sarah down to the river and heard shrieks of laughter from the younger children as they evaded his outstretched arms. He slipped on the grass. Caroline watched as Sarah went back to help him to his feet. Then they disappeared from view among the trees.

She stared, unseeing, at the wintry landscape. Some visions of the past had a clarity that even events of a moment ago could not match. That was supposed to be one of the quirks of old age. Certainly, whenever she wished, she could recreate the past so vividly that she saw the nursery rooms as they had been then, inhabited by a stranger, a youth of astonishing comeliness. Perhaps, she admitted, distance enriched the memory. Perhaps he was not as handsome as she remembered him. It did not matter; to her there had been then and there would remain a conviction that no other creature on God's earth could match him for grace and perfection. She recalled now, without any sense of shame but with a stir of bodily excitement she had thought long since dead, the sight of him as he had been that day fifty years before. She could close her eyes and see him. He had been right when he had said – she could hear his voice clearly over the years – 'There is no shame.' She had not known that then, had tried to suppress the longing roused by the sight of his naked body, had thought it sinful to feel so. Yet nothing so beautiful, so natural, could contain sin, she knew now.

She heard Maud come into the room and opened her eyes.

'I'm sorry, Mother. I didn't mean to wake you.'

'I wasn't sleeping.'

Maud smiled, showing her disbelief.

'I was thinking, thinking back, to a day long since,' Caroline explained. 'Before you were born.'

'All that time ago!'

'I was very innocent. I did not know how innocent. Everyone sheltered me from life.'

'You're still innocent, Mother,' Maud said. 'We only have to look at you to know how blameless your life has been. That's one reason we love and admire you.'

Caroline laughed. 'And still want to protect me, treat me like a delicate ornament − pretty but of no practical use.'

'No, Mother. That's not how it is.'

'I don't mind. I'm used to it. That's how Thomas always thought of me. Something to be treasured, to be shown off to his friends, to be taken from its case every now and again to be fondled and admired.'

'He loved you, Mother. You're not being fair to him.'

'Of course he loved me. He loved all his possessions. And I don't mean that badly. He would let no harm come near me, cherished and protected me. No, I'm not complaining.'

'"With my body I thee worship, with all my wordly goods I thee endow." Are those not the words? Did he not hold to that?' Maud said.

But to Caroline the words brought thoughts of another than her husband. She tried to dismiss the image but it would not be dislodged. 'With my body I thee worship' echoed in her mind.

'What is it' she heard Maud say through her memories.

'Yes, child?'

'Are you all right?'

'Of course I'm all right. Don't fuss.' She looked out of the window again. There was no sign of the children. There was a quiet about the house which she did not like. The young people breathed life into it, and into her. 'Where are the children?' she said.

'I sent them for a walk. I thought you needed a bit of peace.'

Caroline shook her head in exasperation at Maud's concern. 'I like them about me, like to hear them. Peace of the kind you mean will come soon enough.'

'Mother!' Maud protested.

'And how is Prideaux this morning? She hasn't been to see me.'

'She's not at all well. I made her stay in bed and I've called for the doctor. It was for her sake as much as yours that I sent the children out.'

'I'll go and see her.' She got up from her chair, awkwardly because of the pain in her knees, and made her way to the housekeeper's room. It had been a long time since she had come here. She had always respected Prideaux's need for privacy.

The housekeeper was lying in bed and, when she recognised her mistress, made an effort to sit up. It was too much for her.

'How are you, Ada?' Caroline said. She felt a deep concern for her old servant. 'Ada?'

Prideaux did not answer, merely shook her head slowly in a way to suggest she had no strength to speak. She put out a hand and Caroline took hold of it. It felt cold, fleshless, and Caroline moved her own fingers to warm it.

'I ...' The housekeeper tried to say something but could not get the words out. She shook her head again and Caroline was disturbed by the expression in her eyes – a look of appeal? An appeal for what? Forgiveness? She had nothing to forgive. Prideaux had always done her duty and more.

'Don't worry,' Caroline said. 'Lie still. Maud and I will do whatever needs doing. You just have to get well.'

She watched beside the bed until an uneasy sleep came to the woman; her eyes closed and her mouth fell open. Caroline, still holding her hand, stroked it gently before putting it under the cover. Then, without knowing why, she bent to kiss her lightly on the forehead. In her sleep, Ada Prideaux smiled.

Chapter Sixteen

1

'Are you sure it must be you to go to South Africa?' she asked Thomas. 'Is there no one who can take your place?' Could he not see how dangerous it was for her to be left alone?

'I wish I could think of someone,' he said. 'But there's no one I can trust to make the right sort of judgment. I have a great deal at stake in the Transvaal. But six months will quickly go.'

'You said there is trouble there with the Afrikaaners. Can you not wait another year?' Caroline pleaded.

Thomas took hold of her hands and drew her to him. 'I'll be quite safe. You need not worry. And you will be safe too. You're not still anxious about that man Prideaux, are you?'

She hoped he would not notice how she reacted to the name, but he was aware of the change in her.

'That is it,' he said. 'I should have been more considerate. Of course you are anxious with a murderer on the loose. I understand. It was thoughtless of me to think of leaving you. I'll postpone my going until the man is caught or until we're certain he's left the county.' He held her close and fondled her hair. 'There, there, don't worry your pretty little head. I'll not desert you.'

She *was* afraid of Prideaux, but not in a way that Thomas would understand. At the mention of his name, she felt a stir of excitement, a coursing of the blood that she had never before experienced, an anguish and a joy combined. She needed Thomas with her to protect her from that, to save

151

her from herself. With him away, distantly in the Southern Hemisphere, she might yield to the impulses that threatened to destroy her. With him near to give her strength she could perhaps resist.

She could not understand how she could let the image of the young man invade her mind. Whatever she was doing, her embroidery or reading, her thoughts would drift to him, and she saw, so clearly that she blushed at the memory, his naked body stretched before her, legs braced, arms high above his head, lean body strong and firm in the pride and glory of youth. She was afraid she would give herself away, saw Thomas watching her from across the room, smiling, getting up from his chair, coming over to take her face between his hands, bending down to kiss her. If only it was for him her flesh tingled.

She lay beside her husband at night and pictured the young man. When Thomas turned to give her an affectionate good-night kiss she clung to him, desperate to love and be loved, wanting it to be her husband and no other lying there, but imagining, against her will, that it was a young eager body pressing against hers, not the thick-set heavy limbs of Thomas. She gave a sharp cry of anguish, guilt and disappointment, so that Thomas held her close to comfort her, disturbed by her unfamiliar display of passion.

She saw the naked youth, felt him against her and could not believe her shamelessness in allowing so wicked a sensation to flow over her. She wanted to confess her sin, for sin she knew it to be, and opened her mouth to speak, but Thomas spoke first. 'I'll not leave you, not while you're so upset. I'll send Trevena or one of the others. No harm will come to you, I'll see to that.'

The next day she did not dare to visit the young man yet could not keep away. She hovered close to the nursery wing until she felt she might give rise to suspicion among the servants. She went to her room and lay on her bed, a prey to curiosity, a curiosity which became a longing and soon a frenzy of need. She had to see him, just to see him, to speak to him, to hear his voice, to know he was there, the youth who held sway in her mind.

Slowly she got up from her bed and went to sit at her dressing

152

table, looking into the mirror, searching for the meaning of her unquietness. She saw wide eyes, puzzled at the helplessness of her will to deny the young man entrance to her thoughts. There was no displacing him; wherever she turned he was there, drawing her to him, compelling her attendance upon him. She fancied she heard his voice, saying 'I need you,' and she believed him.

She must go to him. She would control her feelings, keep him at arm's length, but go to him she must. For one last time, to tell him she could see him no more. She would not explain why, maybe there would be no need to; he might understand and see how dangerous, for him as well as her, it would be to continue with their meetings. Soon he would be fit enough to leave and that would be the end of their acquaintance; she must pray for that time to come quickly.

She stood at the door of the nursery wing strengthening her resolve, and put the key to the door.

2

George Prideaux stood at the side of the window looking across the expanse of lawn and garden towards the trees that bordered the river bank. It was unwise to stand there, for one of the estate workers might see him, he supposed, and wonder who it was in the house. But he could not deny himself a glimpse of the world outside. He had been cooped up here long enough, needed to get into the open, breathe the clean air, feel grass under his feet. He was ready to go, strong enough to face the dangers of flight. He had put on the clothes Ada had brought and they gave him the look of any working man. He touched his beard; that was enough to disguise him. His hair was long, curling darkly about his forehead and neck where, as a soldier, it had been cropped close. No one would see in him George Prideaux, the army deserter.

He looked a different man, and felt so too, though he did not know what it was that had changed him. Maybe it was something to do with the woman Caroline. She was like no other woman he had known, with her calm dignity, her self-contained assurance, a quality that came, not just from her position in society, but from some inner source. There was a repose to her that he admired. No other woman of his acquaintance would have seen him naked, as he had been, and shown such self-control. He had been surprised at himself. He had stood facing her, without any sense of shame, aware of her appraisal and knowing it meant no more to her than if he had been a child standing there.

Yet, there had been something in her response that made him wonder. She had blushed a little, had not been indifferent to him, indeed had said his body was beautiful. He recalled the simple frankness of her statement and smiled at her honesty.

He admired her and, as he thought of her, he found himself thinking of her with affection, more affection and tenderness than he had felt for any woman in his life. He could not explain his feelings, for they were complex beyond his experience. He admired and respected her, felt warmly towards her, needed her to listen to him, to comfort him, needed to know she cared.

There was more, he knew, had known all along: he wanted her, as he had never wanted woman before, wanted to touch her, hold her to him, make love to her. He wanted her with a hard physical need that made him move impatiently from the window towards the door as if he could go and find her. But it was no use. She would want no part of him in that way; she was a woman beyond reproach, above him. He tried to persuade himself that such desire was the consequence of being pent up here with no outlet for his energies. He must get away before he made a fool of himself over a woman who had no more care for him than she might have for a wounded animal. That was how he had been when she had found him; that would be how she thought of him.

He must get away, tell Ada he was ready to go, get her to help him cover his tracks. Ada and the woman Caroline had risked enough; he must spare them further trouble. He would leave this evening after dark perhaps before Caroline came again.

He heard the key in the outer door of the nursery wing and waited for the tap on the door that told him it was she. The door opened and she came in, closed it behind her and stood with her back to it.

154

'I've come to say goodbye,' she said, her words coming in a rush.

'Goodbye?' He was confused. It was he who had meant to bid her farewell. Did she know he planned leaving? How could she?

'I cannot come to see you again. I must not.' She looked directly at him as if defying him to challenge her decision. 'It will not do.'

'I do not understand,' he said, but he thought he did. She had guessed his feelings towards her and wished to warn him.

'Don't ask me to explain,' she said and turned as if to go. He could not let her leave without telling her of his gratitude and admiration. He could conceal his desire to touch her, to take hold of her hand and bring it to his lips, to stroke her hair, to tell her he loved her. He could conceal that, but he could not deny himself a moment more of her time. 'No,' he exclaimed. 'You cannot go, not yet. I plan leaving tonight now I'm well enough. But I wanted to tell you how I admire your generosity towards me. I can never thank you enough.' His voice faltered. This was not what he wanted to say. He took a step towards her and another so that he was near enough if he wished to reach out and touch her. She recoiled a little and he thought he had frightened her in some way but it was she who then reached out to him, putting her hand to his cheek and touching his beard.

'It suits you,' she said and her hand followed the line of the beard to his mouth and then let a finger touch his lips gently, provocatively, so that he knew she could not hold herself from him if he made a move to her.

He stood for a moment looking into her eyes, seeing himself reflected in the dark pupils. He felt her hand again touch his cheek, softly stroking his beard. He took the hand and held it to his lips and kissed it, then, unable to resist her invitation, he put his arms about her and drew her to him. She sighed, a long drawn-out exhalation of desire, and kissed him, moving her mouth rapidly about his features, holding his face between her hands, then turned her lips to him to kiss him full on the mouth. Their warm breath commingled until he began to feel faint but she would not let him go. His excitement mounted to match hers and, almost without willing them, his hands

155

searched for an opening to her, to reach to her breasts. She moved slightly away from him and loosened a catch so that he could put his hand to her bosom and let his fingers reach to find a nipple. He began to draw her slowly towards the bed, knowing that, whatever his earlier resolve, he wanted her, would not let her go before he had taken her.

She seemed as eager, made no resistance until she lay beneath him, with him fumbling at his clothes to free himself.

'No,' she said. 'No.'

'You want me, I know.' He might have been angry but, looking at her, the deep affection which was at the heart of his feeling for her overcame him. He wanted to make love to her but not in the blind lust that had come to him then.

'No,' she denied, but he knew from the look in her eyes that the denial was false. 'I came only to say goodbye.'

'You want me.'

'I cannot have you.' She lay beneath him, her dress still open at the bosom so that he could see the creamy swell of her breast and the hint of a nipple. He bent to her and took the pink tip between his lips and gently coaxed it to hardness.

'No,' she sighed. 'No.' but she made no move to escape.

'I want you,' he said.

'And I you,' she admitted. 'But it is no use. It cannot be. I should not have come.' She made a slight movement as if to release herself from his hold but it was only a token of resistance. He began to raise her dress and she lay, passive, eyes wide with disbelief at her willingness to allow him.

'Listen,' she said suddenly, raising her head from the pillow.

He heard nothing save a throbbing of his blood.

She moved rapidly away from him, stood and began to fasten her dress when the door of the bedroom opened and Ada Prideaux came in. She stared in silence at them, first at her brother and then at her mistress, confronting them, hands on hips, waiting for one of them to move.

It was Caroline who hurriedly pushed her way past and fled.

'Well?' said Ada Prideaux.

'I shall leave this evening,' her brother said. 'I had always meant to go as soon as I was fit.'

'Yes,' she said coldly. 'It is more than time.'

156

Chapter Seventeen

Caroline sat by her housekeeper's bed, regretting she had never offered the old woman much display of affection. 'The old woman', she thought wryly; I suppose that is what I am too, older than her by a couple of years.

They had lived so closely together all these years and yet had somehow retained a distance between them, never referring to the past, to the time when they had put their differences behind them to protect the man to whom, in their separate ways, they were bound.

There had been times when she felt hatred for the woman, when she felt it was only Ada who stood between her and the young man. Was it jealousy that made Ada behave as she had?

Caroline looked at Prideaux now, lying motionless against the white pillow; she tried to see what lay behind that impassive face. Ada had never been easy to read, had always kept her emotions under tight control.

Looking at her Caroline saw in her features something of that other Prideaux in their lives, but she decided it was only nostalgic imagination misting her eyes. There was little of George in the woman who lay dying before her, merely a trace of his colouring in her complexion.

'Mother?' It was Maud come to enquire after Prideaux. 'You must not exhaust yourself looking after her.'

'I'm only sitting here, merely keeping her company.

'She's sleeping, doesn't know you are here. There's no point in your staying. You look tired too.'

'It's more that tiredness in her case,' Caroline said softly. 'I knew it had to come. I tried to make things easier for her.'

'Come along, Mother.' Maud took hold of her arm and led her away. 'The doctor will be here shortly. You should get him to have a look at you as well.'

Caroline snatched her arm away. 'There's nothing wrong with me, nothing but a few aches and pains in my joints. Don't fuss.'

Her daughter smiled and Caroline saw Maud's father in the sparkle which lit her eyes and the amusement curling her mouth.

She went to sit by the window looking out to the lawns. Of all the views from the house, this was the one that pleased her most. Even now, shrouded as it was by winter, it had a stark beauty; in spring, with the mist of bluebells under the trees, it took on new charm. But it was in the heat of summer that she liked it best. Then she was reminded of those long lovely weeks of the distant past. She closed her eyes now and let the vision of that time fill her memories. Happiness had come to her then and had stayed with her through the years, was with her still, almost more so than ever. She became aware she was being watched and opened her eyes to see Maud, who had brought so much of that content, the child whose arrival had changed her life and the lives of all of them. Maud bent to kiss her on the cheek.

'You're weeping,' she said.

'I was thinking,' Caroline began.

'Sad thoughts?'

'No,' she answered, but there was a sadness, had always been, underlying the content and joy that Maud's birth had brought.

'Tell me,' Maud said. 'We don't often get a chance to talk with the family around. I've always thought ...' She hesitated, looked away and then went to the window and stood with her back to her mother. 'I've always thought you had a secret.'

'A secret? How could I have. My life has been an open book.'

Chapter Eighteen

1

She fled, red-faced, to her own room and threw herself on the bed, not knowing if she wanted to give way to tears of laughter, tears of frustration or laughter from the bubbling joy that welled up within her.

Shame was mixed in her emotions too, shame not at what she had done – or nearly done – but at being discovered by Ada Prideaux. How had the woman arrived so inopportunely?

He was leaving tonight, he had said, and at the thought a cold sense of reality came over here. He was leaving and with his going the dream would end, the dream born of reaction to her fruitless existence. At least in saving him from capture she had done something to disturb the dull pattern of her life, had acted independently of Thomas, been true to herself, following only her own instincts.

He was going tonight. Yet he could not; they had made no plans for him, no arrangements to get him to Falmouth and take ship. Perhaps his sister had already seen to that. She must speak with her to reassure herself it would be safe for him to go.

She went to find the housekeeper and stood outside the nursery wing waiting for her to appear. The wing had been built in such a way that children could not be heard beyond its walls. She found it frustrating not to know what was going on inside. She knocked on the door and waited. A long interval passed and she raised her hand to knock again when the door opened and the housekeeper emerged. She closed and locked

159

the door behind her and stood for a moment against it, eyes closed. Then she opened them and made as if to push past her mistress. Caroline caught hold of her arm and held her.

'We have to talk,' she said.

'What is there to say?' Ada Prideaux answered. 'It is time he went. There is no reason why he should stay and a hundred and one reasons why he should go.' She raised her eyes to stare at her mistress, accusing her, Caroline thought.

'He cannot go tonight.'

'He must and will.' Mrs Prideaux made to leave.

'We are not ready. We've made no plans. You cannot let him go without making sure he will be safe.'

'He will go tonight,' Mrs Prideaux said firmly. 'There's a woman in Redruth will give him shelter.'

'A woman?'

'He knows her of old. She'll see to him.'

'It is not safe. You know that. Why can't you understand? The police will be watching, waiting, ready to take him. He is safe here.'

'But are you?'

Swift anger made it difficult for Caroline to speak but, as the housekeeper walked away, she raised her voice. 'I do not know what you mean.'

'I think you do,' Mrs Prideaux replied and left Caroline standing outside the nursery, nervously aware of the silence that had fallen on this part of the house. It was as if she was the only living presence here, but only a few yards away a young man was preparing to leave, to vanish from her life, returning to his own world, a world remote from hers in every imaginable way.

She could not let him go, not yet.

2

She would not let him go, not like that. She would see him again, not to tempt him or give way to temptation herself. She had had her moment of madness and had put it behind her. But she must see him, give him her blessing on his going.

Perhaps he would not wish to see her, perhaps he despised

160

her for offering herself to him. Was that what she had done? She could not at first believe it but, in all honesty, that was how she had felt, a willingness — even an eagerness — to take him to her. Only the coming of his sister had stopped her surrendering to her instincts.

She could not go to him in her present confusion, guilt struggling with joy, conscience fighting desire. Nor could she risk seeing anything in his eyes other than the love she had imagined there. She would treasure that; it was enough for her, more than she was entitled to.

She left the house and walked across the lawns, down the terraced gardens towards the river. Warmth struck from the clear blue sky. It was rare for the Cornish summer to last so long and to be so intemperate with heat; it was a day for lazing in the sun, a day when families sat on the beaches and children built their sand-castles or sought among the rock pools for anemones. The pleasures of that were denied her; there was no child for her to watch and care for.

She reached the river and sat on the bank gazing idly across the water, letting pleasurable imaginings take over her mind. A ferry boat, worked by a local fisherman, was taking a party to the other shore, a family, parents and two young children. One of the children exclaimed with delight as she trailed her hand in the cool water and her shrill voice carried back to Caroline, sharpening the regret of her childlessness.

She closed her eyes, listening to the lapping of water on the pebbles, hearing the distant voices of the boat party.

A shadow fell across her, startling her. She had been asleep, maybe only for a moment. She looked up and saw him and sat up in alarm. How and why had he come here? It was not safe for him. He would be seen.

But it was not him, she realised. Her imagination had been playing tricks, her dreams too real. It was another young man, a police constable.

'What is it?' She sat up, making no attempt to hide her anxiety.

'A message from Superintendent Groves, ma'am. He wants your permission to search the grounds again.'

'Why? For what reason?' she said sharply.

The young man was taken aback by her brusque manner.

161

''tes only right, ma'am. He do think that there man Prideaux be hiding somewhere hereabouts.' He was a local man, with local rhythms in his voice, like the man he was hunting.

'Just the grounds?'

'And the house, I do suppose.'

'I'll come.'

He put out a hand to help her to her feet but she ignored it, got up and hurried back to the house, tense with anxiety.

Groves was standing at the front of the house, under the columned portico, a bulky figure of threat.

'Well?' she said challengingly. 'Have you not disturbed us enough?'

He raised his eyebrows and gave her a long look, as if surprised at the change from the timid creature he knew to this aggressive, impatient woman. She was surprised at herself, a tigress protecting her young, she thought, and tried to conceal her fear.

'I regret any inconvenience, Mrs Trevarth,' he said, in a tone that denied any regret. 'We have a murderer on the loose, a brutal young fellow who has killed once and may kill again.'

'You have already judged and condemned him,' she accused.

Again he looked in surprise at her. 'I have my duty to do. It is to apprehend him, to protect the Queen's Peace — your peace, your safety.'

'And what do you want to do this time?'

'Search the house and grounds.'

'Again? What makes you think he may be here?'

'I have my reasons. Information. Your housekeeper's strange behaviour.'

'But you have been watching her? You've seen nothing incriminating surely?'

He smiled so that she wondered what else his informants might have told him. He seemed to be watching her reaction with interest. She must be careful.

'We may proceed?' And, without waiting for her agreement, he gestured to a police sergeant who stood a few paces away waiting for instructions. 'Tell the men to start in the stable and the outbuildings. Miss no corner. Go everywhere. If they find nothing outside then we'll give the inside a

162

good going-over.' He turned to Caroline, whose anger was mounting with every word. She had difficuty restraining herself when he said, 'You will warn the household to give us every co-operation,' and took her agreement for granted.

She dared do nothing to oppose him. She nodded curtly and went into the house, dismayed at the suddenness of the danger to them all, to her, to her housekeeper, and, above all, to George Prideaux.

She must act quickly. It would not take the police long to finish their search outside. Ada Prideaux could do nothing to help; the police were too suspicious of her.

She went into the house in a state of near despair, but she would not let herself give way. His safety depended on her and she had no time to lose. She was afraid but she would find a way out. There must be some place to hide him.

The idea came and she rejected it, but it remained. There was only one place Groves would hesitate to search − her own bedroom. She would feign a headache − it would not be difficult − and retire to bed. She could hide him in her room, in the large ornate wardrobe so beloved of Thomas; Groves would not imagine anyone could be hidden there.

With outward composure but inner turbulence she went to the nursery wing. It was only a few strides from there to her own room, along the corridor. With luck no one would see him.

She let herself quietly into the nursery and to his room. He had been looking out to the lawns, hidden from outside view behind the curtain.

'I saw them,' he said. 'They've come for me.'

'They're searching outside. It won't be long before they come inside and search here too.'

'I'll go down and meet them. I'll not be trapped like an animal. I'll give myself up.' He did not meet her eyes.

'No.' She went to him and took his hands in hers, trying to pretend confidence. 'I can save you, I know. You can't give up now, can't admit defeat.'

'You've done enough. It is dangerous for you. I'll tell them I came in and hid without anyone knowing.'

'They won't believe you. They'll know someone helped you. They'll accuse your sister and suspect me, perhaps. We're

163

wasting time. We must get rid of anything that may show you have been hiding here. Help me, quickly.'

Her determination spurred him and he helped her hurriedly strip the bed and stuff the sheets in the linen basket in the bathroom. She took his hand and swiftly led him from the nursery along to her bedroom and pointed to the massive walnut wardrobe.

'In there,' she commanded. 'I'll call my maid and tell her all this has upset me, made me unwell, and that I need to rest. She'll stay with me. The police will never dare to search here then.' He was staring at her with admiration and, in spite of the danger to them both, with some sort of amusement. He bent to kiss her lightly on the brow and slid into the wardrobe. She closed the door on him, sighed and rang for Beatrice, her maid.

She had done her part, all she could. All that was needed now was for fortune to attend them.

She lay on her bed, the headache she had used as an excuse now no pretence. She felt sick with fear as footsteps moved along the corridor. She had heard voices below, the brusque commands of Groves, the protests of Mrs Prideaux at the violation by the police of the household routine. She would think her brother still in the nursery, might reveal her guilty knowledge, give them all away.

She lay in fear, her resolution of the past hour spent, wondering if they had removed all traces of his occupation of the nursery. They might well have left some small thing to make the police suspicious.

The voices came nearer, gruff commands and responses, whispered consultations. Beatrice went to the door to see what was happening and to warn the men to be quiet.

'I must see her,' Caroline heard Groves say. Beatrice was indignant. 'She's not well, I tell 'ee. And 'tesn't proper to go into a lady's bedroom.

'That's all right, Beatrice,' Caroline called. 'Mr Groves is only doing his duty.' She drew her bed-jacket around her shoulders and sat up.

He came in, his eyes narrowed, not liking to be thwarted even for a moment, and looked sideways at her, his mouth

164

curling a little at the sight of her in bed. She reddened at his glance and gathered her jacket more closely about her. She controlled her anger. She must not antagonise him.

'Have you found anything?'

He interpreted her anxiety as concern for the safety of herself and her household. 'Yes, ma'am, we have.'

She could not help a sharp intake of breath.

'Outside in the stables. He's been there at sometime or other. We found a button from his army tunic. He must have slipped in and out. Mrs Prideaux pretends she has no idea what's happened to him but she knows more than she's telling us, that's for certain.'

He glanced around the room and his eyes seemed to pause for a moment at the wardrobe, then he apologised for disturbing her and left. Beatrice followed him to the door and stood for a while, arms on hips showing her disapproval of him and his men.

'He'll be miles away by now, and good luck to him,' she said.

'That will do, Beatrice. You can go now. I feel a good deal better, now the police have finished.' She could hear one of Groves's sergeants barking commands and the tramp of the men's feet as they were marched away. 'Ask Mrs Prideaux to come and see me.'

She waited until sure Beatrice was out of earshot before going to the wardrobe and opening the door. George stood, half-hidden behind a frock coat belonging to Thomas. She smiled. She could never imagine him so dressed.

'They've gone?' he asked, stepping out into the room.

She nodded.

'Why are you protecting me like this? Don't you know how dangerous it is? I've done nothing to deserve it.'

She was tempted to reach to him and touch his cheek, or to take hold of his hands and bring them to her breasts.

'Why?' he repeated.

If he did not see why how could she explain it? She did not entirely understand it herself. Defence of him was an impulse she could not deny.

'I could not think of your being caught, knowing what they would do to you.'

165

'Why?' He was insistent on an answer, as if needing her to admit her feelings for him. She was saved from answering by a knock at the door. He moved behind the door while she opened it enough to see who was there.

'Come in quickly,' she said, seeing the housekeeper. 'He's here.'

'It's a pretty mess,' Ada Prideaux said and turned accusingly to her brother. 'See what you've done. Put us all at risk.'

'I'll leave as soon as it's dark,' her brother said.

'No,' exclaimed Caroline. 'No. The police are still suspicious, but they've finished searching the house. The room in the nursery will be safe again for the time being, until we can make proper arrangements for your passage out of the country. But you must have nothing to do with him,' she said to Mrs Prideaux. 'Superintendent Groves has someone, maybe one of the servants, reporting on your movements. I'll look after him. There's no reason for anyone to suspect me.'

'I can't let you take the risk,' George said. 'I'll go tonight. I'll find my way to the coast and the old mine at Wheal Charlotte, hide there until the hue and cry's died down. That's one place where I'm more at home than any policeman. My mind's made up,' he said, sensing Caroline's opposition. 'You've done all you can. It's for me to act now. I'll slip away as soon as it's dark.'

Caroline wished she was alone with him, perhaps then she could persuade him to stay, make him see how important it was for her that he should be safe. 'We still have to make arrangements for you to get away,' she said and turned to his sister for support. 'Tell him to be sensible.'

Mrs Prideaux seemed content with her brother's decision. 'I know when he's made his mind up.'

'But we must be able to get in touch with you,' Caroline said. 'To let you know what we plan. And we must have a way of keeping you provided with food and whatever else you will need to help you escape.'

George looked steadily at her. She thought she read admiration in his eyes, perhaps the affection she had imagined before.

'There's an engine house on the cliff, deserted now, and an

166

old count house of the mine, derelict, falling into ruin. No one goes there. You can leave messages there. I'll visit it to pick them up.'

'It is foolish,' Caroline argued. 'You would be safer here.'

'He will be better gone from here,' Mrs Prideaux said firmly and Caroline saw the woman's determination he should leave.

He was to go back to the nursery wing until dark. His sister would provide him with a pack of food. But even she agreed it would be unwise for her to be seen going in the direction of Wheal Charlotte.

'I shall take any messages or food there,' Caroline said. 'You can lead them a dance somewhere else.'

'I shall watch for you,' George said. 'But why? Why are you doing this for me?'

She did not answer, could not in the presence of his sister. He would never know, must never know.

3

Groves watched his men march from the grounds of Trecarrow. He had missed something. There was a tension about the house that was not solely due to the presence of the police. Someone, presumably Prideaux's sister, had something to hide. The army button found in the stable loft confirmed his feeling that Prideaux had been here. Unless there was some secret hidey-hole he was here no longer.

Where then was he? Someone in the house knew more than they said. One of the housemaids? Prideaux was plausible and handsome enough to persuade some gullible young woman to help him. But his men had been everywhere, rummaging on every floor, covering every possibility, and had found nothing, nothing but a button from an army tunic.

He turned towards the stable. Why had it not come to light sooner? His men had searched the stables earlier, immediately after Prideaux had been seen on his way to Trecarrow. They had missed him then. Were they still ignoring some vital clue?

He saw the young groom — Glasson, wasn't it? — slipping out of the stables towards the house, trying to avoid notice.

167

'Oy!' Groves shouted fiercely. 'You've some explaining to do.'

Glasson turned.

'Come here,' said Groves and beckoned Glasson with a menacing bend of a finger.

Glasson slowly approached the policeman and shuffled his feet. He was small, slightly built and terrified. Groves smiled.

'So,' Groves said, taking hold of Glasson's shoulder with his great hand and clenching his fingers together until the man winced and tried to draw away. 'He was here all the time.' He let the man go suddenly so that the groom stumbled and almost fell to the ground. He looked up at the policeman with fear and resentment.

'I didn't see him. I knew nothing. He must have crept in and out again in the dark.'

'You let him go.'

''twas nothin' to do with me. I tell you I didn't know.'

The man was telling the truth, that was obvious, but Groves would not admit it to him. 'You let him go. We could have you for that, accessory to a murder.'

Glasson shook his head in helpless denial and looked about him for a way of escape.

'You'll not miss anything else, understand me? Anything different, any little thing, anyone in the household − anyone at all − doing anything unusual, you tell me.' He reached out a hand to grab Glasson again but the groom evaded him, cowering against the stable wall. Groves smiled at the man's terror. 'Any little thing,' he repeated. 'Or it will be the worse for you.' He scowled at the man and turned on his heels and left the grounds.

Someone in the house knew something about Prideaux. There was tension between Mrs Prideaux and her mistress, a suggestion of something clandestine, but he could not guess what. It probably had nothing to do with the wanted man. Certainly Caroline Trevarth would not be party to concealing a murderer. A man like George Prideaux would terrify the woman.

He shrugged his suspicions off, tried to give his mind to the many other cases demanding his attention. He could not.

The man Prideaux obsessed him, so that it was now a matter of pride that he should bring him to justice.

Later that evening he returned to the house, not sure what it was that drew him there. He made an excuse that he wished to explain to Thomas Trevarth the reason for his earlier visit and apologise for having disturbed the household, especially when Mrs Trevarth had not been well.

'We had information,' he explained. 'Thought the man might be on the premises. We were wrong, it seems, or too late rather. He's been here at some time. We found this in the stables.' He handed the brass button to Trevarth. 'From an army tunic. Belonging to Prideaux without a doubt.'

Trevarth held it for a moment then put it on the table beside him. He looked over to his wife with concern before turning to Groves. 'So, what's the next step? I need to know he's been caught or has left the county before I leave my wife for my visit to South Africa. I need to be assured of her safety.'

'I have no worries, my dear,' Mrs Trevarth said, to Groves's surprise. 'I have seen Mr Groves and his men at work and I am sure they have frightened the man away. If he ever was hidden in the stables, he'll have left long since. I should think he's fled the country by now.' She looked at Groves for confirmation.

'No,' said Groves. 'I have a feeling about him. He's still somewhere about, perhaps nearer than we think. He's a Cornishman, and his instinct will be to stay near home and friends.'

'Can such a man still have friends willing to help him?' Trevarth said.

'Some misguided woman will be giving him bed and board.' He looked over to Mrs Trevarth as he spoke, hoping she would understand what he meant by bed. 'Women fall easy prey to a rogue like this one. They tell me he's a personable young fellow, attractive to women of a certain sort. Some lonely widow — and there are plenty of those about — may well have taken him in, and been taken in by him.'

He thought Mrs Trevarth was about to say something but she suppressed whatever it was and dropped her eyes demurely, then got up to go to the window and open it as

169

if the air in the room were too close for comfort. 'Where are your men looking now?' she said.

'I've got men covering the railway stations and someone watching his old haunts under Carn Brea. But it's not easy. There are holes in plenty for him to hide in. We'll wait till that sister of his gives him away. She's the key. My instinct tells me she knows where he is. She'll lead us to him, never fear.'

He left them, both with anxious expressions on their faces, no doubt at the thought that their housekeeper might be harbouring her brother. He saw the woman as he left the house. She might have been handsome, in a frosty sort of way, but for that disfigurement on her cheek. She ignored him and he watched her go towards the stairs.

She knew something, he could tell.

4

At the open window Caroline breathed deeply of the warm evening air. Thank God that man had gone. She had never liked Groves. Now she found herself hating him with an intensity that was difficult to conceal.

Outside the bats had begun to fly. Soon it would be dark and soon George would be leaving. Thomas was saying something but she had not heard.

'Caroline,' he said and jarred her into attention. 'You heard what Groves said about Mrs Prideaux? I am not at all happy at her remaining in our service. Don't you feel uneasy about it, my dear?'

She turned to him in denial. 'Of course not. There's nothing for us to worry about,' she said. 'I have complete confidence in her. She would do nothing to shame us. She must be anxious about her brother, naturally, but I would not want to make the position any more difficult for her by suggesting we don't trust her. I hope you will say nothing to her, Thomas. She does her job, all that we ask. We could wish for no one better.'

Thomas looked at her in surprise and she realised she had spoken with more force than was usual for her.

'Very well,' he said. 'If you are sure.'

'I am. Quite sure.'

Dark had come to cover his escape. She thought she heard a sound outside, a sudden movement and for a moment feared Thomas might hear and see him and give the alarm, but it was her little cat, Claudia, leaping out of the bushes at a moth fluttering at the window, nothing more.

5

At a signal from his sister that the coast was clear George Prideaux crept down the servants' stairs, along the corridor past the servants' hall to the yard beyond. Ada had assured him that the household were occupied with their own affairs and that there was no danger of his being seen, but a natural caution made him keep to the shadows, pausing frequently to listen for the presence of the police. They would not be far away, but he heard nothing, no more than the shuffling of horses in their stalls.

He yielded to the temptation to go to the front of the house, to take a long look at the place which had given him shelter, the house of the woman Caroline. He would probably never see her again and the thought gave him pain, a more that ordinary regret. He had been near to falling in love with her – a folly he had been spared by the need to flee – and he knew she had come within a moment or two of surrendering herself to him. With sudden clarity he recalled the kisses they had exchanged but was startled from the memory by a movement at his feet and looked to see a cat, the tortoiseshell cat to which he owed his safety, leaping up at a moth and catching it in its paws.

A light shone from the window of the house and he moved rapidly into the shadow. Caroline looked out and leaned from the window to call to her cat. He was tempted to show himself to her but in the room behind her he saw the figure of a man, broad-shouldered, thick-set, her husband no doubt, clearly in every way a man of substance and, seeing him, he felt a stab of jealousy.

Silently he turned away. He had no right to feel jealousy of this man. Envy, maybe, of his status and security, but no right to jealousy. He had no claims on the woman, nor

171

she on him. They had shared an instant of madness, but no more.

And he was free, at last able to walk more than the few paces across the carpeted room which had been a sort of prison to him. He would have liked to shout aloud for joy but caution bade silence; he left the house behind him, striding towards the edge of the estate, ears alive to any whisper of danger.

His way again took him near to Perranwell and past the public house. Once more sounds of jollity came from the inn and he was able to slink past unobserved. At one point, on the edge of woodland, he caught a glimpse of two men furtively making their way through the trees. He thought at first they were police shadowing him but they were poachers, as anxious to avoid observation as he. They had not heard nor seen him and he was reassured that his own awareness of danger was even more acute than theirs.

He came at last to the mine, the old workings. The mining equipment, the kibbles and waggons and the rest, had long since been moved. The engine house was stripped of its engine and only the gaunt granite walls were left to mark the once prosperous enterprise.

The building's noble silhouette stood sharp against the night sky. Here he would be safe until the hue and cry died down. He had worked here too for a time before going to Wheal Kitty and knew the drives and stopes, the shafts and winzes. Time would have changed them, with rock falls and the inundation of water, but there were places enough to hide him. His sister had provided him with candles and lucifers, so he would not be lost in the dark. And she had given him food, not the sort of 'croust' he had carried with him as a miner, the pasty and the dry unleavened 'hoggan', but wheaten bread and sharp-tasting cheese and salt beef. He would have no shortage of water to drink for it ran freely down the rock walls, collecting in pools and forming underground freshets.

This was his element, though in truth it was as dank as his cell in Bodmin barracks. But he was free to wander where he would, find the old ways, remember the comrades he had worked with — old Joe Beskeen who had guided him down

172

the ladder way on his first terrifying descent, and Josiah Williams, who had been killed by a misfire the very day the mine had closed. He remembered Josiah saying, 'I'll show 'em. There's lots more tin here if you do but know where to look.' He had looked, and died in the looking.

He took his bearings from the engine house and found the entrance to Taylor's shaft without difficulty. He stood for a moment above ground looking about him. The moon had risen and its silver beams, falling on the abandoned engine house a hundred yards or so away, revealed a stark beauty; it was not so much a ruin, he thought, as a monument to the glory of the men of Cornwall, the engineers, the masons, and the miners.

He was one of those, a miner, would still be one but for the mischance of taking the Queen's shilling. He was at home here and safe − for the present. He looked down the shaft. The metal ladder leading to the drives below was there still. He would go down, several fathoms deep, before lighting a candle. Even in this lonely place a flicker of light might be seen and give rise to questions. So, cautiously, hand over hand, foot reaching tentatively for each successive rung, he moved down, conscious how neglect had weakened the ladder's hold as here and there it swung perilously from its mooring.

He reached the platform at the thirty fathom level, breathless but without mishap, lit a candle and looked around him. The candlelight gave him comfort, its flame glistening on the walls, reflecting a myriad of tinselled gleams. He felt the awesomeness of the majesty about him, the mass and weight above him and all around. But he was safe.

6

He woke, knowing it was day from the circle of light at the top of the shaft. He had slept surprisingly well, wrapped in the blanket Ada had given him, and his head resting on his pack. He sat cross-legged and ate some of the bread and the salt beef. He doused his hands and face in the chill water from a pool and felt refreshed, ready for a day of activity. But it would be a day of idleness, he realised. He had nothing

173

to do but wait for a message telling him it was safe to make his way to Falmouth and take ship.

He had always been a man of action, working with comrades at the rock face or, briefly, with his fellow soldiers in military exercises. He enjoyed the company of other men, was not used to the loneliness which had been his lot of late. But now he was beginning to find some inner resource which allowed him to bear that loneliness with a kind of calm.

Nevertheless he needed the sound of the human voice and began to talk aloud to himself, letting his thoughts wander, speaking them and listening in surprise to them. He heard himself describing the lanes around Carn Brea, that great primeval gathering of rock that had dominated the skyline of his youth, with its anciently picturesque 'castle'. He told of the paths winding up the slope, the grasses struggling for a hold, the giant boulders, the wind-twisted bushes, the occasional golden burst of gorse.

His voice, soft and whispered at first, echoed about the drive, so that he was led to imagine the place was peopled with companions. He raised his voice a little and then a little more, so that these invisible friends seemed to be shouting to him in response.

He became suddenly aware that his shouts might attract attention, though he reasoned that if any farm boy heard sounds issuing from the shaft, he would run in fear, thinking the voices came from dead miners long since lost and left below. He let his voice sink to a whisper.

It was unlikely there would be a farm boy or anyone else wandering over the old workings. There were no pickings there. The land was spoilt from decades of digging for tin and copper, reduced to arid waste. No one would come here, save, in time, the woman Caroline to leave a message of release or to replenish his stock of food.

He slowly climbed the ladder way to the top of the shaft and waited a few feet below the opening, listening. He heard the sound of a lark and, not far off, the surge of the sea. But there was no sound of man to alarm him. He raised his head to peer from the shaft and, seeing nothing to make him suspicious, clambered to the surface but lay, supine, behind a heap of rock, until he was certain there was no one about.

174

Caution made him count slowly to two hundred before he rose to his full height, still ready to slip into the shaft again if need be. But he was alone. He had an almost clear view over a circle of several hundred yards. The only place for anyone to find cover was the engine house, where he had arranged for messages to be brought.

He ran, bent double, over to the ruins, but there was no one there to see him. And no one to meet him. He had not expected her to be there, but he was disappointed nevertheless, though he knew a message was unlikely to come so soon. They would take time to make arrangements for his passage.

He stayed in the ruins for most of the day. He was tempted to remain above ground overnight, but he realised he would be safer in the drives he knew. Below ground he would hear if anyone came close, below ground he was confident he could escape capture. So, when dusk came, he took himself back down the shaft and settling on the platform at the thirty fathom level, wrapped the blanket around him and slept.

7

The house was without life. She had been to the nursery and looked at the empty rooms with a sense of loss. For a few short weeks they had been occupied, not with the children she had once hoped for but with a sort of child, a dependant, someone to shelter and nourish and love.

She was not afraid to admit the word. She loved the boy, not in the way she loved Thomas of course, but with love of a kind she had never known till now, love that changed her very nature, that had a bodily effect upon her, making her nerves newly sensitive, responsive to the tiniest stimulus.

The room was empty, the bed stripped to its mattress, no trace remaining of the young man who had lain there. She shuddered at the suddenness of the image of him that invaded her and stood, clasping her fingers together almost in prayer, not knowing if she wished to dispel the image or hold it closer to her. A voice broke into her thoughts so that she jumped with fear. 'Mrs Prideaux!' she exclaimed.

'I came to make sure there was nothing left to show anyone's been here.'

'There is nothing.' The ghost of a memory only, she told herself.

The housekeeper turned to go but Caroline stopped her. 'We must plan.'

'It need not concern you, ma'am.'

'I am concerned. You cannot help him on your own. He would have been caught already but for me. I still want to help.'

The housekeeper was silent, but shook her head in disapproval.

'You need me. The police are watching you, waiting for you to lead them to him. They have no suspicion of me. So it must be left to me to go to him. You must see that.'

'He should never have come here. He has gone now and we can leave him to himself. That's the wise thing to do.'

Caroline was horrified at the woman's suggestion. 'We cannot abandon him now. I shall help him, with or without you.'

'And how do you propose to save him?'

'There are men leaving every month for America, on cheap passages, miners whose skills are valued over there, who have no work here.' She had heard Thomas complain that all the young men of ambition and ability were leaving Cornwall. 'He could join a group like that. No one need recognise him.' Her mind was racing on. She could find him money. The only problem was to divert the attention of the police, persuade them to give up their watch on Falmouth for another port. 'I'm sure I can see to that. It will be for you to lay a false trail for the police.' She paced back and forth across the room, trying to foresee the difficulties. 'What is it?' she said, seeing Mrs Prideaux shaking her head sadly again.

'He is not worth it,' the housekeeper said. 'You must not do this, must not think of it.'

'How do you think he is now, waiting for us to help him, expecting a message? We cannot abandon him.'

'I gave him bread and meat, and a blanket. You need not bother your head about him. He's used to hardship and hunger.' She glanced from the soft bed to the heavy velvet curtains at the window. 'This isn't his world, comfort of this kind. He'll not miss this.' She seemed to be telling Caroline that the young man she had known here was not the real man. 'He'll make his way without your help. I know him. You don't.'

No, thought Caroline, I don't know the man you imagine your brother to be. The young man I know is another being entirely, one hidden from all but me. He is mine, in a sense my own creation, belongs only to me.

But he was no longer there for her to nurse and protect. He had gone and the room was once again empty, a proof of her barrenness, an affront to her womanhood. She swept past Mrs Prideaux out of the nursery wing, leaving it to its sterile and vacant routine of housemaid's visits.

She would have liked to go to the cliffs where the engine house stood on the fringe of the old workings of Wheal Charlotte but it would draw attention to her if she went without reason. If she took the trap and drove there alone questions would be asked. She must somehow prepare the ground. She could find an excuse again in a charitable visit to some family in need, but Thomas, if he heard — and he was sure to be informed of her movements — would disapprove of her going out unaccompanied, with a 'murderer' still at large.

She gave her mind to the problem. Never before had she had so serious a matter to consider, a matter in which her decisions alone were relevant, where she could rely on no one else to help make her mind up. She enjoyed the feeling of responsibility until the thought came that a man's life depended on her. But even that thought seemed to give her heart. She could not fail him. She was filled with a resolution that surprised her and would have surprised her husband even more. She was not the helpless, fragile, ornamental woman Thomas had married; she had initiative and will.

Chapter Nineteen

Maud came downstairs with the news that the doctor had seen Mrs Prideaux, was very concerned about her, but thought there was no immediate danger. 'He said he'll arrange for a nurse to come in and help.'

'She won't like that. She hates feeling dependent. I'll help look after her.'

'There's no call for you to do anything, Mother, except go to see her from time to time.'

But Caroline felt a responsibility for her old servant. It might have been kinder, years ago, to have arranged for Ada to go into a home, but she would have got few thanks for that. Trecarrow was Ada's home, had been so almost as long as it had been Caroline's, and held as many memories for the servant as for the mistress.

Memories. They flooded back at odd moments for no apparent reason. The breath of a breeze through the rose bed would set a train of thought going, of a day long since when Maud was a small child and had lost one of her 'magic bits and pieces', a button she had found and which, for some reason known only to her childish mind, she cherished. It was there now; she had come across it the other day. Where had she put it? She must show it to Maud, see if she remembered it and the mystery it held for her.

There were other triggers of memory, the most evocative the sight of Joseph in the old stables, probing into the corners, fascinated by the leather harness still hanging there. Only this morning he had said, 'You should keep a horse or two, Grandmama.'

'And where would I find the money to feed a horse or pay a groom?' She laughed at his innocence.

He had climbed up the ladder to the loft to see what else he might find and as she looked up she saw another young man, more muscled than her grandson, but no less handsome. She had caught her breath at the sight and Joseph had said, 'It's quite safe,' misinterpreting her gasp as concern for him.

He came quickly down and put his arms about her. 'It's all right,' he said. 'I'm safe.'

Was he safe? Did he find safety? She still did not know. But she had done what she could; she recalled how the business changed her, made a woman of her.

'Grandmama,' she heard Joseph say, his voice an echo of one heard then, 'you've left me again.'

She smiled. He and his mother were always accusing her of living in the past. It was not true; she only visited it from time to time.

'You must go and see Mrs Prideaux,' she urged. 'She always looks forward to your visits. And when I saw her this morning I could tell she was wanting to see you. Go along now. I'm not the only old woman who needs you.'

He took her arm and together they walked back to the house. 'You're not old,' he said. 'You just have a lot of life behind you. That's different.'

But it was not behind her. It was with her wherever she went.

Chapter Twenty

1

She would find a reason for visiting the village of St Agnes. From there it was not far to the workings and the engine house of the old Wheal Charlotte. She could ask one of the ladies working for the Cornwall Distress Committee for the names of families in the village needing help. Each day that passed with no news of George made her anxious.

Thomas was looking at her as if he had unpleasant news to break to her and was hesitant to do so. The boy had been caught! For the moment she feared the worst and then realised that of course Thomas would not be unwilling to tell her that. It was something else.

'What is it?' she asked.

'I don't know how to tell you,' Thomas said. 'It is very difficult for me to put off my visit to the Cape. There's no one whom I can trust to handle my business, no one with the right mining experience.'

'Then you must go yourself, as you intended. I shall miss you of course, but there's no reason why you should hesitate to leave me.'

'The man Prideaux. I am still uneasy about him, until he's caught ...'

'He's no danger to us. I am convinced of that. You need not worry.'

Thomas was clearly relieved. 'If you're quite certain then I shall keep to my original plans. My passage still stands for next week.'

Caroline felt guilty at the thought that leapt to her mind; his leaving now would make it easier to help George – and easier to see him. With Thomas gone there would be no one to whom she need explain her movements.

'How long will you be away?' she asked.

'Too long, my love, much too long. Maybe five or six months.'

'That long?' She was dismayed. In spite of her new-found sense of independence she would miss Thomas's solid reassuring presence about the house.

'I shall not stay out there a day longer than I need.' He came to her and bent to kiss her. He was always a considerate husband, but normally kept his emotions under firm control. Now in the imminence of his departure he allowed his feelings to show.

'I shall think of you every day. You will be constantly in my prayers and I shall write as often as I can,' he said.

The night before he left for Southampton they made love, not with passion – that had never seemed to be part of their natures – but with gentle affection, husband and wife in the sort of union expected of them.

Her impatience to see George had continued to grow. She was anxious about him, fearing he would think he had been forgotten. As soon as Thomas left she gave orders for a horse to be saddled for her. The groom could not hide his surprise. She rode rarely now; she had taken a bad fall riding with the Four Burrows Hunt two years before and her confidence had been shaken. Now she mounted the bay gelding without hesitation, took the reins and found her old skill as a horsewoman had not deserted her.

'Would you like me to ride along with you, ma'am?' Glasson asked, hand on the horse's neck as if unwilling to let her go on her own.

'No,' she said firmly. 'You have work to do here. Get on with it.'

'I only meant . . .' he began but she was already out of earshot, feeling freedom in the wind blowing through her hair as she rode out of the estate and turned towards the north coast. The time had been when she had begun each morning with a canter, with no more motive than the exercise. Now there was purpose in it, one which filled her mind, making her spur her mount to a gallop.

He will be there, she said to herself, there waiting. I shall see him.

Her horse stumbled over a clump of heather and, startled, she drew it to a walk. She dare not risk an accident now. George was dependent on her good sense, on her planning. She held the key to his safety.

Clouds were gathering. Bright sun had lasted till the moment of Thomas's departure. Now the heaviness of impending storm weighed on the air. In the distance over the horizon the sky lit with a lightning flash and within a few short seconds a clap of thunder followed. There was no rain as yet but she knew it would come and soon. Ahead in the gloom she saw a tall chimney and a great granite-built house tight against it, the building George had described. She dismounted and led her horse the few yards to the shelter of the engine-house just as the storm unleashed its fury with another flash, a roll of thunder and a downpour. The gelding was restive and she spoke soothingly, calming it, and together she and the horse stood within the walls, waiting.

The walls of granite blocks were sound, the roof had slates broken and missing here and there but there was cover enough to protect them, even from this torrent. But, through the gaps of the windows, no longer glazed and frames rotted, blew wind and rain.

There was no sign of the young man, none that he had ever been here. Perhaps he was hiding in the mine still, she thought, and then was seized with sudden dread; he might have fallen or again been taken ill. He should have been looking out for her, have come to her when she arrived, and he had not come.

Anxiety overwhelmed her and, leaving the horse in the shelter of the old ruin, she ran headlong through the rain towards the shaft, crying out with fear. She knew it was foolish to behave so but she could not resist the impulse. He had not come to her and she must find him.

2

Prideaux had exhausted the store of food his sister had

provided but, snaring two rabbits, had skinned and cooked them. He had hoped to find more food left for him in the ruin but though he visited the building daily he had found nothing. He took the risk of going into fields on the edge of the workings to find turnips and the like. At first he kept to the hours of darkness for his foraging but later, becoming restless, had ventured to go in the early morning, before even the herdsmen were about. Then he had been tempted to go down to the sea to bathe. He found a quiet cove, a narrow inlet between jagged cliff faces. There the sea came swelling in at full tide, throwing spume as high as the cliff top, till, at the fall of the tide, the sea's anger abated and, on the surface at least, it became temptingly placid. It was still dangerous to swim here, he knew, but he could not resist the attraction of the green-white waves, stripped off and plunged in.

Afterwards he lay on the sand and let the warmth of the sun dry him. But this morning the sun had retreated behind cloud and, when he came out of the water, rain was falling. He stood with raised arms to greet it, finding pleasure in its stinging assault. Refreshed — and wet from sea and rain — he drew on his trousers and shirt and clambered up the path to the cliff top. A flash of lightning and a swiftly-following peal of thunder made him pause. It was as if the gods themselves had aimed their bolt at him, for the roll was directly above, deafening him. He cowered against the cliff side, waiting to be struck down. Then lightning flashed again and thunder rolled, but this time drifting away so that he knew the eye of the storm had passed.

As he reached the cliff top he saw a woman running through the driving rain towards the shaft. He recognised Caroline and called out in warning to her but the storm drowned his voice. He ran towards her. She could not know the perils of the workings. There were holes everywhere, vent holes, shafts for lowering men to the depths, shafts for drawing ore up, danger at every step.

'Caroline!' he called, stumbled over a heap of waste, almost fell, called again, this time loud enough to be heard even over the storm, and saw her stop and turn. She seemed astonished at his appearing there, waited for him and as he reached her opened her arms to him. They stood embraced, unaware of the rain beating upon them and the lightning flashing across the sky and the thunder rolling, knowing nothing but their own selves and their need each for the other, in sudden realisation that there was no one but them in, on or above the earth. They were all; the rest, the tempest, the swirling clouds, the teeming heavens were as nothing.

He did not speak, could not, for nothing needed saying; he held her close, kissed her wet cheeks, stroked her dripping hair, knew he was mad but cared nothing for sanity.

She was speaking, repeating over and over again words which at last reached his mind. 'My love, my love,' she was saying.

'What is happening?' he said, bewildered at the intensity of his feelings and at the emotion that charged her words. He held her from him to look at her. The rain had bedraggled her fair hair so that it hung wet and darkly over her shoulders. She shook it about her and droplets of rain spattered him; he laughed, hardly knowing why, save that his joy was too great to be contained. She laughed with him, looked down at herself, her clinging clothes, the damp material shaping itself revealingly to her.

'You will catch cold,' he said.

'And you are soaked.' She put a hand out to his beard, black and wiry and bristling with moisture.

They stood a little apart from each other, looking shyly into each other's eyes, as if neither could understand what had taken place between them.

'What is happening?' he repeated.

She did not answer, shook her head again, ran her hand through her hair and shivered.

'You are cold,' he said, concerned for her.

'No. It is not the cold,' she said. 'And look. The storm has gone. The sun is shining.' The sky was swept clean, its blue a deep azure, a steam rising as the sun's heat touched the ground.

'You must get out of those damp things,' he said.

'What can I do?' she said, shrugging her shoulders, then clasping her arms about her against the chill of her wet clothes.

'Come with me,' he said.

184

She did not question him and when he put out his hand to hers she let him lead her from the workings towards the cliff edge.

'Down here.' He pointed to a cleft between the rocks. A path led to a triangle of smooth golden sand stretching to the lapping tide. The sun shone hotly on the little beach and an inviting warmth rose from the narrow cove. He led the way down.

'I come here to swim and lie in the sun.' He gestured to a cluster of rocks, already dry and giving off heat in the baking of the sun. 'Your clothes will dry out there,' he said, stripping his shirt off and spreading it on a rock.

She did not move. 'How can I?' she said.

'I shall turn away.'

'I do not know.'

'What don't you know?'

'What is happening here. To me. To us. Tell me.' But she did not wait for him to answer as she raised her arms to draw off her blouse. It clung to her so that she had a moment's awkwardness, but when she was free of it she put it beside his shirt.

'You're soaked to the skin,' he said.

She looked at her camisole and skirt and ran her hands down her body. She raised her head and looked challengingly at him and then back at the cliff top.

'There's nobody there. No one ever comes this way. We are alone. Just us.'

She shivered and said, 'I am wet and cold now.' She unfastened her skirt and put it on the rock beside her blouse. Then calmly and unselfconsciously she removed her petticoat and camisole until she wore only her drawers and her bust bodice. These too were damp and in their dampness disclosed more than they concealed. She looked at him, again with the directness in her that seemed to challenge him to speak, to say what he was thinking, but he could not, dare not. Then she lifted her arms, unfastened the clasp of her bodice at the back, let it slip to the sand and stood, breasts bared, facing him, only a foot away.

She dropped her head, looked down at herself and then slowly raised her eyes to his. She blushed as she saw him gazing at her breasts and when he closed his eyes and drew in his breath in an effort to gain control over himself, she moved to him and held him to her, her breasts soft against his firm chest. They did not kiss, but stood, close and still, until the touching of their flesh brought them to madness again so that they sank to the sand, lay for a long moment arms clasped about each other, then slowly began to remove each other's last garment, freeing themselves wholly from all sense of the material world.

3

She rode slowly back, almost unaware of the path she followed, unconcerned at the time that had passed, knowing only the feel of him within her, the scent of him clinging to her, the sight of him fresh in her mind's eye, the sound of his voice, soft and urgent. She thought she heard him call and turned in the saddle to look back but he had gone. She had wanted him to return with her, saying she could find another hiding place within the house, but they both knew it would be unsafe. In a wild moment she had thought she might stay with him in the depths of Wheal Charlotte, but he had laughed at her and she had known it was folly.

It was all folly, she knew in her heart, but a folly that had brought fulfilment, in a way secret to her that she could not yet understand. The love she felt was all-enveloping; she longed for his touch upon her and hers on him. She had never felt so before and wondered if she would ever feel so again. She had not imagined a woman could experience so urgent a desire; women were not made like that, save only those of a certain sort. Well, she was that sort, she knew it now; she loved passionately, had given herself willingly, wanted him, needed him, could be satisfied only by him. And she felt no shame, only pride; she was, as never before, herself, Caroline Trevarth, opening to love and finding the meaning of herself in that love. It was as if she had been preparing for this moment all her life, as if it had been inevitable from the start of time.

She had found him.

She was shaken from her reverie by a shout and her mind cleared. Glasson, the groom, was riding swiftly towards her. He drew his horse up in front of her.

'Miss, ma'am,' he stammered, flustered. 'We were that worried. We've been searching everywhere. 'twas feared you'd been thrown. 'tes hours since you left.'

Hours? It had been moments only, and yet an eternity.

'Hours?' she said.

'Six hours, all but. We were some worried, ma'am.' He looked her up and down. 'You had a fall, ma'am?'

She knew her hair was mussed, her blouse and skirt creased, boots muddy. 'I had to shelter from the storm. Nothing more. You need not have been concerned.'

'We were thinking we should send some one to the police to get them to look.'

'Oh no,' she exclaimed. 'There's no need for that. I can look after myself. Do you understand? I needed to be alone. I was perfectly safe. And you must never again think of bothering the police. I shall be in no danger.'

He rode beside her, glancing at her from time to time, as if this woman were a stranger. So I am, she thought. It was not I who rode away six hours ago. That was someone else, in another time.

The household had been alarmed, she could see from the relief on the faces of them all. She went upstairs to bath and change. Particles of sand fell from her as she took off her undergarments and grains were still pressed into her buttocks. She brushed them from her to the floor, glittering reminders of those golden moments. She closed her eyes and saw him stretched upon her and felt a stirring within her, an echo of him, a presence there still.

When she was dressed she sent for her housekeeper. Ada Prideaux frowned disapprovingly as if she knew all, yet she could know nothing. 'You have seen him,' she said, a challenge, not a question.

Caroline stared at her, trying to see in this woman some trace of the man, her lover, but there was nothing, except — for a moment — a look about the eyes that had something of his passion in them. She was imagining it, she told herself. 'Yes, I saw him. I rode out there.'

187

'I knew it. You should not have gone. It is dangerous for you to think of seeing him.'

'I had to know he was safe. And I shall have to go again, with food and another blanket. The nights are cold.'

'He must go. We must get him away.'

It would come to that of course, but for the moment she had not thought of his going.

'We must give our minds to that,' Mrs Prideaux said firmly. 'You must see that, ma'am.'

She knew she would lose him. He must be saved, that was all that mattered, even more than her love for him; indeed, because she loved him.

Mrs Prideaux was going on. 'You had plans of having him join emigrant workers leaving from Falmouth. We should set about doing that.'

I could go with him. The thought came unbidden and took hold of her. Why need he go alone? It would be cover for him to have a woman with him. The police would not be looking for a couple.

'Well?' said Ada Prideaux. 'What have you in mind? I can see you have thought of something.'

Caroline was startled at the woman's sharpness. She must be careful to keep her idea to herself, tell her housekeeper only so much as concerned her.

She paced about the room, impatient now to work out her plan.

'Well?' Mrs Prideaux said again.

'You are still being watched by the police. We'll make that work to our advantage. Go to a shipping agent in Redruth and find out details of sailings over the next weeks — from Falmouth, Plymouth, Padstow. When we see what there is available we can decide what to do. You will book a passage for a single male on one of the boats. The police will know all about that, you can be sure. And I will book a passage on an earlier boat from a Truro agent. No one is going to suspect me of helping him.' She saw it clearly. She would go with him, turn her back on the meaningless life she was leading here and accompany him wherever fate took them.

Mrs Prideaux looked hard at her. 'That is all you have in mind?'

'I have told you. I shall book passage for him on an earlier ship from a port different from the one the police expect.' She was conscious of having gained authority, a will of her own; she was in command, mistress of the house, and mistress of her fate. 'Tomorrow you will go to the agents.'

'And you?' Mrs Prideaux asked.

'I shall go to him,' she said. 'Make up a hamper of food. If anyone wants to know who it's meant for, tell them it's for a family in St Agnes. And,' she added with emphasis, 'no one is to worry if I am gone some time.' She smiled at the thought.

'It is madness to take such risks. I beg you, leave him to himself. We can get a message to him when it's all arranged. Till then it's safer to leave him be.' She was plainly upset.

'He needs help, reassurance, food, friends. Who else but me can give him what he needs? You? You cannot move an inch without the police following you. Your every move is suspect.'

'What has happened to you?' Mrs Prideaux frowned, seeing, as Caroline thought, the new woman in her.

'Happened?' said Caroline. 'What can have happened? I only know he needs me. I don't want him caught. I want him safe, with a future in a new world, with ...' She stopped, fearing she was about to give herself away.

'He will be gone soon,' the housekeeper said.

'Yes, please God,' said Caroline. And please God I shall go with him, she said to herself.

4

He did not come to her when she arrived at the engine house, but she was not anxious. She left her horse by the building, put the basket of food inside it and walked to the cove where they had made love. He would be there waiting. She did not see him at first, only his clothes on the rocks, then she saw his head bobbing in the water as he swam, with long strong strokes, out to sea. She was fearful for him, knowing the danger of these waters, and clambered down the cliff side to persuade him to come out to her. He saw her and turned to

189

shore, and, as he walked naked from the water, she was there on the beach holding out her hands, welcoming him to her.

She undressed, shyly this time, for there was no reason for it other than her desire to be near, flesh to flesh, no excuse as there had been yesterday. He was wet from the sea and there was a salt taste to him, a savour that was all his own. They did not speak, letting their bodies express their love, lying curled to each other, first with her below, then turning so that she was above and looking down at him, love welling inside her at the sight of him and his pleasure at her possession of him.

For a while afterwards they lay without words and then George ran into the sea. Caroline plunged after him to where he stood, water up to his thighs, waiting, godlike in his bronzed beauty so that she caught her breath again in admiration.

'I love you,' she whispered. 'I cannot help myself.' He said nothing but held her to him as desire mounted.

'Here,' he said, but she took his hand and led him back to the warm golden sand. She would remember this for ever, she thought, this very moment, as she looked beyond his shoulders to the sun-filled sky. A gull wheeled above and another as if curious at the strange habits of the humans on the beach below. She heard their mewing and then heard herself rivalling their shrill call in a long exultant cry which echoed and re-echoed about the encircling cliffs.

They slept and she woke to the sound of water beating against rocks at the entrance to the cove. She turned to wake him but hesitated, moved by his youth and vulnerability. In sleep his lips were slightly parted. She bent to kiss them and he opened his eyes and seemed for a moment surprised at her presence.

'We must go,' she said. 'The tide is coming in.'

They dressed hurriedly, climbed to the cliff top and ran to the ruins. 'I have to go,' she said. 'But I shall come tomorrow, at the same time.'

'I shall be waiting,' he said, smiling.

'I have plans,' Caroline said. 'I'll be able to tell you more tomorrow.' She bent from the saddle to kiss him and wondered how she had the strength of will to leave when every second away was a torment.

He was standing at the door of the engine house as she rode reluctantly away.

It was madness, but madness with a sort of reason to it. She lay in the large double bed she usually shared with Thomas, and dreamt of George. She had always thought of herself as a loving wife, indeed still thought of herself in that way; she admired and respected Thomas, felt deep affection for him; but her feeling for George belonged to another part of her, a part which till now had been hidden even from her. George and Thomas belonged to different worlds, and the Caroline married to Thomas and the Caroline who lay with George were two equally diverse women. That was the madness, this separation between her two selves, the one known to her household and her husband − the fragile, weak, dependent woman − and the other, known only to herself and George − passionate, wilful, wanton.

The word came to her and she knew it to be so: she was a wanton. How else could she explain the delight she had in taking this man to her, allowing him freedoms with her body that she could not even have imagined before? Yes, she was a wanton, but this new Caroline cherished the notion, for she was a wanton only for him, for her young god. For him she would abandon everything; home, respect, status, even her husband.

Her mind turned to Thomas, that kind, dependable, protective man who, for fifteen years had spoilt and cossetted her; who, even though she had failed him in her duty to provide him with an heir, still loved her. She loved him, could not deny it, had no wish to deny it. But it was love of a different order from that she felt for George; love of him was a physical ache, so that even now in the small hours of the night, she was tempted to rise and go to him.

Sense prevailed. She lay in her bed, waiting for dawn, for the sounds of the household to tell her it was proper for her to move. She would go to him then. But first she had to visit Truro and the steamship offices. Mrs Prideaux had brought lists of sailings from Falmouth and Plymouth. A liner was due out of Plymouth for the St Lawrence River, in three weeks' time, and a ship was leaving Falmouth for the Spanish port of Santander a week before. Mrs Prideaux would make a booking on the Canadian vessel but, by the time the police arrived at the dockside in Plymouth to arrest their man, he – and Caroline herself – would be in Spain, free to begin a new life.

Doubts crept upon her. She recalled Superintendent Groves's remark about 'some poor misguided woman, easy prey of such a personable rogue'. Maybe that's how she would be seen, but he was no rogue, nor was she a victim. Even if he were to abandon her – unthinkable though that was – she would still not be a victim; she had given herself willingly, out of love, a love that was hers to give. And he had given her more, a gift she had not thought possible. She had no regrets. Whatever happened now, nothing could change what had already happened.

She met no difficulties at the offices of the Truro Shipping Company, remembering at the last minute to give an assumed name. 'Williams,' she said. 'Mr and Mrs Williams,' and paid in cash for the tickets. She was surprised at the ease with which the lie came to her lips.

She returned home and concealed the tickets in a drawer in her dressing table. She told Mrs Prideaux she had booked a single ticket for her brother in the name of Williams for the sailing in a fortnight.

A mere two weeks before her life began anew.

5

She was about to mount her horse to ride out to Wheal Charlotte when she was told Superintendent Groves wished a word with her. She thought of refusing to see him but knew she must do nothing to offend him. She needed to learn as much as possible of his plans and suspicions.

He had a self-satisfied look on his face and she found herself disliking him more than ever. 'Well?' she said curtly.

He was not abashed at her unfriendly reception, pretended to be full of apologies for disturbing her in the absence of her husband. 'Have you news of Mr Trevarth?' he asked.

'By now the boat will have left Southampton, I expect,' she said.

'I may wish to get in touch with him,' Groves said. 'The boat puts in at Cherbourg, I believe.'

She did not know. 'Why should you want to get in touch with him?' She was only idly curious, was impatient for him to leave.

'I'm sure he would like to know when we have caught the man Prideaux. He would feel happier at the news. He asked me to let him know.'

Caroline smiled to herself. 'Have you caught him?' she asked innocently.

'As good as.'

She had a tremor of alarm, looked sharply at the policeman. But Groves could know nothing.

'Indeed,' she said, trying to sound indifferent to the fate of the young Prideaux.

'He's been seen. A farmer up along near Mithian says he's seen someone answering his description near the old workings at Wheal Charlotte.' He rubbed his large fleshy hands together and glanced at Caroline as if to test her reaction to his news, adding 'He's been seen with some young woman down on the sands.' He was watching her so that for a moment she thought he knew, until she realised he was trying to shock her. He would not dare to mention it if Thomas were present. She should show displeasure but she needed to find out how much he knew.

'A young woman?' she asked.

'I guessed his nature would betray him, be his undoing.'

'I don't understand.'

'He can't keep away from them, the women,' he explained. 'Not that sort of fellow. I expect — you'll forgive me for mentioning it — I expect he's taken up with some trollop from Redruth.' He was enjoying the telling, would reveal all the details if she were to encourage him.

'How can you be sure it's him?' she asked.

'The man from Mithian gave us a good description, detailed even, of the woman and Prideaux. He's watched them two or three times on the beach. I wouldn't like to tell you what they were up to.'

Caroline knew she was reddening, partly from humiliation at the realisation she had been watched while making love, but

193

more from anger at the hypocrisy of the man Groves. He was relishing his tale, savouring the description the peeping Tom had given him.

'I want to hear no more,' she exclaimed. 'I don't believe it can be him. He's sure to be miles away by now.' Her mind was in turmoil. She wanted to dismiss Groves there and then and ride out to George to warn him.

Groves had more to say. 'It's Prideaux all right, I'm sure. We've got him now. But I mean to get the woman too. She's an accessory. Deserves all that's coming to her.'

'How do you plan to catch them?' She tried to sound unconcerned but needed desperately to know.

'Give them a bit more rope to hang themselves, catch them at it. The farmer says they have no eyes for anyone but themselves. We'll wait till then. It should be interesting.' His eyes lit with prurient anticipation so that Caroline felt unclean.

She watched him go, then buried her head in her hands. She must warn George. But how? Who could she trust to help? Perhaps Mrs Prideaux was no longer being watched, since they thought they could seize him whenever they wanted. But how could she or anyone get to him without being observed?

There was no one but herself. Whatever the risks she had to go to him, and quickly. She was still beyond suspicion, unless Groves had been laying a trap for her. She had to risk that.

She went to the stables, where she found her horse still saddled, took the reins from Glasson the groom, mounted and rode away from the house towards the workings.

6

Superintendent Groves wondered who the woman with Prideaux was. 'Some trollop from Redruth' he had told Mrs Trevarth. It could not be Irish Molly for she had been under close observation since Prideaux's escape. And the woman was fair, so much had been evident from the farmer's excited narrative. The man had been almost incoherent in his salacious account of the 'bare-arsed whore'. Well, they would soon have her and Prideaux in their grasp, and God help them both.

He trusted his men were alert. He had instructed them not to approach the old workings until the woman arrived. 'I want them both,' he had said. And he had warned Hosken, the man from Mithian, to keep well away from the cove. 'You only get the reward when we've got him, understand?' Hosken had asked if he could be there at the finish. 'Keep away altogether,' Groves had commanded, knowing the man hoped to be witness once more to the coupling of Prideaux and his woman.

He would catch them *in flagrante delicto,* wait till Prideaux and the woman were naked and defenceless. It would be an exploit he could retail for years afterwards. 'Caught in the act.' He felt a quiet satisfaction that things should be working out like this, though regretting that he had not caught the housekeeper, Mrs Prideaux, in the net as well. He still believed she must have had a hand in saving her brother.

He called his sergeant to him. 'Everyone knows what they have to do?'

Sergeant Penrose confirmed arrangements. 'I told them to wait for you before they make their move.'

Groves nodded his approval.

'The groom at Trecarrow wants a word,' Penrose said.

'Glasson?'

'He's back in the stables waiting for you.'

The man could serve no purpose now with his gossip but he might have something to reveal about Prideaux's sister. It might be worth a moment.

He made a detour to Trecarrow and found the little man brushing dung from the horse stalls. 'You have something for me?'

Glasson rested his brush against the wall, looked into the courtyard as if to make sure no one was within earshot.

'Go on, man,' Groves said angrily. 'What have you got for me? And be quick.'

'The mistress,' Glasson said uncertainly, then spoke hurriedly as Groves turned impatiently away. 'You said to tell you anything strange, unusual like.'

'Out with it. I've not got all day.'

'She's taken to riding. Not done that for as long as I've been here. Goes off on her own. Stays away a long time too.'

'Your mistress?'

'Mrs Trevarth, yes.'

Groves stared down at the little man with disbelief. 'You mean to say you've been spying on your mistress?' He wanted to take hold of the fellow and shake him, but he had no time to waste on such trivial business. 'Mrs Prideaux. I want to know about her, you fool. What right have you to question your mistress's movements?'

'I only did what you asked,' Glasson began, but Groves had gone.

7

George Prideaux stood in the shelter of the engine house, crouched against the rough granite walls, barely breathing, aware that an incautious move might reveal his presence. He wondered who the man was, not a policeman that was sure, a local farmer maybe. There was something furtive about his manner that made Prideaux suspicious. He moved crouched, treading warily, looking slyly about him, as if engaged in some nefarious enterprise.

The man walked almost to the edge of the cliff, lay down and crawled the rest of the way to the edge, propped himself up on his elbows and peered over. Then he stood up to get a better look into the cove, looked around him, gave an impatient shrug of the shoulders and walked towards the engine house. Prideaux sank further into the shadows. The man, short and stocky, with slack mouth and mean eyes, walked past George's hiding place without a glance, muttering to himself.

Prideaux was tempted to leap out and challenge him, but held back, sharply aware of danger. The fellow had come with a purpose and it was not his first visit; the stealth of his movements towards the cliff edge and the way he looked down into the cove revealed his expectation, the hope of seeing him and Caroline. Prideaux felt a surge of rage, wanted to run after him, knock him to the ground, beat him senseless; he controlled his anger, shuddering with revulsion at the thought that this peeping Tom had watched his communion with Caroline. He knew it had been so. Everything about the man betrayed it.

If this man knew, so might others. The cove was no longer a private place, a secret, sacred, rendezvous for Caroline and him. It spelt danger for them both. Maybe the man had recognised him; wanted posters were everywhere about the district and a new beard was hardly enough to disguise him. And, if the man had identified him, as was possible, he would not hesitate to claim the police reward.

George knew then the danger he was in and the danger he brought to Caroline. He must get away from here, perhaps even leave the area without waiting to hear the plans she had made for his escape. He must rely on his own initiative, go now before the police were alerted. He dare not even wait for dark and, worst of all, he could not wait for Caroline.

He must leave now, without delay, perhaps aim for Redruth and Irish Molly. She would shelter him. It need not be for long.

He could see no one on the workings, could hear no human sound. A kestrel hovered above the scrub beyond the ruins, out at sea a steamer slowly passed along the horizon, thin cloud drifted high, and all was peaceful, without threat. There were two or three hundred yards of open ground to cross to get to the shaft and recover his pack. He wondered if it was worth the risk. A quick dash in the other direction would bring him to the shelter of a hedge, leading to a small copse and farm land with plenty of cover. The one way led to the darkness of Wheal Charlotte, the other to wooded countryside. He chose the latter. He had had enough of dark and damp. He would take his chance above ground.

He scanned the scene from the gap in the engine house walls and of a sudden ran, bent double, dodging this way and that, half expecting a shout to show the chase was taken up. But there was nothing but the shriek of a mouse caught in the kestrel's talons. He was free. He ducked into the shelter of a hedge and continued running.

8

She drew her horse to a halt. This was folly, but she did not know what else to do. Whatever the risk to herself, she must warn him. The police might already be at the workings or even behind the rocks in the cove. She dreaded to think what might happen if she got there too late; sickness at the thought made her retch.

She could not go on, dismounted, and leaned against her horse to recover her composure. The motion of riding, usually so pleasant, seemed to make her queasy. She took the horse's bridle and led it along between the high hedges. However sick she felt she had to go on; it was her duty. She could not let him be caught.

She tried to remount but had not the stomach for it so stumbled on, keeping a grip on the horse's harness, stopping from time to time to take a deep breath, conscious that despair was only a fraction of thought away.

She was within a mile of the workings, drawing near the waste land surrounding the old mine, when she caught a glimpse of a dark-uniformed man, and another, skirting the edge of the mine, and saw another man running, head down, to take up post on the top of the cliff. He was joined by another and then another. It was all done in silence. She was too late.

The policemen disappeared into hiding, waiting, biding their time, their trap set, and she was helpless.

She waited out of sight at a distance from the shaft and the ruined engine-house, but with a clear view of the workings, waiting for him to appear, knowing she could do nothing to help him now. He was on his own.

She had failed him, could only watch and wait and, as she did, the sickness she had felt before returned.

Chapter Twenty-One

The Christmas tree was still decorated, but needles fell whenever anyone brushed past it. It was almost time to clear the house of holly and paper chains.

Caroline Trevarth had opened her eyes to see Joseph standing beside it and for a moment could not understand what he was doing there.

'Did I wake you, Grandmama?' he said. 'I tried to creep out again.'

She smiled and shook her head to let him know he was welcome.

'I'll be sorry when I have to go back to college,' he said. 'Holidays go so quickly.'

His voice held echoes of the voice she had heard a moment ago in her dreams. Were they dreams? Or was she, in some mysterious way, transported to the past to re-live that blessed time?

Joseph came to sit at her feet and she put out a hand to stroke his dark curling hair. She had done that too in her dream, she thought.

'What are you thinking of?' he asked.

'When do you join your unit?' She dreaded the answer.

'Not till July.'

'I shall miss you.'

'You talk as if you won't be seeing me again.'

I shan't, she said to herself, not if it's like the last time. She had not known it had ended, had hoped against hope he would return, but she should have known; ecstasy such as that could only be fleeting.

It was given to no one to live at such heights for ever.

Her daughter Maud joined them. 'Mrs Prideaux would like to see you, Joseph,' she told her son and he left them to themselves.

'How is she?' Caroline asked her daughter.

'Not well.'

'She has always favoured Joseph,' Caroline said, with a touch of annoyance.

Maud smiled. 'She is not the only one.'

'They're all a credit to you.'

'But you still think Joseph is someone special.'

'He reminds me so ...' She stopped. The memory was sharp, both painful and joyous.

'Tell me,' Maud said. 'You've been wanting to say something for days. What is it?'

Caroline laughed. 'What makes you think there is something? Do you think I have secrets?'

'Haven't we all?'

You too? Caroline wondered but could hardly believe such magic as she had enjoyed could have blessed others too. How short a time it had been and what enchantment it had held. And, though short, it was with her still, in the presence of Maud and her family, in the love they showered upon her and that she felt for them. Without the madness of that time long ago, content and fulfilment would have passed her by. She shuddered at the thought and Maud, observant as ever, said, 'It's getting cold, mother. I'll get you a blanket for your knees.'

The room got chilly when the sun went, and the sun had gone and winter dusk had come.

The sun had gone that day too before she reached home. She had not seen him, did not know what had happened, watched the posse of policemen scour the cliff top, climb down into the cove and approach the shaft where he had been hiding. She could not bear to see him captured and had turned for home, arriving weary and in despair to await the dread news. It did not come and she was left to wonder.

Until the next day when Groves had arrived, angry and frustrated, accusing Mrs Prideaux of having helped her brother escape, but producing no evidence. The police had found a blanket and pack below ground at Wheal Charlotte which they presumed belonged to him, but that was all they found. They searched the drives and unearthed nothing but the skeleton of a dog at the very foot of the shaft, but no human bones, no mangled body, nothing.

He had escaped somehow. He had gone and she had had no notion where he might be, had not even known whether she would see him again.

He had gone, but was with her still, for he had left her a gift, one she could not have imagined, a greater gift than she could ever have hoped for. She had been with child.

She remembered even the fierce pride she felt, knowing it was his child she carried. She opened her eyes to see that child, a woman now, smiling at her.

'You were away again,' Maud said. 'It's been tiring for you, having us all here.'

'It has been rejuvenating, rather.' Caroline said.

'What will you do when Mrs Prideaux goes?' Maud asked.

'Goes?' She did not immediately understand.

'She won't get better, Mother, you must reconcile yourself to that. Doctor Hayes says she can't last much longer. What will you do?'

She refused to discuss the matter. She knew Maud wanted her to sell Trecarrow and move to some more manageable place. It would come to that, she supposed, but she saw no reason for considering it now. The house was peopled with memories, of Maud as a child, of Thomas's delight in her. At every turn there were reminders of the past. She could not leave those.

She felt tired of a sudden, and knew Maud had seen it, for her daughter took her arm and said, 'You must lie down. You've been doing too much.' She let herself be taken to her bedroom and helped into bed.

'I'll come down for dinner,' she said. 'I don't intend spending the evening up here alone.'

'I'll come back in an hour and help you up,' Maud said.

Why did they fuss so? It had always been the same. Thomas had returned from the Cape as soon as she wrote to tell him she was pregnant, abandoning the business which had been so pressing before. He had treated her again like one of his fragile porcelain figures though, after the first weeks of sickness, she had been bursting with energy. She remembered she had felt no guilt or shame in deceiving him by bearing another man's child. The pleasure he got from Maud was unalloyed. The truth would have unmanned him. She went to sleep with the recollected image of her husband and his joy in her pregnancy to comfort her.

She woke to the sound of Maud moving bottles on her dressing table. 'What are you looking for?' she said.

'I'm tidying up. Really, Mother, you do let things get in a mess!'

'I can't be bothered.'

Maud busied herself opening drawers and putting things away, throwing aside empty jars, replacing tops on bottles, clicking her tongue with irritation at her mother's untidiness.

'Don't fuss so,' Caroline said, but Maud persisted in sorting things out.

'What on earth are these?' she said suddenly and held up a couple of pieces of cardboard.

'Let me see,' Caroline said, but she knew what they were. She remembered hiding them there so long ago, had taken them out and looked at them over the years, relics of a long-lost intent.

'Who were Mr and Mrs Williams? And all that time ago. What are they doing here? Tickets for Santander and the year 1889! How curious!'

'Isn't it?' said her mother, holding out her hand for them.

Maud looked at her, eyes narrowed in speculation. 'Is this part of the secret?'

'What secret?'

'The one you've been longing to tell me.'

'Your imagination is running away with you, my love. You always enjoyed a story.'

'And what story have you to tell to explain those?' Maud helped her mother up from the bed, sat her down at the dressing table, and began to brush her hair. 'You look beautiful, Mother,' she said. 'What keeps you so young?'

What could she answer? Love?

'Love,' she said. 'Love of you, your father, the whole family. I have been well blessed.' She was glad Maud's attention had been diverted from the tickets. She had no ready answer. But Maud was not deceived. 'Who were they?' she said. 'And why were the tickets not used?'

Chapter Twenty-Two

1

He was tempted to go back to see what was happening at the workings. Perhaps he had been too hasty in running away. Maybe the man he had seen had known nothing, was a mere passer-by.

He turned back. Caroline would be coming and he would not be there to greet her. He stood, irresolute, at one moment thinking he had taken fright needlessly, at the next terrified at the sound of a rabbit in the undergrowth. It was as if the last feverish days with Caroline had brought nerves to the surface, making him react rawly to every sensation. He was near tears and yet on the verge of laughter. He sat under a hedge, put his head in his hands and tried to think rationally.

Slowly he came to his senses. He needed to know whether or not his fears of a police ambush at Wheal Charlotte were justified. He could return, keeping under cover, and see if his suspicions were correct.

He retraced his steps to within half a mile of the workings without seeing or hearing anything of danger, and had begun to think his fears were groundless, when the sound of a voice on the other side of the hedge brought him to a stop. He crouched below the wall, holding his breath.

'It's a wild goose chase, I tell you,' a gruff, low-pitched voice said. 'The man's away long since. Who would give him shelter hereabouts?'

'The farmer said it was him, said he was sure.'

'What did he see? A man having it in with a maid. You

204

can see that sort of thing any day of the week, if you do know where to look.'

George heard the sound of lips drawing on a pipe, and caught the pungent smell of cheap twist tobacco.

'He'll not come here along,' said the lighter voice. 'We'd better get back. Old Groves'll be hopping mad if he's not caught. I don't want to fall foul of that bugger.'

George waited, listening as footsteps receded. He crept along the hedge away from danger, knowing how close he had been to capture. It was as before; he was every man's enemy, an outlaw, hunted and pursued, fair game for anyone. He had had his few days of happiness. They were gone, Caroline was gone, and he was on his own.

He had survived before; he would do so again.

He had put another couple of miles between him and Wheal Charlotte before finding shelter for the night in a barn on the outskirts of the village of Mount Hawke. He slept poorly, waking constantly at the sounds of rats. They sniffed at him, curious at his presence, and wary. He was fully awake at first light, slipped out of the barn before the farm workers were about, and found his way to a stream at the foot of the valley to drink and douse his face. The water had a familiar taste, the metallic tang of water from the mines. The stream must be fed from adits from the mines at Wheal Rose near Scorrier.

He knew this area of old, every lane and hamlet, had walked to work this way and that meant he might well be recognised. He would need to keep hidden in the day and move only at night. He knew of a coppice this side of Scorrier where he could lie concealed until dark. He worked his way there without seeing a soul, crept to its heart through the weeds and brambles and made himself at home, hoping to sleep and wake refreshed at nightfall.

His mind was too active and his sense of danger too acute for him to do more than take a few fitful naps, so that he was still on edge and impatient to get going long before dusk came. He decided what to do and where to go. He was not far from Redruth. And in Redruth was Molly Sullivan, the sort of friend he needed now, tough-minded yet affectionate, cunning and self-sufficient. She was the sort of woman who had other friends like him, men on the wrong side of the law, friends who would help a man on the run. Irish Molly would be his salvation. He took fresh heart from the notion and, though it was still a long way from dark, he set off confidently towards Redruth.

Irish Molly — Caroline — two women he had loved. Caroline he loved still. He wished he could clear his mind of her. But it was no use wishing; she was there, speaking to him, touching him, letting her fingers play through his beard.

He realised he was not alone. An old man, grizzled haired and grey-cheeked, was watching him from the gate of a cob-walled cottage. George raised his hand in a friendly way but turned away into the shadowed side of the lane, praying the man had not recognised him. He had recognised the man, old Reuben Rodda. Then he recalled that Reuben was sightless, blinded by a gunpowder misfire at the rock face. He was glad now he had not spoken, for Reuben would have known his voice.

He hurried on, guilty at the gratitude he felt for the old man's blindness. He must stay alert; thoughts of Caroline made him careless of danger. Redruth and Irish Molly must occupy his mind now.

Every step held peril and the nearer he got to the town, the greater the danger. He would have to avoid Fore Street, with its taverns and press of people. It would be safer to approach Molly's from the lower end of the town. She lived in a two-roomed cottage in a terrace behind Fore Street, a dank, dark corner of the town. There he might feel safe, as safe at any rate as anywhere in this part of the world. And Irish Molly would welcome him for the fond memories they had of each other.

Hunger and sleeplessness were taking their toll. He felt suddenly exhausted, desperate for a place to lay his head. He thought he was hallucinating when he heard the soft voices of men singing and the sound of boots on the cobbles. Then he saw them, broad, solid men, coming towards him, lifting their voices in a hymn he recalled from the chapel-going days of his youth, 'Nearer, my God, to Thee.'

They must be making their way to Pednandrea mine for the night shift, and he wished he could be going with them.

The drives and gunnises of the mine had always been his element, the pick and gad his tools, not rifle and bayonet.

He stood to one side as the men passed. He recognised them, men of the Paynter family, and thought they might recognise him. He turned his back on them and they went by without interrupting their hymn-singing.

There were other people about, lounging at street corners, gossiping, indifferent he thought to him, but he tried to keep to the darker side of the roads. His nerves were taut and more so when he caught sight of a tattered poster fixed to a tree. 'Wanted for Murder', it announced, 'George Prideaux'. He did not pause to decipher the rest, saw only a crudely-drawn portrait which might have been of any villain. He bent his head and turned into Stratton Yard.

It was dark here in the dingy courtyard. The door of Molly's cottage was hanging loosely on its hinges. He pushed it open and stepped inside, directly into the room.

'Who's that?' he heard Molly call. The Irish lilt in her voice moved him with his memories of her. 'Who is it?' she called again, a touch of irritation at there being no answer. 'Are you playing games, now?' She came down the narrow flight of stairs, holding her arms about her, over a thin shift, her sturdy legs bare. She peered down at him.

'What do you want coming in here?' she said and glared belligerently at him. 'Who d'you think you are, then?'

'I know who I am,' he said in a low teasing voice. 'Don't *you* know?'

She came to the foot of the stairs and gazed at him. 'Oh, Jasus,' she said. 'Holy Mary! 'tis not you!'

'It is,' he said. She pushed past him, shoved the door closed, and stood with her back to it.

'Why have you come here?'

'Is that all your welcome?' He put his arms out to draw her to him but she evaded his grasp.

'You shouldn't have come,' she said. 'You're a wanted man.'

'Don't you want me?' he teased and opened his arms wide. 'I'm here.'

'God help us,' she said. 'They're after you. You're a

207

murderer, so you are. What would I be wanting with a murderer?'

'You believe that?' He was astonished she should think him capable of such a crime.

'You've a temper on you, I know that.'

'I'm no murderer. Believe me, Molly. I never killed him.'

She stood behind the deal table in the centre of the room and stared across at him.

' 'tes true, Molly, I swear. I never killed him.'

'Why me? Why come here? They're looking for you. They've been here asking about you.'

'Will you help me, Molly? For old times' sake?' He reached over the table to take her chin in his hand. She twisted away from him but came from behind the table and drew nearer so that he was acutely aware of the earthy warmth of her.

'Did you think of me sometimes when you were away?' she asked. 'Did you remember me when you took those other girls to bed?'

'Which other girls?'

'I know you, George Prideaux.'

' 'twas never like that,' he said. He rested his hands on her shoulders and looked into her green eyes. 'Will you help me, Molly? Can I trust you?'

Outside there was the sound of boots on cobbled stones. His hold on her tightened.

'Sure, 'tis nothing, just the men come back from work,' Molly said and drew close to him so that he was sharply aware she was clad in nothing but a flimsy shift.

'Can I trust you?' he repeated and, at the question, she thrust him away.

'What is it you want of me?' she said angrily. 'Trust? What's that now? Is that what you give to me with your hellos and goodbyes? Am I yours for the taking, do you think, when and where you want? Do you think I trust you?'

'Molly, I'm in danger,' he pleaded. 'If they catch me I'm a goner. No one will believe my story. I've no one else.'

'I'm your last resort, is it? That's the only reason you come here. Irish Molly will take me in, for she's a good-hearted soul, so she is. Well, you can stay, for the night − no longer. I want nothing of you, for I can see you want nothing of me but a safe place to hide.'

He went over to her and took her in his arms but she refused to be held, thrust him aside and turned angrily on him. 'I'm your Irish whore, am I? Well, if that's so, what is it I'm worth?' She stood in front of him, arms on hips, shift falling off one shoulder, chest heaving, the cotton shaping itself to her full breasts.

He could say nothing. He was remembering the times he had spent with her, the days of his youth and early manhood when he thought she was the most beautiful woman on earth. And beautiful she was, a strong forceful spirit, and he was sorry he could not take her in his arms and do as she wanted, tell her he loved her, that life had no meaning without her. He could have spoken so once, but no longer. Caroline stood between them.

'Well?' she challenged.

'Please,' he said, 'don't cast me out. I need your help. Can you not give it to me for old times' sake?'

'Who is it?' she demanded.

'Who?'

'You've never refused me before. There's a reason for you refusing me now, and it's a woman, I see. Does she mean so much to you?'

'She means nothing to me,' he said. But it was not true.

'So, there is a woman. I knew it.'

'Will you help me?'

'One night only.' Her anger had subsided and there was calculation in her look. 'You'll have to hide upstairs. I don't want the neighbours knowing. You can rest a while and I'll come to you later, so I will.'

She led him upstairs. A thin mattress lay on the floor and blankets were thrown back from it. Gratefully he sank down to the bed and was unaware of Molly looking down on him as she put on a dress and shoes and left him.

2

The house seemed to echo with its emptiness and she too, for all her knowledge that she was pregnant, could not but

209

feel a void. She called Mrs Prideaux to her merely to be able to talk of him. Just to speak his name was a relief, but there was little comfort to be got from the fact that there was no news of him.

Ada Prideaux was glad he had gone. 'It is better that way,' she said. 'He can make do for himself now.'

'Where do you think he will go? Where is he likely to get help?'

'Don't bother your head, ma'am. Be glad he's left us. I was so anxious for you. I could not bear to think it was my brother who was leading you into danger.'

Danger? Was that what it was?

'Have you heard anything from the police?' Caroline said.

'They'd not confide in me.' She turned to leave her mistress but, at the door, she paused to speak. 'He's not worth it, ma'am. I'm glad he's gone. I pray that's the last we hear of him.'

Caroline stared at her. 'Your own brother? That's all you can say?'

'It's you I'm concerned for, not him.' She looked back at her mistress but Caroline could not read what was in her eyes. She knew only that the look in them reminded her agonisingly of George.

'Are you unwell?' she heard the housekeeper say. Indeed she felt faint for a moment, but it was nothing.

'Let me take you up to your bed,' Mrs Prideaux said. 'I'll call Beatrice to you.'

'It is nothing. It has all been a strain, that is all. Let me know if you hear anything.'

But no one brought her news and she was left to wonder.

3

He woke, startled, sat up and looked around. He had been dreaming of a room so different from this and could not at first understand what had happened to the pale painted walls of the nursery, to the soft bed and the clean sheets. This room he saw was dingy and drab and the bed little more than a heap of old blankets stretched on the floor.

Then it came back. This was Irish Molly's home, her bed, the bed he had shared with her at times in the past, a past long gone and best forgotten.

The sound that had wakened him came again, gruff voices whispered below in the courtyard, a scuff of boots on cobbles, a close secret sound.

He knew it for what it was. They had come for him. Molly had betrayed him, or the police had guessed he would find his way here and had been watching for him.

He threw the blankets back and got to his feet. He was still fully clothed and recalled that, in his weariness, he had fallen on to the bed as he was and slept. 'I'll come to you later.' Molly had said. Had she come back? He had heard nothing of her, could not hear her now.

There was a window at the back of the room which gave on to the roofs of neighbouring houses. And there were the stairs to the room below. Two ways out and one took him to certain capture. Perhaps he could sell his life dearly if he stayed and kept the police at bay. The stairs were narrow, giving passage to no more than one at a time. It would be a desperate venture to stay and fight, but he was desperate.

He heard a step below and looked around for some sort of weapon. There was nothing, only a rickety chest of drawers and, beside it, a bentwood chair. The chair would have to do. He seized hold of it and stood at the head of the stairs ready to do battle.

'What's the matter now?' he heard, Molly's voice, soft and seductive as ever.

'Who's that with you?' he said.

'With me? Now what's got into you? Can't you see there's no one but me? Who else would there be?'

For a moment he wondered if he had imagined the whispered voices, the boots shifting on the cobbles, until his ears, sharp with alarm, picked up the sound on a muttered curse, quickly suppressed. They were there, he knew now, waiting to seize him, and Molly was their instrument, using her wiles to disarm him.

'Let me up,' she said. 'Don't stand there blocking my way. I said I'd be back and here I am. I thought you'd be glad, so I did. For old times' sake, you said. In the old times you wouldn't hold me away with a chair now, would you?' She took a step further, but he thrust the chair at her to have her keep her distance.

'I don't know what's the matter with you, I don't. Well, if you'll not let me up to offer you some comfort, you can do without. I'm not so desperate myself.' She took a step downstairs but paused and her voice softened. 'Sure, now, wouldn't it be good to get back to the old days? Do you remember? I've thought of you day in, day out. But I don't suppose you've given mind to me, not for a minute, have you?'

He wondered if his suspicions were misplaced. Dear Irish Molly. They had been friends, more than friends, for so long before he became a soldier. She had a smile to her voice now. In the dark of the stairway he could not see her eyes but he knew the look they held, the teasing warmth of them that had never failed to draw him to her. He lowered the chair and stood away from the top of the stairs.

'I knew you'd be glad to see me,' said Molly, coming up the stairs and putting her arms around him, holding him to her and pressing her lips to his, forcing her tongue between them, probing, so that for a moment the outside world was lost and all sensation was gathered in the touch of tongue on tongue, heady breath to breath.

She was drawing him to the blankets spread on the floor and he was letting her, his will weakened by the closeness of her, the touch of her hand to his groin. 'For old times' sake,' she whispered in his ear.

He wanted to lie with her, as in the old days, his good sense mastered by her practised skills. He was ready to surrender when, through the veil of his desire, he heard the slightest of sounds in the room below. Molly must have heard it too, a hoarse whispered voice of command. She tried to deafen him to it and the danger it held by clutching him to her in a pretence of passion. He thrust her from him so that she fell on the blankets and lay, legs asprawl, eyes wide in fear as if she thought he was about to attack her.

'I could do nought else.' she said softly, appealing for his understanding. 'I tried, but they wouldn't let me be.'

'They're there?' he whispered. 'How many?'

'Too many,' she said, again under her breath, so that he could barely hear her. 'They're waiting for my signal, when you're fit to be taken.'

'Lie still.'

He trod carefully over to the window. Perhaps it offered escape. It was a sash window, held by a catch. Before he could release it, Molly came to him and said, 'The window cord's broken. The window will crash down if you let it go.' He held the upper window while he moved the catch and gently, noiselessly, lowered the frame.

'George, my darlin',' Molly said. 'I don't want to, but I must.' Before he knew what she was about she yelled, 'He's away!'

George clambered out of the window to the roof beyond, fell and bruised his elbow and sent slates tumbling to the street below. He glanced back into the room and saw Molly, lying at the top of the stairs holding her jaw, as if she had fallen at a blow from him, and obstructing the passage of the police who rushed to get at their quarry.

He did not stop for a second glance but scuttled away across one roof and another, aware as he did of shouts, the breaking of glass, another rattle of falling slates. He saw a narrow street below and grabbed a wooden launder to let himself down. It snapped under his weight and he fell to the ground but was up and away almost unaware that he was bleeding from a cut to his head. He knew every twist and turn of these streets from his boyhood and, as he ran, round corners and up backlets, he calculated his chances.

Dark covered him. Behind him came sounds of pursuit, but distant now. They had lost him — for the moment.

He was not far from the cattle market and, a little further on, there were woods behind the brewery and a stream running along the valley to Portreath. There was not much cover there, more to be found perhaps in the other direction, towards the town of St Day and the Downs beyond. But whichever way he went the hue and cry was on. If Molly had turned against him, there was no sanctuary anywhere.

Except ... His thoughts went back to Trecarrow. There, with his sister and Caroline, he had found shelter. Perhaps for a little while, he could find safety there again. He gathered hope to him and ran on, dodging and turning about until he was out of the town and running east.

He climbed over a hedge into a field of rough pasture, where a few scrawny cows slept. They raised their heads and stared at him but settled again to sleep. He listened for sounds of the chase but heard nothing, save the distant clacking of a mine engine. He could lie doggo here to get his breath back and them make his way across country again to Trecarrow.

He wished he could think of another way to save himself. Perhaps he could make his way to a fishing port and take service on some trawler. But the police would have alerted everyone to watch out for him, harbourmasters and coastguards, customs men and ship's masters. They would be ready for him.

There was no alternative, for the moment at any rate, but to return to Trecarrow, throw himself on the mercy of Caroline and his sister, wait for them to arrange his passage out of the country. That was his only hope.

4

Spencer Groves was furious. The man Prideaux had slipped through his fingers again, got clean away. He suspected Molly Sullivan had warned him, helped him escape, but she denied that. She also denied knowing where he had been hiding through these last weeks.

He should be giving his mind to other cases but could not abandon the chase. Prideaux had begun to dominate every waking moment and even enter his dreams. Groves did not like being made a fool of and Prideaux had almost succeeded in doing that. He would have to put more pressure on Ada Prideaux and the household at Trecarrow. Someone in the house knew more than they said; he would find them, whoever they were, and wring their knowledge from them.

He presented himself at the house and asked to see Mrs Trevarth. He was shown into her drawing room.

'Have you caught him?' she asked impulsively on his appearance. 'Where is he?'

'I wish I knew,' he said. 'He got away this time, but, by God, I'll not let it happen again.'

214

He was puzzled at the woman's reaction. She had seemed alarmed before; now, somehow, she was reassured. It must be that she was encouraged by his determination to catch the man. He smiled at her, his harsh features softening at the thought of her reliance upon him. She was a handsome woman, had become so over recent weeks, changed remarkably from the merely pretty and empty woman he had seen first. There were strengths in her he had not suspected.

He became irritated at her leaving him standing and, with a challenging look at her, sat down. She said nothing.

'I'm dogged by stupidity and treachery. But for that he'd be in gaol by now. That idiot farmer went to have a look for himself, I understand. Prideaux must have seen him and taken fright. So we lost him then and his doxy.' Mrs Trevarth got up and went to stand at the window and he wondered if she had taken offence at his use of the word. But how else could he describe the woman?

'And then?' she said.

'We cornered him. We guessed he'd try to find shelter with an old friend of his, a woman well known to us — Irish and just the sort of brazen trollop to appeal to a man like Prideaux. They always go for the same sort, men of his kind.'

He sensed he had gone too far, for she turned sharply upon him and he thought she was going to voice her objection to his frankness, but she held back whatever she had intended to say and merely asked, 'What happened then that you lost him?'

He felt anger returning at the failure of his men to seize Prideaux. 'We knew he'd end up in Redruth. Molly Sullivan's house in Stratton Yard is well known to us. She said she'd help us trap him. She must have warned him somehow, gave him just enough time to get away, after all she'd promised.' She had not so much promised as been driven into a corner by their threats. He wondered how much of that he should tell Mrs Trevarth. But he had not come here to give her news, only to demand her co-operation in his interrogation of her staff.

'I'll get him, sooner or later. Sooner, with your help, I believe. Someone in this house — probably your housekeeper but maybe one of the other women — knows more than they're saying. Is there anyone you think may have been

215

willing to help him? Some impressionable young woman? Anyone who might have been taken in by his so-called charm? Some housemaid, a young servant? Whoever she is I pity the woman. He'll have used her, a man like him. It wouldn't surprise me ... No. I shouldn't say.' Her face, as she looked at him, was blank of expression. He wished he could tell what she was thinking.

'What shouldn't you say?' she asked.

'He'll have left her pregnant, like as not. I'm sorry,' he said. 'Perhaps I ought not to mention it, but if you suspect any of your girls is in that condition I hope you'll let me know. We might still bring him to book.'

'And the girl?'

'Her too.'

'And what do you want of me?' she said coldly, so that he began to think he had outstayed his welcome.

'Your co-operation in my questioning your servants.'

'They know nothing.'

'How can you be sure? Someone knows something. That I'm certain of. Mr Trevarth would expect me to do everything possible to find the man.'

'Let him go,' she said, to his surprise. 'What good will it serve to take him? Let him go.'

She spoke with a feeling that he put down to woman's natural soft-heartedness.

'It's not easy,' he said. 'Duty rules me.'

'Duty? Or frustration at your failure so far?'

His anger began to rise again. He got to his feet and said, 'I expect your co-operation. Will you send for your housekeeper and inform her what I intend doing, or shall I find her for myself?'

For answer she pulled the bell-cord.

'Mrs Prideaux,' she said, when the housekeeper appeared, 'Mr Groves wishes to question everyone. He has the mistaken idea that someone in the household has been helping your brother. I wish you to be present at every interview to make sure he doesn't browbeat anyone.'

She turned to Groves and smiled and he again saw her new strength, a new authority. He was moved to protest.

'That's not good enough,' he began.

216

'If my husband were here he would expect the same. You either agree to what I ask or forget the whole business.'

'Very well,' he said, and added, 'I shall miss no one, no one at all. I hope you appreciate that?' And, he said to himself, I shall question you too, madam, no less forcibly than the rest of the household, little though you may have to tell me. It would be a challenge he would welcome.

5

Groves's visit had disturbed her but at least she knew now George was still at liberty. Yet she could not rest easy until she knew where he had gone. He might even now be trying to reach her, might think he could find sanctuary again at Trecarrow.

She hated Groves, but feared him even more, recognising his obsession with capturing George. Why could he not let him go? Why must be pursue him to the bitter end?

She was confident none of the servants could tell Groves anything. But it was not safe for George to come here. Yet where else was he likely to go? Where else could he turn?

And who was this Molly Sullivan, this Irish woman who had been George's friend and who, if Groves was to be believed, kept a bawdy house in Redruth? And how had she been George's friend? That was in the past, yet Caroline could not suppress an intense curiosity, a need to see for herself what sort of woman this Irish Molly was. And she might know where George had gone. At the least she had seen him, could give news of him.

She had to see her.

There was no time to be lost. The ship for Santander sailed in a week, with berths booked in the name of Mr and Mrs Williams. She had not even had time to tell George her plan. She must find him or some way to get a message to him.

In any case she could not bear to stay in the house where the presence of Groves was so pervasive. She might as well be driven to Redruth as remain here. She could see one or more of the families whom she had been helping with her charity. One had lived in that same Stratton Yard.

She went to the stables and gave orders for a carriage to take her to Redruth. The coachman was being questioned by Groves, it seemed, so it was one of the other stable hands, a man called Glasson, who drove her there.

Stratton Yard, as she recalled, was behind Fore Street, and not far from the station. She ordered the carriage to wait for her at the station while she walked alone to the Yard.

The family she had visited in Stratton Yard occupied a squalid room in one of the terraced cottages. Their circumstances had appalled her, with the realisation that she could do no more than touch the fringe of their need. The woman had five children; her husband, two years back, had gone off to America to 'make his fortune' and had not been heard of since. The woman − Caroline tried to think of her name, but could not − would surely know this Molly Sullivan. Stratton Yard was a small, close-knit community. Everyone would know everyone else.

The doors of the cottages opened on to a fetid cobbled courtyard. A group of children, ill-clad, dirty and cheerful, were sitting on the steps of the home she had visited before. The name came back to her − Mrs Rowe.

At her appearance in the yard three of the children scampered away. They must think she came from the School Board. The two who remained glanced up at her and got on with their game, tossing pebbles into the air and catching them on the backs of their hands. Caroline watched for a moment before bending down to them and saying, 'Molly Sullivan? Do you know her? Can you tell me where she lives?'

One of the children − a girl, thought Caroline, though it was difficult to tell − looked suspiciously at her and shook her head.

Caroline put her hand in her purse and drew out a shiny threepenny-piece. 'Molly Sullivan?' she repeated.

A shadow fell across them and the child looked up. 'I didn't tell 'er nuffin,' she said to the woman standing over them.

'And what do you want with Molly Sullivan, now?' the woman said aggressively. 'Who are you? Stinking rich, I can see that.' She was a big woman, with a broad face under a feather hat, from which wild curls of reddish hair escaped. She wore a long coat that had once been a flamboyant green but was now shiny and almost black with wear. Her eyes, green too, had a hostile look, so that Caroline felt threatened.

'What is it you want with Molly Sullivan then?' the woman said and Caroline recognised an Irish intonation in her voice.

'Molly Sullivan?' she said uncertainly.

'And what if I am? What do you want here? Come to share a little sweetness and light with the likes of us poor folk, is that it? My Lady Bountiful is it? I've heard of you, I have, with your kind words and your old clothes. And what do you want of me? There's nothing I want of you. I've got all I need. I want none of your flaming charity.' She turned away as if that concluded her business.

'It's not that. It's something else.' Caroline said to the woman's back. 'Someone else.'

The woman stopped but did not look round.

'A man,' Caroline said in a low voice. 'I can't say more.'

'A man is it? Well, there's plenty of those. You can have the lot of them as far as I'm concerned. A man, now?' She turned to look at Caroline.

Caroline glanced down at the two children. They had lost interest in her, had returned to their game. They would not understand, anyway, she supposed.

'He was with you, I know. The police told me. They're after him now.'

'He? And who is he? And whoever he is, what's he to do with me?' She walked impatiently away towards the street which crossed the bottom of the courtyard. Caroline ran after her and caught hold of her arm.

The woman turned on her. 'Leave him be. And leave me be. Get back to your own world. There's no place for the likes of you here.'

'Where is he? Where has he gone? Tell me. Tell me something, anything. How was he? Please.' She had not intended to throw herself on the woman's mercy and felt humiliated that she had to ask a woman of this sort for help, but she needed to know. She took hold of the woman's arm again and was surprised at her own strength for, when the Irishwoman tried to tear herself away, Caroline's grip tightened. A surge of anger gave her courage. 'You betrayed him,' she accused.

219

'Betray? Is that it now? And what do you know of betrayal? You with your soft furs and your soft life. Get out of my way.' She suddenly wrenched her arm away and gave Caroline a shove so that she almost fell to the ground.

'Where is he?' Caroline pleaded and her distress must have touched some chord in the woman for she turned back to Caroline.

'So it was you,' she said. 'I knew there had to be someone.'

'Where is he?'

'How do I know? He went, that's all I know, and I never want to see him more.' She raised her head defiantly, as if George Prideaux meant nothing to her, but Caroline thought there was a look about her eyes that belied her indifference.

'Was he all right? Did he not say anything to suggest where he might go?'

Irish Molly looked at her with a kind of compassion. 'You need to know, don't you?'

'I need to know.'

'But there's nothing I can tell you. Nothing at all.' She shook her head sadly. 'There's no comfort for you there. And none knowing that that bastard Groves means to get his man this time. You'd best watch out for him. You know him?'

'I know him,' Caroline said.

'He plays rough with the likes of me. He may treat your sort with kid gloves, but he'll not go easy on you if he thinks you know anything. Watch him.'

Caroline made no effort to stop her when she turned and disappeared into the busy traffic of Fore Street.

Caroline looked about her as if the dismal yard might offer some clue to what had happened to George. I do not belong here, she thought. Molly Sullivan is right. I should get back to my own world. I can do nothing to help him, for I have no notion where he might be. She shuddered for though the sun still shone warm elsewhere, here in the drab shadowed yard the air was damp and chilling. Two women had come to the doors of their cottages and were gazing at her with curiosity and, she thought, with the same hostility Molly Sullivan had first shown. The children who fled at her approach had returned

220

to their game with the two younger ones. An old man, sucking on an empty pipe, head bowed, sat in a corner of the yard, nodding and muttering to himself.

No one here could know anything and she hurried away back to the station forecourt to her carriage. Glasson was waiting there and, eyes curious, almost knowing, he smilingly opened the door for her.

She sat disconsolate through the drive back, unconcerned that her absence might have been noticed. She had forgotten that Groves would be there questioning the servants. But it seemed he had finished for the time being, for Mrs Prideaux came to report that he had gone away disappointed with the lack of information from the household.

'He wanted to speak to you, but no one knew where you were,' the housekeeper said, revealing her own curiosity.

'I went to Redruth to see if the woman Sullivan knew anything.'

'Madam!' Mrs Prideaux exclaimed. 'That was madness. What could you hope to do by that, except show you are somehow involved. Oh, my God!'

Caroline had never seen her so agitated.

'There's no harm done,' she said. 'I hoped to learn what had happened to him.'

'He has gone. That's all we need to know. And there's nothing more you can do. Put him out of your mind. You did what you could for him, more than you should have done. Now forget him.'

'Don't you feel anxious about him?'

'Not as anxious as I am about you, ma'am. I do not feel for him as I feel for you.'

Caroline looked at her in surprise. 'Your own brother?'

'I have given him enough love and to spare. He can expect no more.'

'I am tired,' Caroline said. 'And confused.'

'It has been a trying time, but it's over now and we can get back to our own lives, just as we were before.'

As before? That was impossible. He had gone, but his

coming had changed her life. She would never be the same again.

6

Groves had deputed much of the questioning of the servants to his sergeant for he disliked the idea of having Ada Prideaux watching him, ready to intervene if he seemed to be getting anywhere with his enquiries. In any case there was no need to browbeat the servants; they were already conditioned to kowtow to authority.

Neither he nor Sergeant Penrose had discovered anything of significance. The servants knew nothing, he was sure of that; but when he read the sergeant's report, he saw there was one name missing from the list of staff. He called Penrose to him.

'There's no mention of Bert Glasson, the groom.'

'He wasn't there. He'd taken the mistress into Redruth, so I was told.'

'Go back and see Glasson — no, on second thoughts, I'll have a word with him myself. I want to see Mrs Trevarth again anyway.'

He cursorily disposed of other matters waiting for his attention and rode out to Trecarrow. It was Glasson himself who came to take his horse.

'So,' Groves said. 'You weren't here yesterday when I wanted to question you.' He smiled to himself. Circumstances had given Glasson into his hands without the presence of Mrs Prideaux to hinder him. 'Where were you?'

'Doing my job, that's all,' Glasson replied sulkily.

'Where?'

'That's my mistress's business.' the groom said.

'And mine.'

'You didn't think that the last time.'

Groves raised his hand and the man shrank away. 'Tell me this time,' Groves said. 'I'll ask you again. Where did you go?'

'Redruth.'

'Why?'

222

'The mistress visits families, helps them. You do know that.'

'Forget what I know or don't know. Where in Redruth?'

'How do I know? I waited for her at the station while she went off.'

'What did you do?'

Glasson did not answer but took the reins of Groves's horse to lead it away.

'What did you do?'

'Nothing. Waited.' He was hiding something, no doubt some petty flirtation or something equally harmless, but it was enough for Groves to seize on to show the man who was master.

Groves slowly shook his head. 'No, that's not all you did. Tell me. What did you get up to?' He followed Glasson into the stable and reached out to grip him by the shoulder. The man shrank away.

'Well?' said Groves, knowing he was about to learn what the man had been doing while waiting for his mistress. 'A little pickpocketing, eh?' he said, recalling that was the offence which had first brought Glasson to the notice of the police.

'No,' Glasson said indignantly. 'I've finished with that now I'm in work.'

'You won't stay long in work if you don't tell me what you were up to yesterday.'

'I wasn't up to anything. I only ...' He stopped. 'It's nothing.'

'Tell me.'

The groom took a step away. 'You told me before,' he said, ' not to gossip about the mistress.'

Groves felt a sudden and real interest in Glasson's doings. Was there a chink in Mrs Trevarth's armour after all? Was she keeping some assignation? He could not let this opportunity slip by.

'You'd better tell me. Leave it to me to decide whether it's just gossip or means something.' What good fortune that he had caught Glasson like this, without Mrs Prideaux to intervene.

' 'twas nothing.'

'I'll be the judge of that.'

'I went after her, followed her.'

'Why?'

Glasson pretended concern. 'I wanted to make sure she was all right.'

Perhaps the man had nothing to tell but Groves persisted. 'And where did she take you when you followed her?'

'Stratton Yard, that's all.'

At the mention of Stratton Yard he became more curious than ever to know what could take a woman of Mrs Trevarth's class to such an unsalubrious quarter.

'Well?' he said.

'That's all,' said Glasson. 'I didn't stay, didn't want her to know I'd gone after her. It was only to see she was safe. I went back to wait for her.'

Why Stratton Yard? And coming so soon after his mention of it to her. He could not imagine there was a connection between her visit and the hunt for the man Prideaux, but it was strange, to say the least, that she should go there. Had she some connection with Irish Molly? Groves could not conceive of any such possibility.

He had an opening nevertheless, a chance to make her uncomfortable and he welcomed it. It could have nothing to do with his enquiry but he would not let that deter him; it pleased him to think he might catch her out in some peccadillo.

He left Glasson without another word, his mind now occupied with Caroline Trevarth. He would lead slowly up to the reason for her visit to Stratton Yard, catch her unawares, if he could.

Ada Prideaux met him and challenged him. 'I heard you had come,' she said angrily. 'And that you were with one of the stable hands. Have you forgotten what the mistress said, that you should not question any of the servants unless I was there?'

'Just an idle chat, that was all I had. No questions. It was your mistress I came to see, to report what we discovered yesterday.'

'You discovered nothing, you and Sergeant Penrose,' she said with ill-concealed scorn.

'You'd be surprised,' Groves said, then more sharply, 'Let Mrs Trevarth know I wish to see her.'

224

'You may leave us, Mrs Prideaux,' Caroline said, as the housekeeper folded her arms and stood ready to defend her against the Superintendent's interrogation. 'He won't browbeat me, I'm quite sure,' she added as Mrs Prideaux stood her ground. 'You may go.'

'If you say so, ma'am.' Caroline smiled at the look Mrs Prideaux directed at the policeman, heavy with promise of retribution if he dared to hurt her mistress.

'You must forgive her,' Caroline said. 'She's very loyal and takes her duties very seriously, especially in the absence of my husband.' She gestured Groves to sit. 'And what have you to tell me as a result of your interrogation of my servants? You made them feel very uneasy, you and your sergeant.'

'No one need feel uneasy unless they have something to hide.'

'And did you think any of them was hiding something?'

Groves did not immediately answer but took a hard look at her until she began to feel uneasy. She tried to cover it with a laugh and a careless, 'I can see you're not going to tell me. Well, I've no wish to know. I consider the whole matter closed.'

'Ah,' said Groves. 'I think we'd all like to feel it closed, but the truth is it's still very much open. Prideaux is still on the run, and someone here is very concerned that he stays free. I'm making it my business to find out who that person is.'

'But you're getting nowhere. Why not forget it? There must be lots of other matters pressing for your attention.' She wondered why he had asked to see her if there was nothing to report from his investigation. He was watching her closely, his eyes showing an expression she had seen in them before. She was embarrassed by it, wished Thomas were here. It was a coarse and offensive look, suggestive, lascivious almost, and she resented it.

'If that's all,' she said haughtily and half-rose from her chair in dismissal.

'No,' he said. 'It's not all. There was one servant I had no chance to question yesterday. I saw him today.'

Groves seemed to be expecting a response but she had none to give. She tapped her fingers on the arm of her chair in impatience. What was the point of this?

'It was your man Glasson.' He waited again. She said nothing, but doubts assailed her. Yet he could know nothing.

'He took you to Redruth, I understand.'

'How does that concern you?' She decided that attack was the best defence.

'Not at all, madam, save that Stratton Yard is not the sort of place I would expect anyone such as you to visit.'

She felt a wave of anger and, at the same time, fear. What right had this man to have her followed and spied on?

'Have you been having me watched, Mr Groves? Is that what you're telling me?' Her mind was running through everything she had done or said in Stratton Yard. Nobody could have heard her conversation with Molly Sullivan, nobody could have known her purpose in visiting the place. Groves was bluffing. He knew nothing of her involvement with George Prideaux. How could he?

'I have a duty to keep myself informed of what is happening,' he said.

She interrupted him. 'To have me watched and followed? On whose instructions, may I ask? With whose permission? Have you thought what my husband would say?'

'You were not being followed, madam, let me assure you, but when it comes to my notice that you've been visiting a woman like Molly Sullivan, I start to wonder.'

She held her breath. How could he know? Or was it a shot in the dark? She cast her mind back to the events of yesterday. He was waiting for her to answer his challenge.

'Molly Sullivan?' she said, as if the name meant nothing to her. Was it Molly Sullivan herself who had given her away? She could not believe it. She was aware how closely he was watching her, waiting for her to trap herself, she thought.

'Molly Sullivan,' he said. 'The Irish woman I spoke of. You remember? I happened to mention Stratton Yard as her address. Is that why you went there? To see her?'

Caroline nerved herself to look at him with scorn. 'Are you accusing me of something, Mr Groves?'

'Just wondering, madam. I am allowed to do that, am I

226

not? It is in the cause of duty.' He smiled, but there was no humour in the smile. It was a frightening show of the pleasure he took in cornering his victim. How she hated this petty official for daring to question her as if she were a common thief, or a whore?

'How dare you even think of questioning my movements? I will not be treated so.' She stood up and moved to pull the bell-rope, but he got up quickly and grasped her hand to prevent her.

'Take your hand away,' she said.

He moved his hand but remained close, looming over her as if ready to take hold of her again if she made a move to call her housekeeper.

'I am waiting for an explanation,' he said.

'I owe you no explanation,' she protested. 'I have done nothing to concern you.'

'Then perhaps you would not mind telling me what you were doing in Stratton Yard yesterday.'

Her mind went back to the dim and dingy courtyard and she saw the children playing, the women standing at their doors, the old man huddled over his empty pipe.

'I do mind telling you,' she said, 'because you have no right to be interested in what I do or don't do. I shall make sure my husband hears of this. He is well aware of my visits to Redruth and Stratton Yard. Perhaps you are blind to the poverty of those who live there, or if not blind, unconcerned. I visit those people to take them a little something, food, clothing, hope. Is that a crime? Does that disturb you, that I have a mind to help those poor women?' She spoke with such vehemence that he was evidently surprised. She had defeated him, she thought. He knows he dare no longer question my motives in going there. She smiled with satisfaction.

'That is all?' she said and rang for someone to see him to the door.

'That is all,' he said, but turned as he went and added, 'for the time being.'

She was exhausted and, when he had gone, she went to her bed, afraid her state of mind would not be good for the child she carried. She tried to force herself to relax, but it was useless. She still knew nothing of what had happened to

George, knew only he was somewhere on the run. She began to weep at her helplessness. The tears turned to sobs.

Ada Prideaux came to her, stood beside the bed, held her hand and tried to comfort her. But there was nothing she could do. Nothing but the touch of George's hand could bring her peace.

8

He had got away. He was hungry and tired but he was free. He felt sure now of making his escape. With luck he could reach Truro and, biding his time there, watch for one of the Norwegian timber ships on the wharf side, wait for the right moment, slip aboard and stow away. He was certain it would work.

He had spent the night in a tiny chapel a mile or so west of Truro, curled uncomfortably on a bench, and cold. At dawn he had crept out of the building to find a heavy mist lying in the valley, but, as the sun strengthened, the mist lifted, the damp cold went, and his spirits rose. He even felt confident enough in his freedom to stop and chat for a moment to a cowman.

' 'tes going to be another 'ansom day,' the man said.

George leaned on the gate beside the man and agreed. 'It's been a fine hot summer.' he said.

'Too hot most days,' the farm worker commented. 'And 'tes some dry, but I'd rather that than they long wet days we do have most years.'

George felt safe, relaxed. It was good to be able to pass the time of day with his fellow-men without fear. Yet he saw the danger of being too much at ease. He was still wanted for murder, every man's enemy. He must still be vigilant. He wished the man good-day and walked on, making for the market town of Truro. There he was unlikely to be much noticed. It was always a busy place. He had only once been there, when he had first joined the army and his company had marched through the town for some civic occasion, stepping out at the rapid pace of the Light Infantry. Now he deliberately slowed his walk as if to draw a contrast between then and now.

He stopped, grateful for the bounty, to pick blackberries from time to time, ripe luscious fruit. He might have to rely on that sort of fare for some while, he supposed. A signpost indicated he was within a couple of miles of Truro and he saw the houses of the town in the basin below, and the shining waters of the Truro river, spreading wide and flowing into the Fal. To the east, on the limits of the horizon and almost lost in the haze, were the grey spoil heaps of the clay district; around him hedgerows, oak and holly and elder, elm and blackthorn, wild garlic and foxglove.

Suddenly he hated the thought of leaving the county. This was his home; he belonged here as he would never belong anywhere else. He stood gazing at the landscape, taking his fill of it. The scent of gorse came to him, the sweet honey-rich heady perfume that he would carry with him always. He saw a magpie dipping to a hedge and, high above, circling widely, a noble pair of buzzards.

He sat on a stone at the side of the lane and put his head in his hands, in near despair. Why was he giving up so easily on his birthright? Could he not stay?

It was not to be. He could do nothing to prove his innocence of Rennie's murder. He was already judged guilty. Like it or not, he had to flee the county.

He got up and walked into Truro. He had known it would be busy and indeed it was, for it was market day and the streets were filled with farmers and their women folk, the air heavy with the smell of cattle, and the cobbles wet with cow muck. No one paid him any attention, not even the policeman standing in High Cross, watching the masons at work on the new cathedral.

He strolled, his manner casual, towards the river and the Town Quay. A ship was moored there, a small steam cargo ship. No one was to be seen on deck and, at the quayside, a sailor, probably one of the ship's crew, was in conversation with a woman, from the look of her one of the town whores. The man had no mind for anyone but the woman and was unaware as George slipped aboard the boat, ready at a challenge to say that he was looking for work, but hoping the ship's company were ashore. He guessed the man he had seen had been left as watchman in the absence of his comrades.

He was lucky. There was no one to question him, no one to observe his descent below deck and his concealment behind bales of wool stacked in the hold. The ship was travelling light. He could not guess where she was bound but it would be far away from Cornwall, away to safety and exile. His feelings were confused, regret vying with relief, but regret uppermost.

Till now, in his escape, he had refused to let his thoughts turn to Caroline. To think of leaving Cornwall was bad enough, to be abandoning her was unbearably painful. Never before had he been so at the mercy of emotion. Now, hard though he tried, he could not keep out of his mind the image of Caroline, serene and yet passionate, modest and yet without shame, a woman who, wherever fate took him, would never leave him.

He knew he could not go before he had seen her to take his farewell, perhaps to persuade her to leave with him. She would do that, he knew, would share with him the danger and sacrifice that flight and exile would bring.

He became aware of movement about him, voices, the creaking of the ship's timbers, as if the boat were being prepared for departure. He had changed his mind, needed to go ashore and hastily wriggled out from his hiding-place and made his way to the deck to see that the boat was already well away from the quayside, heading down river.

'Hoy!' he heard a loud and angry voice challenge him. 'What are you doing here aboard my ship? Who are you?' A large, bearded man, fair haired, blue-eyed, with a deeply weathered face, stood before him, clenching his fists, head thrust aggressively forward on broad shoulders. 'Well?'

'I'm sorry,' George said, thinking quickly. 'I was drunk, came aboard to sleep it off. I'm sorry. Put me ashore, please.'

'I'll put you ashore all right, when I want, into the hands of the police. That's what I'll do.'

'I've done nothing,' said George. 'I meant no harm.'

'And you'll do no harm while you're aboard. You'll stay out of my way and when we get to Falmouth I'll hand you over to the Customs men. They'll know what to do with you.' He turned to one of the crew. 'Keep an eye on this fellow.'

The crewman was the sailor who had been engaged in conversation with the woman on the quayside. He scowled at George and made no response to George's smile.

'He's a fierce old bugger, your master,' George said.

'Aye, he is. You'll find that all right. He means what he says. You'd do better to jump overboard, I tell you that.'

George looked over the ship's side at the water.

'You'd better not try it,' the sailor said, grabbing him by the arm.

'Don't worry,' said George. 'I wouldn't dare. I can't swim.' The sailor released him.

Truro was soon lost to sight round a bend in the river as the ship made its way downstream. On the banks trees hung close to the water's edge; here and there a clearing revealed a cottage or the inlet of some secret creek. A heron, broad-winged and silent, glided past to settle high among the trees.

Then, as he gazed, he saw, through a gap in the trees, the shape of a house he knew. Of a sudden he realised he was seeing Trecarrow. There it was, almost within reach, its white front glowing in the sun, the house which had given him refuge, the house where he had found Caroline.

He looked around. The sailor deputed to keep an eye on him was not to be seen, assuming no doubt that a non-swimmer would not go overboard. The ship's master was forward, guiding the ship throught the narrow waters of the channel. George removed his heavy serge jacket. He could do without that. No one saw him stroll to the ship's side and leap from the deck into the water. He struck out for shore and from the ship he had left he heard a shout. With the flow of the tide the river ran swiftly and for several strokes he thought that and the weight of his clothes would carry him downstream. But he was a strong swimmer and slowly he made headway until his feet touched bottom. He dragged himself on to a sandbank and lay, exhausted. The steamer had gone on its way, was lost to view, caring nothing for him. They would forget him. There was no reason for them to report him to the police or Customs. He had tricked the lot of them.

Chapter Twenty-Three

Caroline Trevarth sat with her daughter Maud recalling family holidays, stimulated by the discovery of an old photo album.

'You were always adventurous,' Caroline said.

'No more than you, Mother.'

It was true. With Maud, her child, she had found new resources of spirit. The image Thomas had of her as a delicate and fragile object did not match with the truth and though he had continued to treat her with over-zealous care, she had not let it stifle her.

'Do you remember the Lakes?' Maud asked, coming across a snapshot of the two of them, arm in arm, on the slopes of Helvellyn.

'It was such a long way to go. I never wanted to leave Cornwall. I can't think why we ever did. Summers here were so full of contentment.'

'And that holiday in Ireland,' Maud reminded her. 'Look at this.'

But Caroline did not see the photograph her daughter held out. Of a sudden she was recalling the image of that Irish woman — Molly, was it? — who had once held their safety in her hands.

'Mother,' she heard Maud say.

'Ireland, yes,' she answered. 'I remember.' But she was thinking of Molly Sullivan. She wondered what had become of her — long since dead no doubt.

Maud had produced another photograph, this time of a younger Ada Prideaux holding Maud, a child of four or five, by the hand. 'She always made sure you came to no harm,' Caroline said. 'I sometimes felt jealous of her, the care she took of you.'

'Poor Prideaux,' Maud said. 'I used to resent the way she watched over me, when I was old enough to look after myself. But I know it was well-meant. She has always been so devoted to us and we have not done nearly enough to show our gratitude.'

'I suppose she loves us, in her own way, though perhaps she'd deny it. She's never been one to show her feelings.'

'Except in Joseph's case. She's made no secret of her feelings for him. She's as bad as you.' Maud said with a smile to her mother to show she understood her feelings for her eldest grandchild.

'Where is he?' Caroline asked.

'He's gone exploring somewhere with the twins. They told him they want to do as much as possible with him before he goes to war.'

Caroline tried to close her mind against the time when that would happen. She fingered the silver brooch Joseph had given her, the bugle-horn of the Duke of Cornwall's Light Infantry. She was glad to wear it openly, not hidden away as the bronze bugle-horn badge from the past had had to be. She had wanted to flourish that, to declare her allegiance to the man who had left it behind, but she had not dared. Now the silver badge served to remind her, not just of Joseph, but of that other young man, whose coming had brought unexpected purpose to her life.

'We must find you a smaller place,' Maud broke into her thoughts. 'This great house is far too big for you. You'll be much happier in a smaller property in Falmouth, say.'

'Why bring that up again? My memories are all here.'

'You have always said you take your memories with you wherever you go.'

It was true. Memories were not locked into brick and stone, but in nerve and sinew, flesh and blood. Yet this house had sheltered him and was precious for that. She could not abandon it to strangers, for whom the nursery would hold no magic, no ghosts. She only had to go in there to see him, still as he had been all those years since,

233

strong and virile, while she, with the passing of every year, grew old and weak. She sighed at the sadness of it.

'Share them with me,' Maud said.

Caroline looked at her daughter in surprise. 'Share what with you?'

'Your secret thoughts. I know you have them, from the way you smile to yourself. Tell me.'

'There's nothing to tell.'

Maud shook her head in disbelief. 'There's something,' she said lightly. 'It's to do with Joseph, isn't it?'

'In a way. But more to do with you, if the truth be told.'

'The truth? Are we to hear it at last?' Maud said in jest.

Caroline folded her hands in her lap, closed her eyes and pretended to settle down to doze. She heard Maud gathering the photographs together and leaving the room. She touched the bugle-horn brooch again and let memory people her dreams.

Chapter Twenty-Four

1

Groves was asking again if he could see her. She wished the man would leave them alone. On his last visit she had seen something in his eyes to worry her, nothing to do with George and the hunt for him, but something else, as if the policeman held some personal grudge against her. Perhaps he had; certainly she felt strongly against him, resented his attendance upon her. She wished Thomas were here to deal with him. But then Groves would not have behaved so if the man of the house were about.

'Stay with me, Prideaux,' she said to her housekeeper. 'I do not trust him. What does he want of me in any case?'

'Perhaps that woman Molly Sullivan has told him why you went. Perhaps she put two and two together, guessed you had given shelter to George and told Groves. I hope to God that's not so.'

But Groves made no reference to the Irishwoman when he came in. He looked at Mrs Prideaux as if he wished her gone, but said nothing, and when he spoke it was as much to Mrs Prideaux as to her mistress.

'There's been a sighting of that fellow Prideaux,' he said and seemed to take satisfaction in the news. 'We may well have seen the last of him.'

Caroline pretended indifference but she was afraid she had given herself away when Groves looked at her before going on. 'He got as far as Truro, hid aboard a cargo boat, came up for air and fell overboard.'

Caroline could say nothing. To speak would be to declare her anxiety, for a cold fear clutched at her.

'He couldn't swim, it seems.'

Caroline had a sharp image of George swimming strongly out to sea and then back to her. She hid her smile. 'So?' she said.

'They saw him trying to make for shore but lost sight of him. They think he drowned.'

'Didn't they stop to help him?' Caroline asked, still uneasy, in spite of her knowledge of George's ease in the water.

Groves smiled. 'And lose the tide? They didn't see why they should worry about someone like him. They were only going to hand him over to the authorities in Falmouth in any case. Good riddance, they thought. And so do I. It's saved us a heap of paperwork.'

She must know more, could not be certain George had not drowned. She felt sick, as uncertainty challenged hope. He must have swum to safety. 'You're satisfied?' she asked.

'Not quite,' Groves said. 'I'll feel better when his body comes ashore. But for the moment I can give my mind to other things.' He looked at the housekeeper who stood silent, arms clasped across her, head bowed. 'So, that's that, Mrs Prideaux. You're well rid of him, I'd say.'

The housekeeper raised her eyes, gazed impassively at the superintendent and held the door open for him. He bowed his head in acknowledgement to Caroline and turned to go, but paused on the threshold to say. 'I'll let you know as soon as his body's washed up. Someone will have to identify the corpse. It'll be a few days, they tell me, might surface anywhere between Truro and Restronguet.'

He left and Caroline collapsed into a chair. Her morning sickness was still with her and it had been with the greatest self-control that she had remained calm. Anxiety for George gripped her. But he was a strong swimmer, surely too strong, she prayed, for the river to have defeated him.

His sister returned and stood at the door watching her, eyes filled with compassion.

'What do you think?' Caroline asked.

'Let the police think he is drowned. It's better that way.'

'But you don't believe it?'

236

She did not answer at first, then she said, 'Let him go, ma'am. Maybe he is drowned. Either way he's left your life — and mine.'

'Pray God he's safe.' Caroline said and was seized with a paroxysm of nausea.

'Let me take you to bed, ma'am,' the housekeeper said and she allowed herself to be led upstairs.

'You should let the master know,' Mrs Prideaux said. 'He ought to be told.'

'That George may be dead?' Caroline asked incredulously.

'That you are with child, ma'am. He will want to be with you throughout. And he'll be so proud.' She stood by the bed looking down at her mistress, eyes revealing nothing.

2

Ada Prideaux made her way through the trees towards the river then turned along the bank. She knew the police had given up their watch on her, in their confident belief that George had drowned. But George was a survivor. He had come ashore, but not as a corpse, and had found his way to the old boathouse on the creek.

She could not say what instinct had taken her there. She did not often go for walks on the estate, but yesterday evening she had wanted solitude. She had been concerned for her mistress, fearing that, by her visit to Irish Molly, she had endangered herself. She had sought in her mind some way of rescuing Caroline from the consequences of her folly, but had found no solution.

Finding the house oppressive, in the quiet of the evening she took herself into the beech woods, bringing to mind, as she walked, those distant days when she had had charge of her young brother. He had been a dear soul as a child, but always devil-may-care. Now his recklessness threatened her mistress, and she found it impossible to forgive him that.

She was glad he had gone, though she longed to know what had happened to him. The past still had some hold over her.

The path she had followed took her near to the old boathouse, a ramshackle building beside the creek. It was falling into disrepair and Mr Trevarth had thought of having it demolished, but it had remained, forgotten in this remote corner of the estate, with no children of the house to take an interest in sailing.

She was walking past it, heading along the path which would take her back to the house when she heard a sound, little more than a whisper, so that at first she imagined it to be the rustling of a creature on the bank.

It came again, clearer than before. 'Ada!'

There was no mistaking it, George's voice, coming from within the boathouse. She glanced behind to reassure herself she was not under observation. No one was within sight. She raised her skirts and treading carefully found her way up the bank to the steps leading into the upper floor of the boathouse.

'Here,' she heard and in the shadows saw the crouched figure of her brother.

'Why have you come back?' she asked accusingly, concern for Caroline again overwhelming her.

'I could not leave without saying goodbye.'

'To me?' she said with disbelief.

'To you — and Caroline.'

'Caroline, is it?'

He was silent for a moment. 'You must have known how it was.'

'How could I know? I didn't wish to know. I have no wish to know now. I only want you gone, out of her life.'

'I love her. I cannot go, not without knowing she wants me to, not without her telling me to go.'

'You are a danger to her and to yourself.' She looked through the gaps in the wooden building towards the other bank of the creek. There was a small cottage there and a light appeared inside as candles were lit.

'Give her a message from me,' he said.

'What do you want me to say?'

'Tell her where I am. Ask her to come and see me.'

'How can you ask this of me?'

'Please tell her. I'll wait. And bring me some food.'

She had left him then, and now, with food, was coming back. She had a message for him, but not from Caroline.

238

He was waiting for her, stood to greet her with an embrace and a kiss on her cheek. She told herself she must harden her heart against him. He has charmed her as a boy; she would not let him charm her now.

'Is she coming?' he said.

'She dare not. She had already put herself at risk for you.'

'Does she know I'm here?'

'I told her.'

He looked closely at her and must have seen something in her eyes to make him question her.

'You love her too?' he said with dawning understanding.

'Is that so strange?'

'Then you must want what she wants. You must know what she means to me. Help us. Bring her to me.'

'The police think you drowned yesterday. They are expecting your body to be washed up somewhere in the next few days.'

'What does that mean?'

'It means they've relaxed their watch on the ports. You can get away, provided you waste no time over it.'

'She will come with me?' he said urgently.

'She will follow. It would not be safe for her to leave with you.'

He took hold of her again and kissed her on the lips. She could close her eyes and see him as a lad again, but for the bristliness of his beard. She found herself laughing at the incongruity of it.

'What is it?' he said.

'You were always wanting me to do something for you, helping you out of a fix.'

'Will you help me now?'

'I shall arrange things. Promise you will do as I tell you and everything will be all right. Trust me,' she added and hated herself for her deceitfulness.

'I trust you, Ada. I always have.' He kissed her again and said. 'Tell her I love her and will do whatever she wants me to.'

'I'll be back tomorrow. Be ready to leave then.'

'She'll follow?'

'Trust me.'

3

He was so near her that he was tempted to leave the shelter of the boathouse and find his way to the house. He knew it was madness to think so and tried to forget the fact until the need for her became so acute that he left the ramshackle building and set out along the path which led to her.

He heard someone walking towards him and tried to take cover in the bushes, but he was seen. It was Ada. She seized him by the arm and dragged him back to the boathouse.

'Are you mad?' she said, eyes blazing with anger. He had not seen her so since he was little. 'Have you no thought for her?'

'I think of nothing else.'

'Then come to your senses.' She threw the bundle she had been carrying to the floor. 'There's a new jacket in there and some food, a shirt and other things. And I've booked a passage for you with a party of miners on the *Aurora* out of Falmouth tomorrow.'

'So soon?'

'The sooner the better. The police might start the hunt for you again.'

'Caroline?'

'What of her?'

'What does she think?'

His sister hesitated, so that he exclaimed: 'She knows? You've told her?'

'She's unwell.'

'Then I must go to her.'

'That would do her no good, nor you either. Take ship from Falmouth. You'll be safe at the Cape in a couple of months and she can join you there.'

He took hold of his sister by the shoulders and looked into her eyes. 'She'll join me? You're sure?'

'Trust me,' she said. 'You're a miner from Dolcoath, Harry Curnow. Remember that. We want no slip-ups. The boat leaves on the evening tide. Be sure you're aboard on time.'

He watched her go and, as dusk fell, he again thought of finding his way to the house in the hope of seeing Caroline, but secure in the belief that his sister knew best, he kept hidden

240

until first light. Then he set off on foot to Falmouth, swinging his bundle over his shoulder, ready to take his place with his fellow miners, Cousin Jacks like him, and make a new life in South Africa.

He had heard tales of the mines there, had seen men return, lungs eaten away. But some had made good. He would make good too. For Caroline's sake. Make a home fit for a woman such as her.

He stepped out with confidence, walking to a future of freedom and hope and life with his Caroline.

4

She waited for news, dreading that each dawn might bring word that his body had been washed up on the banks of the Fal, but days went and there was nothing, nothing to distress or reassure her.

She asked Mrs Prideaux to make enquiries of the police to see if there was news of her brother. 'They will think it natural for you to want to know,' she pleaded. She could not understand the housekeeper's apparent indifference. 'I need to know,' she said. 'Something, anything.'

'Perhaps it is better to know nothing,' Mrs Prideaux said.

'I do not understand you.'

'Whatever has happened to him, he has gone. Out of our lives. For ever.'

It was not so; he had gone maybe, but not out of her life, for he had left part of himself with her in the child she carried. She was grateful for that blessing, and longed to be able to tell him of it, share the wonder with him.

Then a message came for Mrs Prideaux from the police, a message that drove all thoughts of wonder from Caroline's mind, replacing it with a dull despair.

'They tell me a fisherman has pulled a body out of the Fal. They want me to see it to tell them if it's George.' Mrs Prideaux spoke matter-of-factly. Caroline admired her self-possession, wished she too could pretend indifference.

'I'll come with you,' she said.

'You cannot.'

'You may need a woman with you when you see him,'

241

Caroline said, thinking she herself would want to see him too, to say goodbye.

'It would not be fitting.'

'I shall come with you.'

Groves himself was there at the door of the stone-built mortuary. He looked in surprise at Caroline.

'My housekeeper needs my support,' she said in answer to his glance. She had dressed in black, as if she already knew the worst.

Groves led the way into the small chill room, in the centre of which was a slate table, on it the shrouded figure of the drowned man.

The attendant, a fisherman by trade, drew back the sheet.

'Well?' said Groves.

Caroline stared with relief at the corpse. There was, thank God, nothing of George about him, save a beard. His face was grey and puckered and his open eyes showed light blue in their vacant stare. She sighed, with sorrow for the man and his family.

'Is it him?' Groves said brusquely, unfeelingly. 'Look at him, woman. Do you recognise him?'

Mrs Prideaux turned on her heels and walked towards the door. Groves took hold of her and turned her round and drew her to the table and the corpse.

'Well?' he said. 'Is it him, your brother?'

'I almost wish I could say it was, then you'd stop hounding us. But it's not, it's some other unfortunate.'

'Damn,' said Groves. 'I'd been hoping.'

They drove back to Trecarrow in silence, with Caroline half-way between tears and laughter. It was not George, but where was he? Why had there been no news of him? No news from him? Surely he would try to reach her, to get word to her. Wherever he was he would think of her, whatever danger threatened him, he would not lose sight of her need of him — and his of her.

Mrs Prideaux went with her into the drawing room. 'You should not have come with me.' she said. 'If you had not been there I might have been tempted to tell them it was him, after all.'

'Why?'

'To end the business. As it should be ended.'

'Where can he be?'

'Beyond your reach, wherever it is. You must put him out of your mind. You have the baby to think of now.'

5

Daily she expected to hear — a letter, a message of some kind — and daily she was disappointed. Yet daily she found content in planning for the future, in preparing the nursery which had harboured him for a new occupant, his child.

As the weeks passed and no word came she knew she had lost him. Groves was right. George had used her. She should have hated him for it, but she forgave him, for she too had used him, had brought him to her to make this child of theirs. In giving her a child he had given more than she had a right to expect.

She wrote to tell Thomas she was pregnant. He would have no suspicion that the child was not his. The news would come as a surprise, but would bring him no less joy than it brought her.

'We have been blessed at last,' she wrote. 'I cannot express my joy at knowing I am with child. I am already well advanced in pregnancy. By the time you return I shall be only a few months away from my confinement, only a few months away from being a mother.' But she was already a mother, could feel the child lively and active within her.

Thomas hurried back to her. She had known he would and was glad of it. She loved him deeply, not with the intensity of the love she had for George, but with a love as real.

Thomas held her from him to look at her when they were alone. 'We have waited so long for this miracle,' he said. 'And it makes the moment all the more precious.' He was near to tears. He was no less fulfilled than her, no less proud.

6

The voyage to Cape Town had been long and unpleasant, so that he and his fellow miners began to wonder why they were willing to risk their lives on the high seas. When he had embarked at Falmouth George had been afraid he would be seen for what he was, a fugitive from justice, but he held his head high, looked everyone in the eye as if he had nothing to be afraid of and was accepted as Harry Curnow, from Dolcoath mine in Camborne.

Until the tenth day out, when, as he lay on his bunk in the hot and fetid steerage, a man in the bunk above leaned over and said in a soft conspiratorial voice, ''tes George Prideaux, I do reckon, under that black beard.'

'Who's he?' said George, as if only mildly curious, but heart thumping.

The man laughed. 'You've nothing to fear from me. I'll say nothing. I've my own reasons for getting out, same as you, though not so desperate maybe. Just a maid in the family way and a wild old man of a father. But I do know 'ee, all right, from the old days.' He stopped as the vessel lurched and he had to hang on to the wooden rail to keep from falling to the deck.

'Tom Pascoe,' he said, when he had recovered his balance. 'From down along Carn Brea village.'

George held out his hand and Pascoe gripped it.

'A new life,' said Pascoe. 'That's what's in store. A rich new life, by all accounts.'

'A new life,' echoed George. 'Please God.' A new life with Caroline. The image of her was fresh in his mind, so that when he walked on deck, or lay in his bunk, whatever he was doing, she was with him. As he thought of her he knew she was thinking of him. As he planned for the day when he would welcome her to their new home, so he knew she would be making her own arrangements to leave Cornwall and join him. In his mind he wrote to her, but it was not till he reached Cape Town that he put pen to paper to tell her of his hopes.

He did not dare to address the letter directly to her but enclosed it in a letter to Ada. She would see that Caroline got it when it was safe. He could trust his sister; she had never let him down. She would help him now, and help her mistress, for she loved her too.

He could have moved up-country to the mines straight away, for there was need of men like him, but he did not want to leave Cape Town before he had heard from Caroline or, as

244

he planned, met her there. He found work in a warehouse as an under-manager, unfamiliar work but paying well enough and needing no skill beyond common sense and honesty. He could bide his time there until Caroline arrived.

He wrote again, and again, and waited for an answer. He got into the habit of going down to the docks whenever a ship from home was due. He would stand on the quay searching among the passengers lining the ship's rail for a glimpse of that fair and beautiful woman.

He would wait until the last passenger had come ashore before turning away, telling himself that another boat would come and she would be on that. He met the next boat, and the next, not letting hope die, knowing she had promised to join him. Ada had said so and he trusted her.

Ada wrote but with no news of Caroline, and hardly any of herself, a bare conventional greeting that left him unsatisfied and anxious. He thought of taking passage back home, but knew he dare not do that. The law had a long memory. She would come in time; love such as theirs could not be denied.

He waited for her to write, to tell him she had made her arrangements and would be arriving soon. She did not write and he began to wonder if, for some reason, Ada had been unable to give her his letters.

At last he wrote to Caroline, not through his sister, but addressing the letter directly to Mrs Trevarth. Surely she would answer that.

No answer came, nor did Caroline herself. He was left to believe that she had no care for him, that her love had been a fiction, their meeting no more than a chance and meaningless trick of fate. He tried to sweep her out of his mind but failed. She still haunted him and, though he tried to deny the impulse, he found his way to the docks whenever a ship from home arrived.

At length he forced himself to admit defeat, left the Cape of Good Hope and went north to the Transvaal to work in the mines, trying to find forgetfulness in the hard and dangerous work there.

He could not forget, but, with hope gone, he became increasingly careless of his life, indifferent to his future. When he wrote to Ada, as he continued to do, he made no mention of his love for Caroline. That was a thing of the past.

7

There were moments when the absence of news of George drove Caroline almost to despair, so that she wandered about the grounds, distracted, sometimes calling his name in the vain hope that he might be somewhere within hearing. But of course no reply ever came.

On one such day, when she had walked along the river bank as far as the creek, she met Mrs Prideaux, her face filled with concern, coming to look for her.

'Have you had news?' Caroline exclaimed.

'News? Of what?' Mrs Prideaux replied. 'I came only to take you back. You must look after yourself.'

Caroline persisted. 'Have you heard nothing?'

Mrs Prideaux pretended not to understand and Caroline grew impatient. 'Of him, of your brother?' She could not trust herself to speak of him by name. She would burst into tears, was almost ready now to give way.

'I've heard nothing, perhaps never will. You must not think of him. You have only one thing to give your mind to now, your baby. What happens to my brother can be of no possible interest to you.'

She did not contradict the woman, but she could still dream. She did not know what she would do if he ever did get in touch with her. From time to time she got out the steamship tickets in the name of Mr and Mrs Williams and let her imagination play tricks. Now she allowed Mrs Prideaux to take her arm and lead her back to the house.

She was heavy with child and her time was near. With the birth, she would have a new weight of responsibility, a new sense of purpose. It was a time she should look forward to, and indeed she did. She had every reason to be happy, she told herself.

In the spring, when the bluebells carpeted the grass with a soft mist, she gave birth to a daughter, and was content.

Chapter Twenty-Five

It had been a long and delightful holiday. Caroline always enjoyed having the family about her and at Christmas this was a particular pleasure. She was sad it had to end.

'The children have to leave,' Maud said. 'But I shall stay for a while.' They had brought a nurse in from Truro to help look after Mrs Prideaux, but Caroline was glad Maud was remaining. She needed company — living company, not just the ghosts who walked increasingly with her. She was sorry to see the children go and especially to say goodbye to Joseph. The next time she saw him he would be in uniform and after that, no one could say what might happen. 'What, I wonder, will 1940 bring?' Maud had said when they saw the New Year in. 'I dread to think,' Caroline had answered, but they toasted the New Year with the same hope as at the opening of every year.

Part of each day, after the children had gone, Caroline spent sitting by Ada's bed, but the two women had little to say to each other, and Ada, with each passing day, was less and less able to concentrate. At times she too seemed to be living in the past, but it was a more confused and confusing past than the one Caroline recalled. To Caroline the details were sharp, the memories all of moments of surpassing joy, whereas Ada seemed restless, anxious and full of guilt. She muttered in her sleep and when fully awake, held out her hand to Caroline for comfort, but, when Caroline took it and pressed it reassuringly, she snatched it away. Once she tried to get out of bed and reach under it for something but fell back exhausted.

'She's trying to tell you something,' Maud said.

'There is nothing,' Caroline said. 'Nothing that we haven't already said to each other. I know all there is to know about her, and she knows everything about me.' But it was not true. They had lived together all this time keeping their private thoughts secret from each other.

'I'm afraid she's fading fast,' Maud came to say. Caroline closed the book she had been pretending to read and stood up. 'I'll come to her,' she said.

The nurse left them alone together. Ada opened her eyes and, seeing her mistress, made an effort to sit up. It was too much for her and she sighed. Caroline took her hand and stroked it gently. She felt closer to her now than she had ever done and she knew that neither could have existed happily without the other. Love takes many forms, Caroline thought, and we have lived so closely together that a kind of love has developed between us. She wanted to tell Ada so but could find no word capable of expressing her strangely complex feelings.

'We have been through a great deal together,' she said at last.

Ada did not speak but Caroline felt her fingers move, tighten, and relax again.

'It would all have been very different without you,' Caroline said. 'Different and so much the poorer.'

Ada opened her mouth to speak but could only sigh.

'Do you want to tell me something?' Caroline said.

The hand moved but again the effort seemed too much. Ada opened her eyes wide, pleading, it seemed to Caroline, for understanding.

'What is it?'

Ada slowly moved her head from side to side.

'I understand,' Caroline told her. 'Don't concern yourself. I know. There is nothing for you to worry about.'

Ada seemed reassured, closed her eyes, and with her hand still gently held by Caroline, passed peacefully away.

Maud came, stood for a moment in silence, took her mother's arm and led her to her own room.

'She had something to say and did not say it and I could not help her.' Caroline said, feeling she had in some way

248

failed her housekeeper. 'We were together a long time. Part of my life has gone with her, part of me is dead too.'

'You must not let the past have so big a hold on you,' Maud said.

'It's not that the past has a hold on me, it's that I have a hold on the past.'

'Then let it go.'

'But you do not understand,' Caroline said. 'It was a past of love and beauty and joy, and I have it with me still in you, as well as in my memory.'

'Was it all so magical?' Maud said.

'From that first day,' Caroline said. And that day was the day she had seen him free and proud and god-like in his nakedness. 'From that first day,' she repeated.

She tried to give her mind to the arrangements for Ada's funeral, but was glad in the end to leave the details to Maud.

'Is there any family we should get in touch with?' Maud asked. 'You once mentioned a brother, but said you knew nothing of his whereabouts.'

Caroline was silent for a moment, then she said, 'No, there is no one. Just us. We were her family, Thomas and I, you and the children. Some of the old servants would like to be told, though. They all respected her.'

It was a small group which saw her buried in the quiet churchyard, in a plot next to the Trevarth family vault. Ada would have been grateful for that; having given her life to the Trevarths it was only proper she should be near them in death.

When they returned home Caroline was so aware of Ada's absence that for once her customary content left her. Maud found her later in the curtained blacked-out drawing room.

'Mother,' she exclaimed. 'Let's have some light, for heaven's sake.' She sounded impatient and Caroline realised that the last weeks had imposed a heavy strain on her.

'You must go back to the family now, Maud,' she said.

'Not until you make up your mind what you are going to do about this place. You can't keep it on.'

'Where will the children go for their holidays?'

'Holidays will be the least of our worries with the war as it is.'

How everything changed: people you loved came and went, came and went. She would have to do as Maud said, sell the family home; it was far too large for her; it belonged to a world that had gone for good, with its servants' wing, its nursery rooms, its rambling corridors, its spreading grounds and landscaped gardens. It needed a fortune to maintain and she had none to waste on it. If she left she could take her memories with her; they would be as vitally present in a modern house in Falmouth as in this great mansion.

She tried to convince herself but did not succeed. It would never be the same anywhere else.

'I shall have to go home, I'm afraid, some time soon.' Maud said. 'But when I come back I'll expect you to have made up your mind to sell, so that we can put it on the market in the summer.'

'Don't hurry me, Maud.' she said. 'I am surprised you can think of seeing the place go when it has meant so much to us all.'

'Times change,' Maud said. 'And we must change with them.' She had brought a battered leather suitcase into the room. 'I found this under Mrs Prideaux's bed. It's full of photographs and letters and such things. I thought you might like to go through it. It didn't seem right to throw it away without someone seeing it.'

'Put it by the window,' Caroline said. 'I'll have a look at it in the morning.' But curiosity was too strong to leave it till then. That evening, tired though she was, she opened the suitcase to see what was in there. On the top were photographs of Maud and Thomas and of herself. Ada had kept every snapshot and studio portrait that had ever been taken of the family. There seemed an almost complete record of Maud's childhood and that of Maud's children.

When Maud came to say good-night she found her mother surrounded by photographs. 'It was just as I told you,' Caroline said. 'We were her family. She always wanted a copy of everything we had taken. And here they are, every one.'

'Leave them there, Mother, and come to bed. I'm leaving

early in the morning. I'll tell Rachel not to move them. She's a good girl.'

Rachel? Of course. The names of her present servants became confused with those of the past. Now there was a mere handful of them. In the old days there was a cohort to satisfy every need.

In the morning, when Maud left, she settled down to look at the family photographs from Ada Prideaux's collection, pausing constantly as memory was triggered, first by a view of Truro Cathedral, its building half-completed, then by a snapshot of her and Maud on the beach at Swanpool, then by a picture of herself standing in the doorway of an engine house. She had forgotten that, but the sight conjured up an image of Thomas, who had become an enthusiastic amateur photographer, bent under his hood, waving directions at her until he was satisfied with her pose.

She spread the photographs on the carpet and wondered if Ada had had any private memories, any souvenirs of her life apart from service with the Trevarths. She turned over more photographs of the family and then came upon one that caught at her memory with a suddenness that made her draw sharp breath. She held it a moment, eyes misting, before raising it to her lips. It was George, a photograph taken in a studio and showing him in the uniform of the Duke of Cornwall's Light Infantry; George holding his head high, staring fixedly into space, proud in his new role as a soldier. The photograph carried the name of a Bodmin photographer and on the back was pencilled, in Ada's copperplate hand, the words, 'George Prideaux, June 1888, after enlistment.'

Caroline held the photograph to her, surprised so stiff a portrait should hold so much meaning. She looked at it again, seeing the man she had taken to her, her lover, Maud's father, and Joseph's grandfather. It had been no mere trick of memory which had made her see George's likeness in his grandson Joseph. He was there in the studio, looking at her, Joseph to the life.

She was impatient to see what other treasures were contained here, what other precious keepsakes of Ada's brother. But there were no more photographs. There were letters, however, a bundle of them, addressed to Ada at Trecarrow,

251

bearing the distinctive triangular stamps of the Cape of Good Hope. The top one was postmarked with the date 17 November 1889.

She knew, without opening the envelopes, that the letters were from George. His sister had had news after all and Caroline felt a moment of dark hatred for the woman for denying her the comfort of knowing he was safe. She put the photographs and letters back into the suitcase and thrust it away. She had not strength enough to enquire further into the past. It was closed. She would tell Maud to take what she wanted of the photographs and to burn the rest. She went into the garden and walked across the lawns to the river's edge, trying to hold back her tears. I am too old for that sort of thing, she said aloud. But she was not. She could still be moved, could still feel the love that had changed her life. If only she had known where he was. Would she have gone to him? Would he even have wanted her?

She returned to the house. She had decided. When Maud returned she would tell her she was ready, ready to leave Trecarrow.

She tried to ignore the presence of the old suitcase, but it was there. She meant to tell Rachel to have it moved out of sight, but curiosity could not be stilled. It held mysteries, unresolved questions, and she could not let them go unanswered. She had to know.

She opened the case and took out all the photographs of the family and put them on one side, but the photograph of George in his uniform she kept by her. Her eyes constantly turned to it until it seemed he was there in the room so that if she spoke to him he would answer.

She must not let such foolish notions enter her head. If she was going to put Trecarrow on the market, she had work to do to get rid of generations of clutter and decide what furniture and paintings to send to auction. Maud would want Thomas' Dresden collection. She herself would keep only one piece, that of a shepherdess which Thomas had bought because it reminded him of her.

She was trying to put off the moment when she opened George's letters to his sister. She should not read them, for

252

they were private to Ada, and she had no right to pry. Yet she could not resist the impulse.

She took them from the suitcase and untied the ribbon wrapped round the bundle. She picked up the first and held it for a long moment. It was addressed in a strongly distinctive hand to Miss Ada Prideaux, Trecarrow, Cornwall. She took a sheet of paper from the envelope and read, 'Dear Ada. Please give the letter I am sending with this to Mrs Trevarth, I beg you. I know you will do as I ask. It is important. I am well and safe. Your loving brother, George.'

Caroline felt inside the envelope and took from it another envelope, folded to fit into the first. It was addressed simply 'Caroline Trevarth' and was still sealed. She tore impatiently at the envelope and then clasped her hands in front of her, desperate to reach back over the years yet afraid to know what was written there.

She took the sheet of paper from the envelope. The ink was black and unfaded, the words fresh as if penned only that day, their message unmistakable.

Caroline, my love,

I came back to find you, but Ada thought it wiser for me to leave without seeing you. She was right but it was not easy. I took ship at Falmouth and no one questioned me. I was a miner, with miners, and that was enough.

So, here I am, in Cape Province and safe and waiting for you to come to me. It has been this thought and this alone — that you will soon be here with me — that makes life bearable.

It will be hard for you to leave the comfort you enjoy at Trecarrow but I shall work day in, day out, to make a fit home for you here. Write to tell me when you will be joining me. I shall wait here in Cape Town until your letter reaches me.

We can trust Ada to be discreet. I shall write to you through her.

A thousand kisses. I have never written anything like that before, but a thousand kisses and more, so much more,

George

253

She had read the letter in fits and starts, putting it down from time to time to wipe the tears away, to tell herself she was an old woman, had no right to think like the impassioned lover she had once been. Yet that was how she felt. Time should have eased the pain of his leaving, but it was with her still, a wound reopened in the knowledge that he had wanted her to join him, thought of her with love, a love that roused in her sharp memories of his tenderness and strength.

What had made Ada deceive her so? Why had she not given her the letter? And how had she had so little curiosity as to leave it unopened? What a strange sense of honour the woman had. She saw now why Ada had seemed to want forgiveness. They had trusted her, and she had betrayed that trust. How can I forgive her that? she thought.

And what would I have done? Caroline asked herself. At one time she would have had no doubt. She would have gone to him. It had not worked out like that and she should have no regrets, for even without George life had been blessed — by the precious gift he had left her.

She could not have ignored his pleas, she knew. But it had come too late.

It was no use repining. Advanced years had brought a kind of wisdom and she should put such nonsense away from her. She told herself she should leave the other letters unread, but decided they could not upset her more than the first had. She opened the next.

> Dear Ada,
>
> I have settled here in Cape Town for the time being and am living well enough. Your letter took a long time to reach me and was very disappointing. You gave me no news and have left me wondering. What is happening to you and to Mrs Trevarth? You do not tell me if the police have found out who helped me and kept me safe. I dread to think she may be in danger. Write to tell me. And please give her the letter I am putting in with this one. Please, I beg you, Ada, do as I ask.
>
> Your loving brother George

Another unopened letter remained in the envelope. Caroline

254

took it out to read but wondered why she should torture herself so. It would be wiser to leave all the letters as they were, unread, a closed book. But she could not. She had to know.

Caroline

Write to me. I am waiting for you to tell me when you will come. I am lost without you. I think of you wherever I am and whatever I do. And everything I do is for you, preparing for your arrival. I go down to the docks whenever a ship from home is due, thinking you might have taken passage without letting me know, escaping as best you could from England. I shall wait here, in Cape Town, until you do come. I know you will. My love tells me.

My love for you is too great for me to put into words. There are not words enough.

I love you,

George

She saw him on the quayside, searching for her among the passengers lining the ship's rail. And she pictured herself raising her hand to wave, calling, making her voice heard even over the shouting of the ship's crew and the stevedores. But he did not hear. He had never heard.

She could not bear to read more, not at the moment, and when Rachel came bringing her mid-morning tea, she declined it and went into the garden, trying, in the barrenness of the wintry borders, to close her mind to the recollections of those hot summer days. But, wherever she turned, they were there; there was no forgetting. He had sent for her, expected her to join him, and she had made no answer.

She had to know the whole story, if she ever could. She went back into the house and opened the next envelope. The letter to Ada was brief, saying merely, 'Please give this letter to Caroline. Please.' The enclosed envelope was again unopened. Before reading, Caroline hesitated, holding the letter in her hand a moment, imagining that in doing so she could make contact with the writer, but she was no psychic. It was her memory that kept his image sharp, nothing more.

Caroline,

Write to me. Even if only to tell me you will not come, if you will not. I wait here, hoping against hope. Is it against hope? I cannot live without knowing.

I thought you loved me. I know you do. Such love as we had does not fade at a parting, it remains as strong as ever. Mine does. It keeps me in hope, in hope that you will come — and soon.

If you are prevented from coming here, write and tell me so, and, whatever the danger, I shall come back for you, come back to you.

Write, I beg you. I wait for your news.

Her anger against Ada flared. How could she have kept the letters from her? How could she have failed her brother so? Such treachery was unforgivable. Caroline certainly could not forgive. Ada had always done all in her power to keep them apart. And she had succeeded.

She picked up the next letter addressed to Ada. There was no enclosure.

You tell me nothing. Why can you not give me news of Caroline? You say you love her. Then you should understand why it is I need to know. What is happening to her? I do not even know if she is still alive. Three times I have written to her, but have had no answer. Does that mean you have not given her my letters? I cannot believe you would be so cruel. Or does it mean she has no wish to hear from me? For pity's sake, tell me. Tell me.

Tears blinded her to his signature. How could the woman Prideaux have behaved so, to leave unanswered so heartfelt an appeal? What did it mean: 'you say you love her'? Maybe it was true. In a way Ada's loyalty and concern had never wavered. But what sort of love could be so pitiless?

She could read no more of his distress. He must have believed she had rejected him, had been merely making a pretence of love. And even over the years she was touched with guilt at the thought that she had, though unknowingly, deserted him.

256

She put the letter back intending to throw the whole bundle in the fire when she saw the next envelope lying facing her. It was addressed, not to Ada Prideaux, but to her, Mrs Caroline Trevarth, again in George's unmistakable hand. Again it was unopened.

Sorting and distributing the household's mail had always been a duty Mrs Prideaux reserved to herself. And this was how she had fulfilled that duty. Caroline's anger flared again. She tore the envelope open and took out the single sheet folded within.

> I have waited for an answer, waited for you to come and watched every day in hope. But you have not come, you have not written, and I must believe you will not come, that you no longer have any thought of me.
>
> All I have left is a memory − of sand and sea and rocks − a memory of days − only days, not the months and years I hoped for − mere days, of love. I see it still, the blue sky, the golden sand, the blue-green water, and I see your ivory skin, touch your warm flesh, let my hands caress your silken hair. Does not this remind you? Do you too not feel the magic of it?
>
> I cannot believe you have forgotten.
>
> I have taken a risk in writing to you so openly, addressing my letter to you. I meant to be discreet but in the thought of you all my good intentions and good sense vanish. It is no use trying to hide my feelings. I am tormented by them. I love you, love you. How can you be deaf to that?

She was not deaf. She heard him, his very voice, as if he was in the room with her. She looked around, half expecting to see him at the door, but of course she was alone, alone with a handful of letters and a store of memories.

He had written with a power and feeling that surprised her. He had been as intensely moved by their love as had she. She knew it now, had always known it in her heart, could not have doubted him.

There were no more letters to her, either enclosed in letters to his sister or addressed directly to her. The remaining letters to Ada were brief, mere acknowledgements of hers to him,

257

giving occasional brief glimpses of life at the Cape and in the Transvaal, but asking no more questions about life at Trecarrow or its people. It was as if he had erased all that from his mind.

And he had never known about the child that was his. That seemed the final cruelty. Ada had never mentioned Maud in her letters, that was evident. She had kept her brother in ignorance of all that happened to her mistress.She had decreed that her brother should have no part in their fortunes. There was to be only one Prideaux in Caroline's life, herself.

Caroline felt as if the walls of the room were closing in on her, was suddenly breathless. She had to get away from all these echoes of the past. Memory had filled her with joy, but there was a bitter flavour to it now in the thought of how Ada Prideaux had deceived her. 'You say you love her,' George had written. Love? Was that love?

She walked in the garden. It was cold there, with a biting wind coming from the river, a harsh relic of winter. It would soon be spring and the grass carpeted with bluebells. But she shivered, for winter had not yet gone. She heard someone call and turned to see Rachel coming over the grass to her, bringing a shawl against the cold.

'You're a good girl,' Caroline said and allowed herself to be taken back inside as if she were an old lady.

So I am, she thought, though I have the mind and heart of a young woman.

'Shall I clear this up for you, ma'am?' Rachel asked indicating the open suitcase and the contents spread on the carpet.

'No, leave it, my dear.' There was still one envelope she had not pried into. 'Come back later.'

The envelope was addressed to Miss Ada Prideaux, but not in George's handwriting. It bore a stamp of the Cape of Good Hope, postmarked with the date November 1893.

Dear Miss Prideaux,

I am writing to you as I think you may well be the relative of a young man who was recently admitted to our hospital. A letter bearing your name was found in

258

his pocket when he was brought to us. I fear I have bad news for you and wish I could convey it in a more sympathetic way than by mere letter.

The young man, George Prideaux, was admitted to the hospital last week in a state of dreadful neglect. He was brought to us by a coloured family who found him in the bush near their home, in a high fever. They helped him as best they could but when they realised they could do nothing to save him they brought him to us. We could do no more than they. He died yesterday.

He seemed to have lost the will to live. His constitution would have been strong enough to pull him through, but he seemed to have resigned himself to death and we could not fight against that.

You may know of someone called Caroline who seemed to mean much to him. Her name was on his lips when he passed away. Perhaps she too should be told of his death, but I have no means of knowing who she is or where she might be.

Please believe me when I say the nurses and doctors here did everything they could for him. I am only sorry it was not enough.

James Hosking,

Administrator to the British Hospital, Cape Town.

Chapter Twenty-Six

Caroline had taken the decision to leave Trecarrow, difficult though that decision was. She had found it irksome to go round the house identifying the pieces she would like to keep and those she must send to auction. She would not go to the sale when it came up for she could not bear the thought of strangers pawing over the things which had been part of her life for so long.

They were only material things, of course, and so meant nothing by the side of the memories she had, but nevertheless they all had their secrets, even the large walnut wardrobe, ornate and big enough to hide a man — too big for a modern house.

'What is it, Mother?' She looked up to see her daughter, come back to take responsibility for the move from her. 'What is it?' she repeated. 'You look as if you've seen a ghost'

So I have, thought Caroline, but she shook her head and said only, 'I'm just tired with all the clearing up in readiness for leaving.'

'I'm glad you decided to go.'

'I know I have to, but it's a wrench.' She wondered how Maud could say she was glad when the house had held such happiness. Or had she been deluding herself all these years?

'I shall be sorry too,' Maud said. 'We were all so happy here.' She left her mother to wander down to the river and Caroline watched her cross the grass and disappear into the woodland that ran as far as the water's edge. The bluebells had gone; a haze hung over the garden, a haze such as she remembered in those sunlit days of years past, when the magic of summer love had cast a spell over her.

There was no purpose in regretting the past. It had gone, never to be recalled. Yet she recalled it constantly, lived with the people of her past, let them enter her mind, listened to them, talked to them, touched and caressed them, and was caressed by them. She tried to clear her mind of them but it was no use, nor was there any point in denying them entry. The images of Thomas and George became confused, so that she was not sure who it was she summoned to keep her company. Thomas had occupied so many years of her life and reminders of him were everywhere about her. Yet it was George whose image was the sharper. How could so brief a passage of time have left so clear a picture?

She had loved him. But she had loved Thomas too, and if the love for Thomas had not held the passion she felt for George, yet there had been something lasting to it, a secure affection that gave a firm foundation to her life. And he had been the best of fathers to Maud.

George too would have been a good father, had providence allowed him. But he had been denied that blessing.

She became impatient with herself at her constant hankering for a world that could never be and, getting up stiffly from her chair, she walked after Maud. She found her standing beside the river looking out to the bay.

'I shall miss this,' Maud said. 'I remember seeing my first heron here. Father had brought me down to watch one. We waited a long time, so quietly.'

'You were just four. I remember how excited you were when you came back. I don't know how Thomas persuaded you to be still. You were always so full of energy, like your – .' She stopped. What had she been going to say?

Maud looked round at her, waiting for her mother to finish the sentence.

'Like your Joseph,' Caroline said. 'He's just the same.'

'Where does it come from, I wonder, his restlessness and his gypsy looks? From your side or father's? I often wondered. Simon and Sarah both have a look of their father, but Joseph isn't like anyone in either family. Do you know who he takes after? Are there any old photographs that might tell us?'

261

She took her mother's arm and they walked slowly back to the house.

I shall hide the portrait of George, make sure Maud doesn't see it or she might guess. Would it matter if she did? Caroline let her mind turn to the problems as they made their way across the lawns, pausing from time to time to let her get her breath. Age was catching up on her.

'How long is it before Joseph joins his unit?' she asked, dreading the answer.

'A couple of months.' Maud sighed.

'He will come to see me before he goes?'

'I'm sure he will.'

'He'll be sorry we're selling Trecarrow.'

'They all are, but they all know it's sensible to do so. You'll be much better off in a smaller house. You must make sure you take the things that matter most with you.'

What did matter now? A photograph? A collection of letters? Memories? She turned to her daughter. 'Will you do something for me?' she asked.

'Of course, if I can.'

'Take me for a drive. There's a place I want to see.'

Maud drove north, to her mother's instructions, along the road that led to St Agnes and then turned off to skirt the Beacon. The sky was a clear azure and the land shimmering with heat; cattle lay in whatever shadow they could find. Maud drove with the car windows down to let in the breeze and, along the narrow lanes, the air was heady with the scent of gorse.

'Along here,' Caroline said, pointing to a rough track leading from the road through clumps of heather to bare ground beyond.

'We'll have to get out. I can't drive over that,' Maud protested.

'You stay here. I'll walk,' Caroline said.

'You're not going on your own. And why do you want to come here? What is there but a ruined engine house and old men's workings?'

'Memories.'

'Of what?' Maud helped her mother from the car.

'Of a long time past.' It was coming back to her with such

262

vivid detail that she thought she might hear that dark velvet voice and his soft entrancing laugh.

'The secret?' Maud suggested. It was strange that she had not noticed it before, Caroline thought, but in Maud's own voice there was something of the quality of George's, the same warmth and depth.

'A secret,' she admitted.

She needed the support of Maud's arm to help her over the path with its potholes and strewn boulders. She had not remembered it so, but then she had approached the place on horseback from another direction, across country.

'There,' she said. 'Wheal Charlotte engine house.'

'Is that what we've come to see?'

'Part of it.' She stood admiring the majesty of the building, recalling how she had taken shelter there waiting for her lover.

'What is it?' Maud asked.

'Why?'

'You sighed with such feeling.'

'Stay here,' Caroline said. 'I'm going a bit further.' She left Maud and went hesitantly past the other ruin, the old count house. It had fallen further into decay, slates stripped from its roof, its walls showing great gaps where stone had been taken for building by local farmers.

She went on limpingly, her knees protesting at the unevenness of the ground, and drew near the edge of the cliff. She heard Maud call and turned to see her daughter come rushing towards her.

'Mother!' she said indignantly. 'What on earth are you doing? It's not safe. You frighten me going so near the edge.'

Caroline smiled. She was quite safe. She could feel George's arm holding her elbow. She would not stumble while he held her. But it was Maud who had taken hold.

'Careful, Mother. Where do you want to go?'

'Not much further. There's a lovely little cove down below.' She peered down. It was there, the golden sand, the rippling waters, the sun-baked rocks, all there and the same as then.

'Mother!' she heard Maud protest again and wished she had been able to come here alone. She would like to climb down but

263

it was out of the question. There were footsteps, the imprint of bare feet crossing the sand below, running into the water, and she wondered who it could possibly be. But even as she watched a wave came further in and swept the beach clear.

'Mother,' she heard again, more distantly and felt herself swaying dizzily towards the edge. Her daughter seized her arm and pulled her back.

She allowed Maud to lead her back to the car. They sat for a while with Maud waiting for an explanation. 'Well?' she said. 'Are you going to tell me?'

Maud insisted on her going to bed immediately they returned home, but Caroline, though physically weary, was restless with memories and found it impossible to sleep. At times she imagined she was back in the days when Maud had been a child, lively and demanding; at others she saw herself in the barren years before Maud came; at others still she saw Joseph as a boy, reckless and devil-may-care, like his grandfather.

His grandfather – she saw him as he was in the photograph he had sent his sister from Bodmin, proud in the uniform he had later rejected; then the image changed and she saw him as she had seen him first, that splendid moment of truth that had changed her life. She cried out as she had then and was aware someone had come to her.

She heard her daughter's anxious voice and felt her hand on hers. She opened her eyes and said, 'It was nothing. I was dreaming.' But it was everything. 'You are like him in so much,' she said, recalling George's touch and feeling it in her daughter's gentle hands. 'If only – .' She stopped. She could not tell Maud. It would serve no purpose, for she already loved the father she had known.

'If only?' Maud prompted.

'It doesn't matter now.' She felt a weight at the foot of the bed and knew her cat Samson had joined her. Maud wanted to take him downstairs but Caroline insisted he should be allowed to stay. 'He's getting old,' she said. 'He deserves a little comfort.' He purred loudly as if he understood and approved.

Later she got up and went along the corridor to the nursery wing, ready for use by Joseph whenever he should come. She must make sure that in her new house she had room to put him up and anyone else from the family who came to see her. But it would not be the same. Here they knew every corner, every stick of furniture, the view from every window. Here all the paths within the grounds were known and loved, each tree and shrub a familiar friend. Nowhere else could hold such intimacies.

She must not weaken in her decision to leave. Maud was right: this house, their home for so long, was much too big for her to maintain. It needed an army of servants to keep it in the condition it deserved. Someone else would love it as much as they had done, even if for them it held a different magic.

'Are you properly rested?' Maud asked.

'I want you to come round the house with me,' Caroline said. 'We can decide what you want, what you have room for, what we should send to auction and what bits and pieces I might take with me.'

They went from room to room but after half-an-hour Caroline found the task so dispiriting that she had to give it up. 'It's not that I'm tired,' she explained to Maud. 'It's that it's hard to see a life dispersed so easily.'

'I understand,' Maud said comfortingly.

But Caroline did not, could not understand. It was not her life that was being broken up, but Thomas's. It was he who had taken pleasure in material things, he who had prided himself on his Dresden collection, on his acquisition of fine furniture. Thomas had taken such joy in it all that she felt disloyal in surrendering it now.

'It has to go.' Maud said. 'We'll find you a pleasant house within gentle walking distance of the beach.' But there was only one stretch of sand that meant anything to her, and there were no houses near, only ruined mine buildings, relics of a past beyond recall.

During the next weeks Maud drove her to look at houses that might suit. Caroline had little interest in them, was willing to leave the decision on a new house to her daughter. 'You know what will appeal to me,' she explained, to Maud's annoyance.

Each day exhausted her a little more, so that Maud promised she would do as Caroline asked and let her know when she had found something suitable.

265

The month of June passed and a hot humid July followed. As often as she could, Caroline sat outside on the terrace, drowsily enjoying the scents of summer, hearing distantly the sound of children on the river bank, watching the blackbird bathing in the puddles left from the dawn rains. She took pleasure in the moment, not letting her mind too frequently indulge in the past. There was satisfaction to be found in the here and now, in the company of Maud and in the knowledge that Joseph would be coming to see her soon, and the rest of the family later in August for their last holiday in Trecarrow. She would make sure their final visit was one to cherish in the memory.

But she could not prevent the past from seeking her out. When she least expected it a vision would come to her, a sudden sharp realisation of the dangers she and Mrs Prideaux had faced, of the crime they had committed together in hiding a man wanted for murder. She had never believed George had killed a man, was certain it was not in his nature, but what did she know of him truly? Their time together had been so short.

She opened her eyes and was not surprised to see him coming to her across the grass. It could only be him. He was tall, walking with that proud springing stride she had known so well; he was in uniform and she was surprised at that. He had the smile he always kept for her and her alone. He carried his cap in his hand and waved it as he walked. He has not changed, she thought; he is as he always was, the most beautiful being on earth and I love him. I must tell him so, take him to me as I did in those early days. But he does not need telling; I can see in his eyes the certainty that we belong each to the other; he knows, has always known.

She tried to get up from her chair to go to meet him, but her legs would not move. She tried to open her arms to welcome him to them, but they remained in her lap. She opened her mouth to call his name, but no sound came. He is coming nevertheless, she told herself. He is here and I can feel his hand on mine, his lips to mine. George has come back to me.

'Grandmama,' Joseph said and bent to kiss her. 'Grandmama,' he said again, and then turned and ran

266

to the house. 'Mother!' he called. 'Mother, you'd better come. It's Grandmama.'

Maud hurried out and knelt at her mother's side, took the cold hands between hers and tried to warm them. She heard a sob from Joseph.

'I promised to come and see her and I was too late,' he said.

'She knew you loved her. That was enough.'

'If only I had told her.'

'She never doubted it.' She put her hand to straighten her mother's hair as she had done so often for her before.

'It will never be the same again.' she heard her son say.

She stooped to pick up something which had fallen from her mother's hand, an old photograph, and she wondered what significance it had. She did not know who the man in uniform could be, though there was an oddly familiar look to him. Turning the card over she saw a pencilled note. 'George Prideaux, June 1888, after enlistment.' She was still puzzled and looked up to see Joseph, smart in his new khaki, gazing sadly at her. How strange, she thought.

'No,' she said. 'It will never be the same again.'